Facing the World

By the same author

Time to Move On
The Runaway

Facing the World

Grace Thompson

ROBERT HALE · LONDON

Typeset in 10.5/13.5pt Sabon
Printed in Great Britain by the MPG Books Group, Bodmin and King's Lynn

Chapter One

THE SMALL GROUP of onlookers moved aside as two vans drove slowly through the double gates and over to the factory entrance. Today the demolition would begin. What had once been a business making kitchens and small items of furniture would disappear and houses would replace it. Two years since it closed and as the heavy machinery arrived all hope of its reopening had gone.

Although the work hadn't yet begun, the place already had that dejected air of defeat. The walls had become stained with mildew and paint was peeling from its walls. Guttering had become disconnected and formed a crazy pattern of zig-zag lines.

Sally Travis arrived later than the rest and looked around at the sad faces, aware of the disappointment the final end to their dreams was bringing. So much had changed in the small community of Tre Melin since the factory had closed. It had employed so many of the local people and the effect had been wider than imagined, with two shops closing, and local deliveries of fish and other commodities sold from a van reduced to once in two weeks instead of more frequently. Even the community centre was closed for much of the time as, with less money about, fewer activities were arranged. Bus routes had been changed as fewer people went into the nearest town to shop or to meet friends for coffee. Once-familiar faces were missing as families had moved away to where employment was offered. Others had found less well-paid jobs, but many had refused to accept work that was different from the occupation they had known, and spent their time wasting day after day, unwilling – or too lazy – to seek another situation. For them, the dream of the place reopening was gone now the demolition was about to begin.

Although I didn't work there, the changes were just as dramatic for me, Sally thought, although I can see an end to my two years of waiting. Holding the handle of Sadie's pram, she watched with the rest, her thoughts too on the sad end to the factory, but she was thinking specifically of Valmai and Gwilym Martin, and their absent son, Rhys. Gwilym had suffered a serious accident soon after the closure and hadn't walked since and their son, Rhys, had run away, leaving her to cope with the birth of Sadie and the gossip that entailed. Soon their daughter would be two years old and she wondered whether Rhys would mark the occasion with a visit.

Valmai Martin stood with her neighbour, Netta Prosser, and Eric Thomas, and others who were reminiscing about the years of full employment the factory had given them.

Sally overheard Valmai say to Netta, 'Some managed to find other work, mind, but not your Walter. Given up trying, he has, hasn't he?'

'We manage on what I earn,' Netta said, 'but I sometimes wish I'd stopped working when Walter lost his job. That way he'd have had to find work. All he does now is flop about and moan about how unfair life is.'

'Gwilym had an excuse really, him being so badly injured.'

'Maybe, but many have managed to cope with worse than losing a leg, Valmai. Let's be honest here, your Gwilym and my Walter gave up trying. Even poor Eric managed better than them. He worked until he was too old. Bless him.'

Valmai reluctantly agreed. Gwilym and Eric had both been injured in a road accident. Eric had been left with a limp and a weak ankle but Gwilym had been more unfortunate and lost part of a leg. Although help was available, Gwilym hadn't been out of the house since, refusing to be seen in a wheelchair and even more determined not to use crutches. No pleading or lecturing or downright anger had made him change his mind.

Sally turned away from their discussion as the group was pushed aside. A huge lorry loaded with tools, followed by a crane, made its way through the entrance and stopped close to the factory wall. Men shouted instructions and vehicles moved around the area. Then a man carrying a clipboard and wearing a hard hat came towards them.

'Sorry, ladies and gentlemen, but I have to ask you to move away.

There'll be a lot of coming and going soon and we don't want anyone hurt.'

David Gorse – another ex-employee of the factory – was just passing and he stopped and came to join Sally as the man began edging them back on to the road, his arms spread as he coaxed them to leave. 'Like a shepherd herding reluctant sheep,' Valmai muttered.

'Hello, Sally,' David said. 'How's little Sadie today? Starting on the demolition, I see. I hope they can sleep nights!' David stood beside Sally and gave the little girl a small chocolate bar.

'Thanks, David, but you shouldn't spoil her.'

'It's a pleasure, she's a lovely little girl. Her father is missing so much, isn't he?'

Sally didn't reply. People were always prying, trying to guess who the father could be – or have their guesses confirmed – but she refused to satisfy their curiosity. One day they would know and that day wasn't too far away now. Two long years were almost over.

The small crowd dispersed, Eric heading for the old watermill where he was sleeping that week, having spent his rent money on new shoes and a few extra clothes. David walked a little way with Sally, holding Sadie's pushchair, leaning over, talking to the child. Then Valmai said, 'We'd better get on, Sally, love, Gwilym will be wondering what's happened to us. I've got the leeks I promised you. The last of them unfortunately. Stay for a bit of lunch, will you?'

'Just a quick cup of tea. I have to be at Mrs Glover's in half an hour. She has some extra cleaning for me this week.'

Reluctantly David waved goodbye to Sadie, now smeared with chocolate, and promised, 'See you soon. Sally,' to which Sally gave a vague reply.

'He means well, but I do wish he wouldn't keep appearing. I don't have time for company these days,' Sally whispered as she turned the pushchair for Sadie's final wave.

'I think Eric's sleeping in the mill again,' Netta said as she caught up with them. 'Guilty I am, poor man, but I don't have a spare room.'

'Neither do we,' Valmai said. 'Two bedrooms are all we have and you have young Jimmy and I have to keep Rhys's room ready for when he comes back home.'

Sally said nothing. She hoped that Rhys's return home would be temporary, just until they could find a home, then they would marry and the three of them would be together for always.

Netta also avoided a reply. But the expression on her face suggested that Valmai would wait a long time before her runaway son returned. After two years it was time she faced the fact he was gone for good, unable to face the police and their accusations.

Sally put away the last of the cleaning equipment and gave a sigh. Her daughter was playing in the garden and she always complained when they had to leave Mrs Glover's house. Three more cleaning jobs before six o'clock, after which she was free to go back to her two modestly furnished rooms. There she would prepare a meal and play with her two-year-old daughter Sadie for an hour before putting her to bed. Then the loneliness was at its worst. Closed in the small living room, the wireless on very low as she listened for any sound from Sadie, watching the hands of the clock move, oh, so slowly, waiting for sleep that would take her away until the morning came. Twelve dark hours before she would see another soul. The winter seemed never to end.

Being the mother of an illegitimate child had cut her off from most of her friends and although many people sympathized, in 1960 there were still plenty who openly disapproved and relished the opportunity for snide remarks. After the incident that changed everything, she hadn't told anyone, not even Rhys's parents, where he was or what he was doing. As far as neighbours knew, she had slept with a stranger who disappeared, leaving her shamed and unable to keep her position in the fashion trade. There was little criticism for the mystery man but plenty for herself.

Sally had worked as a fashion buyer for a chain of department stores but had given up when her daughter was born. Rhys Martin had been a very persuasive lover and although he seemed thrilled at the thought of having a child, he was determined to continue with his plan to train as a teacher. It was something he'd considered for a long time but he'd lacked the confidence to give up a well-paid job. The closing of the factory meant the decision had been made for him – but only because of Sally's generous support. She had helped financially and more importantly she had helped by denying he was Sadie's father and coping with the criticism alone.

Sally's parents had died when she was fourteen and had left her a large sum of money but she had vowed never to touch it, convinced that she would be celebrating their deaths. Then, when Rhys needed money to help him through his studies, it seemed a better way to use the inheritance and she willingly offered to help. She had given up the smart flat she rented and moved to two small rooms. Then it had all gone wrong.

A spate of burglaries had taken place around the area and Rhys had come to her late one night explaining that he had to get away.

'I can't tell you why but I know they'll accuse me. If there's any suspicion of criminality I'll lose my place at college.'

'But that's ridiculous! Why would they suspect you?' She stared at him. 'You aren't involved, are you?'

'I promise I've had nothing to do with any of it.'

'Then why run away?'

'Someone will tell a different story from mine so I have to go. Please, don't tell anyone where I am. I've told Mam and Dad I've lost my place and I'm going to try to get into drama school.'

He had refused to explain further and she was filled with doubts, but on the following day the police had called and questioned her and she was convinced he had been right to leave.

The baby's birth had been a terrible time with few offers of help and plenty of unpleasant remarks. Only Valmai supported her. Sally knew she suspected the baby was Rhys's but had never confirmed her suspicions.

Since a brief and secret visit, soon after the birth, to see Sadie and reassure her of his love, Sally had seen him rarely and only at night when he would come to the back door after a given signal. She had kept to her word and helped him financially but alone she'd had to face the hardships of work and the unkind remarks of people who had once respected her.

Her money was vastly reduced and she was thankful that the period of Rhys's absence was almost over. In July, he would have finished his exams and surely then he would at last come home and face the critics as she had done for more than two years?

She had needed to work, and had to work where she could take her child. Cleaning other people's houses seemed the best solution and she had succeeded in building a business doing weekly cleaning, for business people mainly, people she rarely saw.

Mrs Glover was an exception. She had never worked and had always enjoyed running the home she had shared with her husband and their children. Now widowed, and with the children moved on, she welcomed the weekly visit of Sally and her small daughter. She happily cared for Sadie while Sally cleaned.

Tomorrow was Tuesday, a day Sally went to the butchers and a day she dreaded. It was always busy at the time she was able to call and there were often a few who made some remark on her single mother state, even after more than two years. She shrugged the thought aside. Better to enjoy today and worry about tomorrow when it came. She cheered herself by remembering that it was only a few more months before Rhys came home and everything would be out in the open.

The rooms where she lived were in School Lane in a house owned by Mr and Mrs Falconer. She had the use of the bathroom and the kitchen, the times arranged and strictly adhered to with the help of a washing bowl in the corner and an outside lavatory – which she hated, being dark, and with a collection of spiders' webs which she hadn't dared to brush away. She could cope with most things after years of being on her own, but not spiders!

The butcher's shop looked empty and she gave a sigh of relief as she went in and placed her order. The doorbell tinkled and she held her breath, afraid of hearing the voice of one of her critics. The continuing conversation told her there were several people entering. Her heart began to race and the temptation to leave, to come back later, was strong. She didn't move: there would be no time later, she would be busy all day. To her consternation a voice said loudly. 'There's pretty that little girl is getting, *Miss* Travis.'

'Thank you,' Sally whispered.

'Dark hair she's got. Like her father's, is it? Or didn't he take his hat off?'

A few people laughed in an embarrassed way and Sally felt her face redden.

'Enough. Milly Sewell,' muttered the butcher, 'or you'll have to go into town for your meat. Right?" He gave Sally her order and whispered, 'A couple of sausages and a few pieces of liver. Not a word, mind.' He took the money for the other items and she smiled and nodded her thanks.

Pushing the pram, she went back to the rooms, put the meat in the pantry and went straight out for her third job that day. Thank goodness it was the flat above the post office where she didn't have to see anyone. If only Rhys could come home. He'd soon stop the gossips.

Mrs Davy was waiting for her and she braced herself for complaint. Kindly but over fussy, she sometimes reminded Sally of the occasional jobs that needed doing.

'Sorry I am to give you extra, dear, but when you've finished in here would you help me to get some of this rubbish down to the gate for the rubbish collection?'

Hoping it would mean an extra few shillings, Sally agreed. It looked as though Mrs Davy had been emptying her garden shed: broken tools, an old deckchair, rusted paint tins, pieces of worn carpet. She set to with Sadie watching from her pram. It was as she lifted one of the large paint tins and realized it was almost full that the idea came.

'Mrs Davy, do you think I could take this tin of yellow paint? There's an outside lavatory that I have to use sometimes and it's dark and full of spiders. If I could somehow clean it out and paint it I'd be less afraid of going in. I'm sure Mrs Falconer wouldn't mind, if it didn't cost her anything.'

'Of course you can, dear. I'll ask Eric to drop it off for you. It's too heavy for you to carry all that way. But how are you going to get rid of the spiders?'

Sally smiled, her blue eyes widening and lighting up her face. 'I haven't thought about that yet. This tin of paint could be waiting a long time if I have to do it!'

'Ask Eric.'

When Eric had lost his job at the closing of the furniture factory, he had just cleared the debts left by his wife when she had walked out on him and taken their daughter Julia. Instead of spending the next few years saving for when he retired, he had been unable to find another opening for a carpenter and had managed for a while doing odd jobs – many of which he did for nothing – but now he lived on a small pension. He lived in a room in a rather neglected boarding house with only a small stove to both heat the place and on which to cook his meals.

Just before the factory closed he had been cycling home with Rhys's father, Gwilym Martin, when a lorry knocked them down. Gwilym had lost a part of his leg but he had been more fortunate and apart from a limp from a damaged ankle he had little of which to complain. The room at Mrs Godfrey's was damp and inconveniently situated on the top floor, thirty-five stairs plus the outside steps leading to the front door, but he never moaned about his misfortunes.

He often wondered about his wife and daughter but after all the years that had passed he no longer tried to find them. He was sad to have missed watching Julia grow from a baby into a young woman and hoped that wherever she was she had been happy.

He was a pleasant man, friend to all and always willing to help with tasks needing an extra pair of hands. With little to do he spent many hours each day wandering around the village, stopping to chat here and there and calling occasionally to scrounge a cup of tea and a bite to eat. Calls to Rhys's parents, Valmai and Gwilym, were a regular part of his week. One of his delights was when he met Sally and little Sadie in the park feeding the ducks.

It was several days after the paint had arrived before Sally asked permission to paint the dismal place and a few more before she saw Eric and asked for his help. In the middle of March, when the sun shone surprisingly brightly, Eric arrived and Sally, dressed in an overall and trousers and with a towel wrapped around her head, handed him a long-handled brush and the work was begun.

'You don't mind if I stand well back, do you?' she said nervously. 'I've got my running shoes on and I'm ready to flee at the sight of an eight-legged monster coming my way.'

Eric laughed. 'Go and make us a cup of tea and I'll get it done in no time.' Gladly, Sally agreed.

An hour later, Eric declared the battle was won and there wasn't a spider or a cobweb to be found. Nervously Sally peered inside. She still felt uneasy, jumping when a leaf moved at her feet and an outside branch touched the small open window.

'You'll be all right once it's painted,' Eric said. 'Easy to see they'll be and they'll keep right away knowing you're on the warpath with that.' He laughingly pointed to the brush she carried. 'When do you plan to start?'

'Don't know.' A shiver of apprehension wriggled through her. 'If no spiders return in the next few days, maybe I'll feel brave enough. I have to go to work now and that's a relief. A reason to forget it for today.' She shivered again. 'I get a squiggle down my back even thinking about the creatures.'

Eric handed her the empty cup. 'I'll come and help when you're ready.'

She thanked him again and went inside to get rid of the extra clothes she had worn and set off for the first of her day's calls.

It was four o'clock when she finished her final task, giving an extra polish to a spare room for a client who was preparing for her son's return. Soon Rhys too would be coming home, she thought with a smile. Then her life would be transformed.

The bright sun had lengthened the day and she bought a bun at the baker's shop for Sadie and one for the ducks and set off for a walk around the park. Their days were spent going from house to house, the evenings passed in their small room and the opportunity to walk in the fresh air was too good to miss. When she reached home she went first to glance nervously towards the outside lavatory. If she saw just one spider she'd never be able to go in there and shut the door to paint the walls. The door was marked with a 'Wet Paint' notice and stood open. Puzzled, she began to walk past, averting her gaze, but she went back and peered in. Everything was clean and the walls had been painted in the bright yellow paint. 'Eric!' she said aloud.

'Eric had some help, mind,' Mrs Falconer said, laughing at her amazed expression. 'Mr Falconer painted the door. Shamed we were by the smart look inside so we had to do something about the outside too.'

Sally felt ridiculously happy. How empty my life must be, she chuckled to herself. A coat of paint on an outside lavatory and I feel like I've been given a wonderful present.

The remains of the factory walls were piled in assorted heaps around the perimeter of the plot and already men in suits carrying the inevitable clipboards were walking around checking that the footings were in the correct place. The sounds of the excavating and the rumble of heavy lorries filled the dusty air and every day a group of elderly men stood watching the progress. Soon the houses would begin to grow and memories of the factory and the hopes of many would fade and die.

Valmai Martin struggled to get her bicycle out of her over-full garden shed, muttering to herself about having to do a 'proper sort-out' one of these days. She couldn't resist picking up oddments she found and although the shed was full to bursting, and in no apparent order, she knew what it contained and where to find it. Local people often called to beg a piece of wood or a certain sized screw or nail and rarely went away disappointed.

She called back to Gwilym, who sat in his wheelchair, a blanket covering his legs, hiding the sound one and the one partially lost in the accident. He smiled, ready to wave as she set off along the road on her way to work. 'Back around two as usual, love.'

'I'll have everything ready,' he promised, blowing a kiss.

March 1960, she mused, as she began to push her way along the road, and still he won't leave the house. She had tried to coax him to face up to his situation every way she could but despite having a decent wheelchair he refused to go further than the garden and only that far when he was fairly certain not to be seen. At least Eric – injured at the same time – had made the effort and was not restricted by stupid pride. Being a sportsman had exacerbated Gwilym's problems: going from a runner, cricketer and rugby coach to living his life in a wheelchair had been too much for him. But if only he'd try.

The morning was dull, the sun refusing to make its way through the low cloud, but the air was warm and there were flowers to admire in the gardens she passed. At the house where the Waterstones had lived she saw workmen moving tools from their van, obviously about to start work on the house for its new owners. She wondered vaguely who would be moving in. Someone from town she'd heard. A couple without children. She smiled, hoping they would be friendly and would settle into Mill Road without trouble.

They couldn't cause more distress than the Waterstones had with their cruel gossip. The Waterstones and their friend Milly Sewell were the reason her son Rhys had been suspected of robberies and the cause of him running away. A twenty-year-old boy forced to run from home by their vicious tongues. She decided to call on the newcomers at the first opportunity and introduce herself. Start right and perhaps they'd be friends.

Mill Road was a pleasant place, on the edge of town but some distance from the mill that had given it its name. She looked up and there, in the distance, high on a hill, was the ruin of a windmill. Beyond the wood, out of sight in the valley below, hidden by overgrown trees and shrubs, was a watermill. Rhys used to play there as a boy, even though he had been warned of its dangers. Once the town had been surrounded by cornfields and the millers had been kept busy. Now only houses grew and factories had taken the place of the ancient craft.

The hotel where she worked came into view and although it was daylight, the place was brightly lit, coloured light offering a welcome. She freewheeled the last few yards and around the building, stopping by dragging both feet on the ground. She parked the bicycle against the wall of the kitchen. 'Mornin' all,' she called as she opened the door. Then she reached for her overall, scrubbed her hands and began to cook breakfast.

Helping with the dishes after the guests had finished eating and cleaning the cooker kept her busy for a while, then after a break she began on the vegetables. She had some time left so she emptied and washed out a couple of cupboards for which she was rewarded with an extra couple of shillings.

Lunch was a simple meal for a few of the guests and she didn't need to stay and serve. It was twelve o'clock when she left and on the way home she was further delayed by the sight of a skip outside the empty house, still called the Waterstones' place, even though the Waterstones had moved away some time ago. Skidding to a stop – she'd really have to get the brakes fixed – she peered over the side hoping to see a few things for which she could find a use.

Books. They'll interest Gwilym, she thought, tugging to release them. She spotted a slightly rusty watering can which she hauled out. Lovely that would be, planted with a few marigolds, or with nasturtiums tumbling down the sides. She stuffed the books in her saddle bag and hooked the watering can over the handlebars but as she set off she stopped and gripped the rusty side of the skip, her feet still on the pedals and able to see more easily, unable to resist a second look. Beneath a few broken bricks she saw the leg of a chair and, grunting and puffing with the effort, she pulled it out and saw it was in good condition, but how on earth was she going to get it home? Constable Harvey had warned her several times about precarious loads.

'Hello, Valmai, want any help?'

'Eric! Am I glad to see you! Hide this for me, will you, till I can come with the wheelbarrow to collect it?'

The clean but poorly dressed man lifted the chair experimentally, judging its weight. 'I can do better than that. I'll deliver it for a piece of your seedy cake.'

'Thanks, Eric. Stay and have a chat with Gwilym, will you? Glad of a bit of company, he is.'

'Of course, but sometimes he seems less pleased to see me. Too much time on his own hasn't been good for him, has it? No sign of him going out yet?'

'I've tried everything.'

'Try again. He's been hiding away for too long.'

With Gwilym helping by sitting in his wheelchair and using the long-handled hoe, the afternoon was spent clearing weeds from an area where they planned to grow onions and carrots and some greens, but Valmai's mind wasn't on her work.

'Gwilym, love, why don't we go for a walk? Just down the road to the corner. The spring flowers in the end garden are beginning to make a real show. We can wait till dark if you like – we'll still see them by the lamplight.'

'Not today, Val. Not today.'

'Gwilym, love. It's years since you and Eric had the accident. Years since you and I went out together. Don't you think it's time we did?'

'Soon, but not yet. Now what about me making us a cup of tea? It's getting chilly out here. Any of that seedy cake left?'

'Yes, but Eric will be coming with the chair soon and I promised him a slice.'

'I hope he won't stay long. I want to look at those books you found.'

'I hope you'll find time to look at the brakes on my bike too. They aren't working and I'm wearing out shoes like a ten-year-old football fan!'

'You should have told me sooner. You mustn't neglect things like that. We can get the bike propped up on the bench and replace the blocks as soon as you buy some – unless you have some in that shed of yours.'

'Here's Eric now. Wait here and show him our plans for spring planting.' As she knew he would, he hurriedly dropped the hoe and pushed himself back into the house. He couldn't bear to be seen struggling to do something, with a blanket where his right leg should be.

Leaving Gwilym and Eric with the remains of the cake, she risked the bike again and, once out of sight of the house, she bent over the handlebars and picked up speed, turning into School Lane. Sally would be at home and she could spend a little time with her, play with little Sadie, as well as give her the ten shillings she managed to give her each week.

Eric went into the house where Gwilym sat with his knees tucked under the table. 'Put the kettle on, shall I?' he asked, not waiting for an answer. 'I brought the chair and a rusty old watering can for your Valmai and she promised me some cake.' They chatted easily as Eric set about the tea-making but it wasn't until he was seated on the armchair that he asked, 'Any news from your Rhys this week?'

'No. Nor last week.'

'Out of the army then, is he?'

'Months ago, I suppose. I can't understand it. What could have happened to make him cut himself from us like that? We pretend he's working at a theatre but we don't know what he's doing or where he is. Apart from an occasional postcard we know nothing about him. How can that happen? A son you've cared for, for twenty years. How can he suddenly walk away and vanish?'

'He was terrible hurt, mind. All that gossip and so many accusing him of burglary, violence and heaven knows what else.'

'Milly Sewell and the Waterstones, you mean. They were the cause of him leaving. And he didn't do it. None of it.'

'I know that and most people around here know that too. But it only takes one or two to spread rumours. He should have stayed and brazened it out. Damn it all, he was only a boy. Don't give up hope.'

'I'd be letting him down – and Valmai too – if I did.'

They talked about the people they had known when they had worked at the furniture factory. Some had stayed and found other work, some had moved away and news filtered back of their successes and failures.

'Pity it closed,' Eric said. 'If I'd been five years younger I'd have started again.'

'Not with half a leg missing you wouldn't!' Gwilym said bitterly.

'Ex-servicemen had to adjust to far worse,' Eric reminded him quietly. 'Besides, it's eyes and hands that make a good carpenter – as you were. It's such a waste of your talent, Gwilym. You were good, and even now after being out of work for so long you'd find it easy to get work if you wanted it.' He stared at his friend. 'What are you waiting for?'

Gwilym didn't reply. How could he when he didn't know himself? There would be a day when things would change but he couldn't imagine how. There was this incomplete dream in his head of suddenly walking alongside Valmai, going to the station to greet his son returning from his self-imposed exile, but how could that ever be? The first half of the dream was a blur and he had no idea how he expected it to happen. His dream consisted only of the happy ending.

He knew the change had to begin with himself but something was twisted up inside and he was waiting for something wonderful to happen. His leg wouldn't miraculously return and he couldn't imagine learning to walk on a false one, so a change, a wonderful event, would never happen and the sooner Valmai gave up hope, as he had, the better.

Valmai sped up the slight incline towards the Falconers' house where, in the fading lights, Sally was hanging clothes on the line.

'Mrs Martin! Lovely to see you.' Dropping her voice she asked, 'You haven't heard anything from Rhys, have you?'

'No, dear, not a word. Come on, I'll give a hand with these, you put the kettle on. There are some cakes in my saddle bag.' She held up a baby dress. 'Tiddly little clothes they are.'

'Not so small now. She'll be two next month.'

'Two precious years of her childhood Rhys has missed. I wish he'd come home.'

'Have you heard who's moving into the Waterstones' house?' Sally asked, pretending not to have heard the comment.

'Only that it's a couple. Amy and Rick.'

'Any children?'

'They aren't married yet according to her in the post office. Wedding planned for the autumn, so I'm told. Workmen are there and it looks as though they're having a lot done before they move in.'

'Good on 'em. Lucky for some.'

Before she left, after reading a story to Sadie, Valmai slipped a ten-shilling note under the sugar basin. 'A little treat for Sadie, eh? Now, I'm off but I'll try to come again soon.'

'Did you see anyone interesting while you were out, love?' Gwilym asked when Valmai handed him the brake blocks she had found in the shed.

'Not really, I just went into work to check on what time I'm wanted tomorrow.'

Gwilym smiled. He knew she had visited Sally and slipped her a few shillings as she did every week. Although Sally had denied it, the baby was Rhys's and one day he'll come home and they'd be one happy family. If only the police could find out who had really committed those burglaries. Then Rhys would come back.

It was a month before the new owners, Amy Seaton-Jones and Rick Perry, appeared at the Waterstones' old place and at once they began to annoy the neighbours. While alterations were being done and Rick had started on the garden, Amy complained about the trees overhanging their fence and about neighbours who didn't brush the pavement outside their houses and the milkman who made too much noise and the postman who sang. So it was with some trepidation that Valmai stopped outside and alighted from her bicycle when she went to deliver an embroidered cushion she had made as a welcoming gift for the new neighbours.

'You can't leave that there!' a voice called, as Valmai propped her bike against the garden wall. She looked around and saw a woman standing in the doorway shaking a yellow duster. She was small, barely five feet tall, and she wore a scarf around her head and an all-concealing apron, both in bright pink.

Valmai quickly decided to pretend not to have heard. 'Mornin'. Welcome to Mill Road,' she said with her brightest smile. 'Pleasant people around here. I'm sure you'll be very happy.' There was no reply; she had obviously confused the woman. 'I'm Valmai Martin. Gwilym and I live at 42. Come and say hello when you have time.'

'I don't think so. You're the mother of that criminal who ran away from the police.'

Outrage flared but Valmai once again decided to avoid trouble. After all, the woman would be easily avoided. Adjusting the bike to confirm her intention to leave, she waved. 'No cushion for you,' she muttered as she stuffed it back into her capacious shopping bag and hung it on the handlebars. 'There's plenty who'll be glad of it.'

'I'll kill her!' she shouted to Gwilym as she practically threw the bicycle down and burst into the house. 'The Waterstones obviously passed on all the gossip, true or otherwise. As if they hadn't caused enough damage while they lived here, they're causing more!'

Gwilym comforted her, soothed away her anger and wiped away her tears. 'If they start by quarrelling with everyone, there won't be anyone to listen.'

'Why doesn't he come home? They'll never catch the man who did those burglaries now, and by running away like he did he looked guilty. I doubt whether the police even looked for anyone else. Why doesn't he come home and face it?'

'He's still hoping the real culprit will be caught.'

'After more than two years? And without any repeat?' She picked up her embroidery on its frame. Working on pictures soothed her.

The spate of burglaries had taken place late in 1958. There had been very little crime in the area and doors were left open, people went into neighbours' houses sharing news, swapping recipes, helping with sewing, and there were plenty of opportunities for someone to go in and out and decide on places to rob.

The offences all took place within a couple of weeks, although some items weren't missed until much later. Rhys was one of the suspects. He was a very outspoken young man and some of his clever remarks were taken literally. No charges were brought but when he saw two policemen coming from his house the morning after the most recent thefts had been discovered, he ran.

Valmai and Eric had searched for him, exploring the fields and the old watermill where Rhys had played as a youngster but there was no sign of the place being recently used. Rhys had been turned down for National Service owing to less than perfect sight but Valmai and Gwilym spread the rumour that he was in the army and had been posted abroad. Then later, when he still hadn't returned, they told everyone that he was working at a theatre, which was the story they still told.

For a while people believed them. A few weeks after his disappearance, Sally admitted she was pregnant but denied that Rhys-the-criminal was the father and although questioned by the police, she insisted she had no knowledge of him or his whereabouts. Valmai had guessed that the suspicions were true but she said nothing. Gwilym also knew the truth but to protect Sally and his son, he feigned ignorance too. As he pretended now not to notice the doll Valmai had bought and spent hours dressing, for Sadie's second birthday.

Sadie's birthday warmed Sally's heart as many people arrived with cards and small gifts for the two-year-old. The critics were silenced; even Milly managed to hand her a card without any unpleasant remark. Mrs Falconer had arranged a party with a few of Sally's friends and their children invited. Music from the gramophone, party games and much laughter: it was a day to remember, made less than perfect only by the absence of Rhys, Sadie's father, who hadn't even sent a card.

A few days later, Sally found an extra job and used the money to place Sadie in a day nursery. It was a wrench to leave her small daughter with strangers each morning but Sadie adapted well, quickly recognizing several of the children she had met in the park.

On the second day Sally greeted her chubby little daughter as she ran from nursery, proudly carrying a painting she had done. Chatting happily. they walked back to their home. On the back porch Sally saw something that made her heart leap. A round pebble she had carried home from the beach some time ago was in the centre of the step. Rhys was here!

She played with Sadie until six o'clock then began getting her ready for bed. Thank goodness she went to sleep without complaint after a bath and story. With Rhys's imminent arrival, Sally's thoughts sped back to when they had first met, when everything was going to be perfect. Rhys was planning to train as a teacher and they would be married as soon as his training was completed. It had all gone so terribly wrong when he had been accused of theft.

On the night of his brush with the police, Rhys had been in the recently closed factory intending to pick up some wood for his parents' fire, something many people were doing as the building was cleared ready for sale. David Gorse, a man he had known from school and had strongly disliked, called him over.

'Look at this,' David hissed into the darkness. 'D'you think it's valuable?'

Rhys used his torch to see that David held a beautiful silver bowl. Rhys admired it curiously. 'Georgian so I'm told. Put it down there,' David instructed. 'Here's something even better.' He opened a sheet of thick brown paper and showed him an oil painting of a young woman.

'Where did you get that?' Rhys asked. 'It's beautiful.' He took it and examined it more closely, running his hands over the features of a young woman dressed in Victorian dress nursing a young kitten and with a small dog sitting nearby. He turned it over and began to read the information on the back.

'Give it back, we have to get out of here,' David said. Holding the sheet of brown paper, he wrapped it and took it from Rhys without touching it. He picked up the silver howl with some tissue and ran off into the darkness.

'Where did you get it?' Rhys asked, beginning to follow him.

'Tell you later,' was the reply.

The following morning the papers reported a theft from a house in a nearby village and the picture was described in detail. The valuation was in five figures and Rhys went to find David, to warn him and demand that he hand it back. 'You stole it, didn't you? If you don't give it back I'll tell the police that you have it,' he warned.

'No, I don't think you will. Your fingerprints are all over it, see. None of mine, only yours. Explain that to the police, will you? They'll be on their way to your house any time now. I told them you had it, that you boasted to me about stealing it. Gave them the time of the robbery down to the last minute, I did. Saw you coming out and showing me what you'd taken. Upstanding citizen that I am.'

'You wouldn't! They wouldn't believe you!'

'I would. In fact I did and they believed me without any hesitation.'

'Why, David? Why would you do something so despicable?'

'Because I dislike you and now they think you were responsible for all the robberies and the attack on that stupid man who tried to stop me, they won't be looking for anyone else, will they? I can enjoy the money I've made without a worry.'

'But I can tell them exactly what happened.'

'You can try but prison is a nasty place to live. Take a chance on it, will you? Better you get right away. See, I haven't actually told them yet. But I will. Don't doubt it. But, sport that I am, I'll give you till tomorrow to get away.' As Rhys grabbed at him, David ran off. 'You've got till tomorrow, sad loser!' Rhys heard his laughter echoed back, mocking him.

He didn't sleep that night but spent the hours thinking, then packing ready to leave before first light. He wrote a letter to his mother and Sally explaining that he had to go away for a while then after delivering Sally's, he went back home to pick up his belongings and it was then that he saw the police. He turned and ran across the fields towards Cardiff. He thumbed a lift from three different lorries, making his way gradually in an irregular way towards London and eventually Bristol.

His first action was to get a job. Just part-time in a bar. Sally had agreed to finance him and she promised not to change her mind now the police wanted to talk to him. He'd already been offered a place in a college. It was difficult but he eventually found a place to stay and it was his intention to complete his training before going home and hopefully proving his innocence.

He was convinced that further robberies would take place and that would go a long way to convince the police he was innocent. But to his alarm, he learnt that the theft of the picture and the silver bowl had been the last.

Two weeks after Sadie's second birthday. Sally was filled with excitement. Two years had passed and he was coming to tell her it was over and he was coming home. They would marry straight away and she'd be able to hold her head high. She took out a dress she had bought, before Sadie had begun to alter her figure, and held it up. It was to have been her wedding dress but she doubted whether it would fit her now. Never mind, she would keep it as a memento. One day she'd make a special dress for Sadie from its generous skirt.

Rhys cut across the fields and, as it was after dark, he entered the back door of the house convinced he hadn't been seen. David Gorse was walking in the opposite direction on his way to spend an hour at the Farmer's Arms. He had heard someone approaching and had stayed perfectly still, hidden by the burgeoning bushes of the hedgerow. He almost gasped when he recognized Rhys. So what was he doing in Tre Melin? Not visiting his parents, that's for sure. Wrong direction completely. Cautiously he followed.

It was hardly a surprise when he saw him entering the house of Mr and Mrs Falconer, the house where Sally lived with her daughter. Rumours had been denied but this confirmed them; Rhys was the father of Sally's daughter and he was obviously in regular touch.

His first impulse was to go and bring Valmai here to face the son she hadn't seen for two years. But he changed his mind. There might be a better way of using the information and he still had the picture and the silver bowl bearing Rhys's fingerprints.

David Gorse was a bitter man. Like many of the people who lived in Tre Melin, he had worked at the furniture factory. When it closed its doors, he and almost fifty others had lost their jobs. Unlike most, David hadn't found alternative employment. He had been so angry that every attempt to help him had been spurned. He had been a supervisor, no longer working with tools, and he felt that as it was clear he was superior to the rest he couldn't accept work in a lesser capacity. A manager or nothing was his insistence when anything was offered.

Some found other jobs, some had retired, David passed the days in frustrated idleness. People no longer listened to his complaints, sympathy had been exhausted and now, many avoided him. He was a competent worker and he could have earned money doing small jobs around the area, designing and making items, dealing with small repairs, but he always declined. A small advancement from bench worker to supervisor had ruined his life. He believed his skill working with wood was a lowly one. He was management and not one of the several men who were proud of their skill, and his tools lay neglected in his mother's garden shed.

Now, he watched as Rhys hid in the shadows until Sally opened the door, two barely visible shadows in the almost complete darkness of the porch. Then the door opened wider and the light from within revealed the shadows merging as Rhys and Sally hugged before slipping through the door, which closed softly behind them. Envy rose in his throat and he turned away, wondering how best to use this new knowledge.

Rhys hugged Sally, breathing in the sweet scent of her, so longed for, and for so long. With their baby in the bedroom, they made them-selves comfortable in the overcrowded living room and spent a blissful hour.

'I long for the day when we can be together – no more snatched moments and painful partings,' Rhys sighed.

'We will. Surely the police must have given up? The trouble is there haven't been any more burglaries since you left. Running away like you did convinced them they were down to you. But you'll have completed your course soon and then you can come home and face up to any accusations. Only a few more months,' she said.

Rhys hadn't told Sally of the false evidence held by David Gorse; he didn't want to worry her further or risk her telling someone. 'I still think it might have been Keith Waterstone.' he said. 'The Waterstones were an unpleasant bunch.'

'He is the most likely. Didn't you say he was a thief when you were at school? The Waterstones have moved away, new people are moving in and the police will never question him now.'

'I wonder whether a new spate of burglaries has happened where they now live?'

'I'll try to find out,' she promised. Then she added, 'Rhys, can't you tell me when you'll be coming home? It must be soon and I want to count the days on the calendar like a child at Christmas.'

'I'm not sure yet, but as soon as I know I'll come and tell you and we can celebrate.' She was disappointed but not alarmed. He had to complete his course and perhaps wait for the results of the finals.

They peeped down at their sleeping daughter, on her back, arms relaxed on the pillow behind her head, her face rosy in the warmth of the small room. In whispers they shared news of the weeks they'd been apart. Rhys left before dawn and slept for a few hours in the old watermill where he had played wild and innocent games as a boy, remembering some as he crept in, and later out, of the old building just as he had during an imaginary adventure with homemade bows and arrows.

Sally lay reliving the past few hours, committing them to memory to replay them from time to time until Rhys came again. It wasn't until much later that she realized, with a surge of alarm, that they hadn't taken precautions.

'I was thinking,' Gwilym said one morning. 'If we can set up a bench in the shed I could start making children's toys. Eric was telling me that wooden trains and wheelbarrows and pull-along toys are still popular even though lots are now made with plastic.'

'Wheels come off, see,' Valmai said. 'Plastic and metal bits don't stay together. Wheeled wooden toys to sit on, trucks and tractors and trains will always be favoured by boys. We still have a few you made for Rhys! You could copy them for a start.' She tried not to sound too excited but this was the first time he had even considered trying to work and if she could get someone to help her clear the shed and fix up a bench she'd get it ready in a very short time.

'What about electricity?' she asked casually. 'A fire for a bit of warmth and you'll need some light, for definite, and maybe a few more tools.'

'Steady on, love. It's only an idea!'

'I know. And it'll be expensive, but there's no harm in asking a few people. Eric'll help clear the shed.' She laughed deprecatingly. 'I admit that would be a good idea even if you don't open your own factory! It could do with a good sorting.'

On her way to work she dropped a note in to Eric, asking if he'd help, and the electrician who did work at the hotel agreed to come and look at what they would need. Their next-door neighbours Netta and Walter promised some muscle and by the time she returned home she had more or less dealt with everything.

'Muscle and a bit of electricity, that's all it'll take.' she said, her eyes sparking with excitement.

'A whirlwind you are, Valmai Martin. I wish I hadn't said anything!' But his eyes were glowing too.

*

Amy Seaton-Jones and Rick Perry were cleaning up after the latest workman had left. They had knocked down a wall between a bathroom and lavatory, creating one large complete bathroom. The rubble had been removed under Amy's imperious instructions but the walls had not yet been repaired and dust was thick over the whole house. Rick was trying to lay the dust on the floorboards with wet sawdust and a large brush. Amy was preparing to scrub the kitchen floor.

'I don't see why we have to clear up this thoroughly every night, Amy dear. Surely it's pointless to scrub floors when they'll be back to do some more bashing in about fourteen hours? Then there'll be cementing, then plastering. Tidy up certainly. But washing floors? Might as well wait until they've finished and give it a good do, surely?'

'It's a matter of standards, Rick darling. Mummy says letting them see how particular we are will remind them to be that much more considerate.'

'Another thing. They'd be faster if you weren't hovering around. It's a small house in a small town, not a palace.' He smiled, to take away the hint of criticism. 'I want to see it finished. I'm longing for the time when you work your magic and make this house into our perfect home.'

'Oh, the magic will come but not before the men have finished their work and every trace of their presence has been removed.'

'Only a couple of weeks, then I can start on the garden.'

'Well, there is another slight delay, darling.'

Rick stared at her, a frown increasing the lines around his dark brown eyes. 'Another delay?'

'It's the wardrobe. It's rather old-fashioned and I thought we could have it taken out and a new one built. We can ask him about the summer house as well while the carpenter's here. We'll put it right at the end where we'll get the most sun. It shouldn't take long. Only a few more weeks. And while the carpenter is busy I thought we might as well arrange for the garden to be paved and the fish pond installed.'

'But I thought we'd agreed that the garden was my province? That I could plan it, leave room for some vegetables?'

'It is, darling. You can do exactly what you want, chose the flowers, everything. But I do need a dry area, I do so hate walking on muddy grass and I've always wanted a fish pond. Mummy thinks water in a garden is so peaceful.'

Rick sighed but said nothing. He sometimes wondered why they even pretended to discuss anything as all the decisions were over-ridden by Amy and her mother.

Amy was at the window when Eric strolled past. 'Look! There's that awful tramp again. He walks past slowly just so he can look in the window! We'll have to have thick net curtains at all the bedrooms and the ground floor.'

In vain Rick protested. 'He isn't a tramp and I hate nets. We agreed that we're far enough away from the road to make them unnecessary.'

'I agree, darling, but having someone like that dirty tramp wandering around changes things, doesn't it?'

Rick walked outside and looked at the garden in the light escaping from the kitchen. A fox slipped through the neglected hedge and stared at him. 'I bet she'll call it a patio,' he whispered. 'And the summer house will be a gazebo.'

The fox walked across the garden and before going through the opposite hedge stopped and stared as though in sympathy. 'I don't recommend you visiting once we're living here,' he called after the beautiful creature. 'Amy's mother wouldn't approve.'

He was smiling as he went back inside. He was being petty about small things. Once they were married and settled, Amy would run things her own way and her mother's influence would fade. It was a difficult time with the wedding to arrange and the house to make into their home. He knew just how much Amy depended on her mother both for planning the wedding and the finances. Once he was solely responsible for their living expenses, everything would be perfect.

Chapter Two

SALLY WAS WALKING to the park with Sadie in her pushchair, armed with bread with which to feed the ducks, a favourite activity for the little girl. Amy, the new tenant in what was still called the Waterstones' house, was coming out of her gate and Sally smiled and greeted her with a remark about the weather.

'We're off to feed the ducks, aren't we, Sadie?' she said.

Amy gave a stiff smile and was about to walk on, but undeterred, Sally said, 'Are your alterations to the house nearly finished? When are you and Rick tying the knot? I hope it will be finished in time – so much to do with the wedding to arrange as well as sort out builders.'

'We have everything in hand,' Amy replied rather pompously, and this time Sally allowed her to walk on. Pointless trying to befriend her. She was clearly uninterested in getting to know her neighbours. Then she heard a call, and Rick appeared. 'Hi, how is little Sadie? Two years old, that's quite an age,' he said as he approached them. Amy had hurried on and he shrugged apologetically and ran after her.

'Come on, love,' he encouraged. 'If we're going to live here we have to be polite to our neighbours.'

'Some of them certainly, darling, but definitely not all.'

Philosophically calm after the attempt to speak to Amy, Sally was convinced that the young woman would eventually come round to accepting the local people. They were friendly and kind and she would soon learn that, whatever Milly Sewell had told her. She walked on to the park, chatting cheerfully to Sadie, trying not to feel hurt. Amy's attitude must be due to that woman's gossiping tongue. She wondered why she took such pleasure in upsetting others.

After watching the ducks for a while, Sally went to the bank. It was time to send more money to Rhys. A balance reminded her of how little was left. She wondered whether they would be able to put a deposit down on a house. If he came home soon, got a job, earned a reasonable wage then they might just manage. His two years at college had cost more than they had expected and it still wasn't over. She folded the statement and hid it in her pocket.

Buying a house wasn't the end, it was just the beginning. Living in two rooms had meant she had practically no furniture or even kitchen equipment, as she had used that belonging to Mrs Falconer. Even the bare minimum would be costly and she unfolded the statement again, stared at it as though it would magically change for the better, and wondered just how they would cope. Buying everything on hire purchase was a recipe for disaster.

As those thoughts were filling her mind, she saw a notice on the community hall doorway advertising a sale of unwanted furniture. Perhaps, if Mrs Falconer didn't mind, she might look for a few bargains. After all, it wouldn't be long before Rhys was home and she would be moving out.

She went to the post office and bought postal orders, which she put in brown business envelopes and sent to Rhys care of a café he regularly used. Surely there wouldn't be many more payments? His second year would end soon and he wouldn't need to stay in his digs once the exams were over. He could be here with her and Sadie while he waited for the results. 'Oh, Rhys,' she muttered aloud, 'Please tell me you're coming home.'

'Talking to yourself, Sally?' David Gorse asked, taking the handle of the pushchair from her and talking to Sadie.

Startled, Sally wondered if he had seen her push the postal orders into the brown envelope. She relaxed. Even if he had, he would have been unable to see the name or the address. She was unaware that it wasn't the first time he had watched her buy the postal orders and had guessed the reason for the regular arrangement.

She approached the gate in School Lane and saw Mrs Falconer at the door. David Gorse helped her lift the pushchair inside.

'Cup of tea?' he asked, winking at Mrs Falconer. 'I've got some biscuits, plenty for four of us.'

He sat talking to Sadie while Sally made the tea and Mrs Falconer brought cakes to add to the biscuits. When they had finished and Mrs Falconer had returned to her part of the house. David stared at Sally and said, softly, 'I do admire you, Sally.'

'Me? Why?'

'The way you support Rhys. Oh, I know you pretend not to know where he is, but you send money, don't you?'

'It's none of your business what I do.'

'Knowing he committed those burglaries, and that the police want him for questioning, you still support him.' Sally said nothing, and he went on, 'He's a lucky man and I just hope he knows it. You deserve so much better than a weak man like Rhys.'

'Stop this,' she said and she stood, implying that he should leave, but he stood with her and held her arms.

'Sally, I know what he's like. We've known each other all our lives and he's weak. And you can add cowardly to that, sheltering behind a strong and brave woman like you.'

'Please go, David. And keep your suspicions to yourself, There are enough gossips in Tre Melin without you starting.'

'Don't forget I'm here when you need a friend.'

She didn't reply.

Valmai spent most of the following weekend trying to sort out the contents of her shed. She struggled to get in and push out some of the contents so she could at least see what she had kept all these years, 'Just in case.' She dragged everything she could move into a pile and had to climb out of the shed, having thrown it too close to the doorway. Each afternoon she did a little more and on Saturday morning, after struggling for an hour with a tea chest filled with boxes of screws and assorted nails and oddments of metal that she no longer remembered the use of, Netta from next door came out and offered help.

'No use me asking my Walter to help. It's as much as he can do to dress and feed himself, lazy so-and-so,' she muttered. 'Our Jimmy might enjoy giving a hand, though. Jimmy?' she shouted and a tousle-headed ten-year-old boy appeared in the doorway, a round of toast in his hand, jam decorating his freckled face.

'Mornin', Mrs Martin,' he called. 'There's a mess you've made in your garden.'

'Be'ave,' Netta scolded, but he grinned, unrepentant.

'Eric's coming later,' Valmai said. 'He'll soon tell me what to keep and what to throw away.'

'All of it, I'd say,' Netta muttered.

'Can I have that old toboggan? Your Rhys is too old for it now.'

'It's April. You'll wait a long time for some snow, young Jimmy.'

Jimmy came over, having wiped his sticky fingers on his jumper, and began helping her to sort out the muddle into various piles. There were lots of pieces of wood ranging from large planks and tree branches to small offcuts stored ready for firewood, but now Valmai piled the best of the small oddly shaped pieces, knowing that if she could persuade Gwilym to start making small toys they would be useful.

Eric came as arranged and when most of the contents were spread across the top of the garden he went inside to check on the building itself. He came out and shook his head. 'Rotten all along the bottom,' he reported, 'and the roof could give way if we had a storm.'

'It can be mended, though?' Valmai asked.

Again the shake of his head. 'Sorry, Val, but it's too far gone and the expense wouldn't be worth it. It'll never make a workshop. It's a bit too small too. You need a new one, I'm afraid.'

'Tea, anyone?' Gwilym called from the doorway.

Valmai hid her disappointment and instead said, 'I'll go to the timber yard. Sectional sheds are the cheapest, aren't they?'

'Not if we get some of the men together and make it ourselves.' He looked at Gwilym, who was watching from the doorway, sitting in his chair, a blanket covering his legs, waving a tea-cup. 'You'll have to design it, mind, Gwilym. Only you know what you'll need.'

'Too expensive,' Gwilym said, turning his chair to go back inside. 'Nice idea, but there's no way we can afford a new shed.' He was half-smiling, as though relieved that his idea had been vetoed by economics.

'We'll see about that,' Valmai muttered. She followed her husband back into the house with Eric and young Jimmy Prosser following. 'We'll have a cup of tea while we think about the best way to go about it,' she announced. She filled the kettle then turned to Gwilym. 'It's no use putting on a pout. A new shed you need and that's what you'll have.'

When Eric left, having promised to try and get a work team together, Jimmy went with him.

'Where are you off to, young Jimmy?' Eric asked.

'Don't know. Down through the wood to the old mill, probably. There's a pair of wrens nesting down there and would you believe a duck has made a nest on the paddles of the waterwheel. Lucky it no longer works, eh?'

'Be careful down there. That building is in a poor state.'

'A hundred and fifty years old and still stronger than Gwilym's shed!' Jimmy said.

'True enough,' Eric agreed with a laugh.

'Someone's been sleeping there.'

'What, recently?'

'I found some paper and a few crusts, and an apple core, and they weren't there the day before.' He put a hand in his pocket and showed Eric a small brass disc that at first looked like a coin. 'I found this too. What d'you think it is?'

Eric looked at it. It bore a number and the name of a coal mine. 'When the miners go down to start work they take a disc like this from the foreman and when they come back up they give him the disc back. That way the foreman knows how many men went down and knows that all the men are all safely out.' He was frowning as he handed it back to Jimmy, who examined it with interest. The mine was the one where Gwilym's father had worked. He was almost certain that the disk was the one proudly owned by Rhys. Did this mean Rhys had been there? Sleeping at the old mill? If he had then Gwilym and Valmai didn't know. He was their trusted friend and he would have been told.

'The new shed is the subject of one-sided discussions in our house,' Valmai complained to Netta. 'I'm determined we'll get one and Gwilym is insisting that we can't afford it and he isn't sure he'd work in it if we did. I point out a solution to every problem he comes up with and I'm talking to myself! Oh, Netta, why is he so defeatist?'

'Pride. Must be. After all, he was a cross-country runner, he coached the local under elevens rugby team, cricket in the summer. To have to give up all that is bound to have changed the poor man.'

'The rugby team would still like him to help but he won't pass through our gate. What do I have to do to make him face the world? He's done nothing wrong yet he's acting like a—'

'A criminal? Like your Rhys but with even less reason? They both faced trouble but dealt with it in opposite ways. Gwilym won't move and Rhys moved too far! They both gave up. Heard anything from your Rhys?'

Valmai shook her head. 'There's a card occasionally, usually from somewhere up north. Blackpool, North Wales, even Scotland.'

'Walking was his favourite pastime like his father, so perhaps he's just wandering.'

'If only he'd come home. The police haven't anything on him. They wanted to question him but he wasn't a suspect, yet he ran off before they could interview him. If they'd really wanted to talk to him you can't tell me they wouldn't have found him. They aren't stupid. But,' she added sadly, 'perhaps my son is.'

'There might have been some other reason he chose to leave, nothing to do with the robberies.' Netta was thinking of Sally, left to face the criticisms and bring up her baby on her own. Nothing had been said, but she'd always believed Rhys was the father of two-year-old Sadie. 'Good heavens, Valmai, I've just realized it's more than two years since he left.' Pointedly she added, 'Little Sadie was two a week or so back. Doesn't time fly?'

Valmai didn't reply.

When Netta went inside, Walter said, 'Still making excuses for that son of theirs, is she? Leaving that girl to cope alone. What sort of a man does that?'

'Not much better yourself,' Netta retorted. 'Leaving me to keep the family fed. Lazy you are, Walter Prosser. Time you got up and shifted yourself. Plenty of work out there for those who want it.'

'I've tried. There's nothing for me and you know it.'

'I know nothing of the sort. Idle, useless waste of breath you are.'

The argument went on and young Jimmy approached the house with his heart racing, aware that it could go on for a long time. He covered his ears and ran back along the path and out into the street.

Valmai was setting off for work and she called to him. 'Go in and have a piece of cake with Gwilym, why don't you?'

His footsteps slowed. 'Rowing again, they are,' he said. 'I hate it when they row. I'm invisible when they row.'

Valmai went back with him and had a quick word with Gwilym, who asked the boy if he fancied a bit of toast. Jimmy stayed until the shouting had subsided then went home. He picked up a chunk of bread, an apple and some crisps and went back out.

Jimmy spent a lot of time out of the house. He wandered around the fields south of Mill Road and spent a lot of time watching the activities around the stream that had once fed the huge wheel of the watermill. He took bread and an apple from his pocket and ate, throwing the crusts where the ducks would find them. Aimlessly strolling through the fields, he joined the main road not far from the Waterstones' house, where he sat on the wall and watched as men went in and out with discarded bricks, old and new wood. A few of the men stopped to talk to him, and one gave him a couple of sweets from his pocket.

Amy appeared at the window and she banged on the pane and made movements clearly telling him to go away. Pretending not to understand, he waved back cheerily. The front door opened and she came running out, flapping her arms as though he were a strange animal.

'Evenin', Mrs,' he said, amused by her behaviour and the peculiar headdress she wore. 'Why are you wearing a net curtain on your head?'

'Go away, you cheeky boy, and don't sit on my wall like that.'

'I wasn't hurting it!' he grumbled as he jumped down. He didn't move far, just a few inches away from the wall, and she continued to shoo him away.

She eventually went inside and Jimmy could hear her complaining to someone. Rick came out and walked towards him, but as Jimmy prepared to run he saw the man was smiling. 'I was only watching the men,' he protested.

'Of course. I understand that. I used to love to watch workmen myself. And the milkman and the postman, and when the gas or water board dug a hole, well, that was something that made me mitch from school once or twice,' Rick confided.

Jimmy stared at him. His jaw dropped in surprise. 'You aren't mad at me?'

'Don't worry about Amy. She's so busy at the moment, dealing with the workmen and arranging our wedding, she gets easily upset. She'll be fine once we're settled in.'

'You hope!' Jimmy said and hurried off. Perhaps Mum thought the same about my dad once, he thought sadly, as he headed for home.

His father was sitting at the table when he got in, his newspaper spread over the plates and condiments and bread set out for dinner. Walter didn't look up and Jimmy stood looking at him, trying to assess his mood. Walter wasn't very prepossessing. Bald, thin and wearing only a sleeveless vest with braces holding up a baggy pair of trousers. He needed a shave, his eyes darted from side to side and his lips moved as he continued to read the newspaper, but he looked calm enough. 'Want to see my painting, Dad?' Jimmy asked, fingering the disc he had found at the mill as though it were a talisman.

'What painting?' His father's eyes didn't leave the paper.

'I came second in a competition at school last week.' He ran to his room and took it carefully off the wall and ran back down. 'See?' he said, as Walter still didn't look up. 'Dad?'

Walter turned his head and glanced at the painting. 'What's it supposed to be?'

'Sheep, in a field with the mill in the distance.'

'Sheep? Funny sheep, boy. Big as cows they are. Better if they taught you something useful. Waste of time scribbling on paper if you ask me.' He turned back to his newspaper and Jimmy returned the painting to his room. It didn't go back on the wall: he stuffed it carelessly in a drawer.

He went next door and asked Gwilym if he'd help him make a wooden car for Sadie.

'Girls don't want cars,' Gwilym said. 'What about a doll?'

''Course they do!'

They made a simple shape and Gwilym carefully carved the wheels and the grille and Jimmy took it and played with Sadie for a while, then reluctantly, he went home. The only good thing about home was food, he decided.

For a week it rained every day and the contents of Valmai's shed were a gloomy sight. A gusting wind reduced the orderly piles into one confused scatter and Valmai began to wonder if the garden would ever return to normal. The rows of vegetables were lost to sight and the sticks ready for the runner beans were leaning drunkenly. Eric came between showers and promised help once the rain stopped.

Walter next door told them they were wasting their time even thinking about a new shed. He waved an arm towards the scattered oddments. 'You'll never have room for another shed. Where will you put that lot? For a start you'll have to have a bonfire and burn the lot of it, then you'll have a lot of clearing up, then you'll need a proper cement base, and where are you going to mix concrete, and then—'

'Come on, Walter, your tea's ready,' Netta shouted, with an expression of frustration on her sharp-featured face. 'They've got everything in hand. There's nothing Gwilym can't do when he sets his mind on it.'

'What d'you mean? Are you saying that I—' The rest was lost as the door slammed behind them.

Valmai stared at the chaos of her garden. Was Walter right? It did seem an impossible dream. She closed her eyes and imagined the new building with the strong workbench and the tools all set out conveniently, the lathe nearby, and Gwilym sitting on his chair patiently working on the figure of a small animal. It would happen. It must be possible. 'Gwilym,' she said as she shrugged off her raincoat, 'I think we need two sheds.'

'Don't be daft, love.'

'All right, one new one but something can be done about the old one, surely? Just for storage. I can't throw that lot out.' She gestured at the window where rain was running down and completely blocking the view of the chaos of her treasure. Flower pots, paint tins, picture frames, curtain rails and lasts of many sizes from when her father used to mend shoes. Panes of glass from a long-gone greenhouse. Nails and screws and drills of every imaginable size. 'I can always find something I need. It's a muddle to you but I know what's there and usually how to find it.'

'Hush now, love, the news is coming on.'

'Netta and Walter are having a television. They say we can go and watch it when there's something we'll enjoy.'

'No need. The wireless is good enough for us. Besides,' he added with a smile, 'I don't fancy sitting listening to Walter moaning for hours. I don't know how Netta puts up with him, d'you?'

Valmai could have replied that Netta didn't know how she managed to live with a man who had given up on everything. But she didn't.

Eric walked away from the post office with his pension. As usual he had divided it up into two envelopes. One paid his rent for the room, the rest was what he had to manage on for the week. He put the two envelopes in his jacket pocket then set off for a walk. The rain had finally relented and a weak sun was drying the ground, making misty patches in places. He felt the warmth on his back and slipped off his jacket, tucking it carelessly under an arm.

David Gorse was watching as the envelopes slipped out and fell to the ground. He was smiling as Eric wandered over the field towards the stream. There was no one in sight as he picked them up and turned away. 'Serve him right, the stupid old fool,' he muttered. 'Perhaps his bad luck will be my good luck.' He made for the betting shop and a search for a coincidental name.

It wasn't until he reached home that Eric missed the money. He called the landlady and put his hand in his pocket to pay her, then gasped when the pocket was empty.

'I – I seem to have – um lost my pension, Mrs Godfrey,' he said, taking off his jacket and searching fruitlessly in every pocket. 'It must have fallen out. I took off my jacket and carried it because it was so nice and warm, you see.'

Mrs Godfrey's expression hardened. 'I'm very sorry, Eric, but you know the rules. No money, no room. I've been kind to my tenants in the past and later found out the missing money had gone to the local pub or the bookies. I remain firm. No, I'm sorry but whatever the excuse the rule remains.'

'Until next week then, Mrs Godfrey.'

'I'm afraid so.'

Eric wasn't too upset. He had blankets in his room and extra clothes. Thankfully the weather was warmer and it was far from the first time he'd had to sleep under the stars. Food was the problem. He had very little money left from the previous week's pension but he knew that calling on friends would keep him from starvation and the bakers often gave him a few leftover pies and cakes. He went to see Gwilym but determined not to tell him about the loss of his week's money. People soon tire of moaners, even good people like Valmai and Gwilym, he thought.

David Gorse was attracted by the commotion around the back lane behind the Martins' house. The banging of hammers, chatter and laughter, plus, as he drew closer, the unmistakable sound of tea-cups on saucers.

He went to the end of the lane and looked towards the source of the activities. Must be important. Even Walter was there and actually carrying something! 'Morning,' he called as he walked towards the scene. 'What's happening? Not moving, are you?'

He saw Gwilym at the back door, sitting in his chair, a blanket covering his knees. 'Morning, Mr Martin. You the foreman then?'

'We're trying to sort out this lot and make room for a new shed,' Valmai explained. 'We could do with a hand if you're offering.'

'Can't the old shed be repaired?'

'Have a look,' Walter said. 'Too far gone, I reckon.'

David looked at the walls of the wooden shed. The base was rotten although the rest of the walls seemed fairly sound. The roof timbers needed a few replacements. The felt had rotted right away. 'I reckon I could fix it up if you get the timber,' he offered. 'It needs a good strong base and some replacement timber. The roof isn't too bad and if it's protected with a new felt—'

Valmai was surprised at David's interest; more so when he actually offered to do the work. She wondered what he'd ask in return. David Gorse wasn't one to help with favours. Better she paid him, keep things straight. The repaired building wouldn't be any use for Gwilym's workshop but it would be very useful for storage. Worth spending a little money on it.

The discussion continued for a while as Netta and Valmai provided tea and cakes, David and Gwilym drew plans and made lists, and Walter found a wheelbarrow, sat in it and fell asleep.

With a list of requirements prepared by Gwilym and David, Eric went to the timber merchants and ordered all they needed. Days passed and there was no sign of David Gorse. Eric called at his mother's house early one morning and she roused David from bed. Reluctantly he agreed to be at the Martins' place in an hour. Two hours later he arrived and rain prevented him from doing anything.

He looked at the wood and sneered. Waste of time trying to fix this, but he'd be sure to get a few pounds for his trouble – he'd protest at first but would take it, insisting it was to make them feel better.

Eric managed to survive the week without any money, mainly thanks to young Jimmy. It was on Monday morning when Jimmy was *mitching* from school, having decided that the day was better spent walking around the fields, that they met. Jimmy was at the edge of the shrubs and trees that had grown around the mill since it had fallen into disuse, when he heard a sound. There were the usual murmurings of the trees and the chuckling of the water past the unmoving wheel, but there was an air of stillness that was unusual. At this time of the year there should have been birdsong and they were silent.

He moved quietly through the trees, careful where he placed his feet and avoiding moving the branches until he was at a point where he could see the doorway of the mill. It was open, and he could hear someone whistling. He grinned. That sounded like old Eric.

He moved closer and joined in with the whistling of 'Que sera sera, whatever will be will be—'

'Good morning, Jimmy. No school today?'

'No, didn't feel like it.'

'That's a pity. You'll have an easier life if you work at school and get a good job.' Eric cleared away the evidence of his breakfast, and tucked his blankets behind a pile of wood.

'Yeah, yeah,' Jimmy sighed. 'I'm ten years old. How can I worry about when I'm twenty? Old that is, and ten is for having fun.'

Eric chuckled. 'I'm off to see Mr and Mrs Martin – coming my way? Or is that too close to home?'

'You said it!'

Eric waved goodbye and went to call on Gwilym. Valmai was always good for a piece of toast or a slice of cake.

Jimmy ran like the wind and staggered, puffing with the effort into Valmai's kitchen. 'Old Eric's sleeping rough again. Someone pinched his pension money.' Valmai thanked him for telling them and added a couple more sausages to the frying pan.

Jimmy was satisfied. She'd make sure the old man didn't go hungry. At the time school would close he went home and insisted he was starving. He planned to hide some food and, after dark, take it to the mill for Eric. Satisfied he had done a good deed, he threw his satchel on the floor and went to change out of his rather muddy school clothes.

That night, when his parents were asleep, Jimmy went to the old mill and left food for Eric, who was snoring contentedly in a corner of what had once been the room where the flour sacks were filled, the sound of the stream his lullaby.

At the end of the week, Eric returned to Mrs Godfrey, but to a smaller and less comfortable room right at the top of the stairs, which was all she had available.

It was May before David actually made a start on the repair to Valmai's shed, and Gwilym, who went up after everyone had gone to see what progress had been made, was worried. The structure didn't look safe and he didn't want Valmai to risk going inside. The sound base they had discussed hadn't been added and the replaced wood wasn't attached firmly to the strongest of the original. Some of the posts bought for strengthening were unused and thrown behind the shed. During the night after David declared he had done all he could, the whole thing fell down. David hid his pleasure well as he commiserated.

Sitting on the wheelbarrow beside Gwilym, staring at the untidy pile of old and new wood that had cost them so much money, Valmai wanted to weep. In a rare explosion of anger she turned to Gwilym. 'You could have prevented this! If you'd been there instead of staying out of sight, seen what he was doing, made sure he was making it safe, this wouldn't have happened!'

Gwilym held her in his arms, hid her face against his shoulder. 'I'm sorry, love, but I just can't.'

She relented then. 'I know, Gwilym, I know.'

It was Rick who rescued the shed. He called to ask a question about local deliveries and saw Eric trying to gather the best of the timber. There were piles of unused planks at Waterstones' old house, and together with one of the lorry drivers he delivered it.

With Eric and the lorry driver helping and Walter sitting on a wall and offering advice, they arranged for the lorry driver and his mates to repair the sad building and make sure it was safe.

Eric slept in the mill again so his pension could pay some of the cost, without Valmai being aware. Besides, he hoped that the following week would mean he'd have his old room back. The present one was up thirty-five steps and seriously dreary.

'There's that tramp again!' Amy said, pointing through the window to where Eric was strolling past. To her outrage he stopped, waved, then sat on the garden wall. 'Tell him to go, Rick. I won't have him coming around here.'

Rick walked to where Eric was sitting. 'Hello, again,' he said. 'Do you live near here?'

Eric pointed along the road, 'I have a room in a small boarding house. I've lived there since I lost my job at the furniture factory,' he explained. 'The rent is cheap and she gives me a good breakfast.'

'But you have to stay out during the day?'

'Mostly. Except Thursdays when she visits her daughter in Cardiff.' Eric stared at Rick, his blue eyes shrewd and his lips beginning to smile. 'Wants me to clear off, does she? Your wife?'

'Well, she's a bit stressed at present. The house and the wedding plans, you know how it is.'

Eric nodded. 'I'm off to see young Jimmy Prosser. Know him, do you? He's a bit of a wanderer too.'

'That's the young boy about eight or nine who lives next to Valmai and Gwilym?'

'Ten he is. He's a good lad. He helped me when I lost my rent and had to sleep in – somewhere else,' he amended. 'Well, I'd better go.' He smiled. 'You can tell your wife I've been told off good and proper!'

Rick saw Jimmy later that day and went out to talk to him. 'Hello, where are you off to, young Jimmy?'

'Who wants to know?'

'Only me.' Rick smiled. 'I'm not MI5! I was talking to Eric and he told me your name.' He began to walk alongside Jimmy and asked a few questions. 'Nice place to live, is it? I mean, we're moving in in a few months and we don't know anyone.'

'It's all right, I suppose. I like it round here. Everything except the school. It's years yet before I can leave. Daft if you ask me.'

'Mmm. I've noticed you wandering around during school hours,'

Rick said. 'Look, I'm not encouraging you to mitch, but if you want something to do at the weekends, come and see Amy and me. Any time, just give a knock and if we're there you'll be welcome.'

Jimmy didn't feel too sure about his wife, but he nodded. 'If I'm not too busy,' he replied.

The following weekend Jimmy visited twice. The first time he helped in the garden, for which Amy rewarded him with a bar of chocolate, and the second time Rick introduced him to some of his favourite books. He soon realized the boy was not a very good reader so he read to him, then listened patiently as Jimmy read. As soon as Jimmy was bored with struggling to read, Rick took over again for a while and Jimmy began to enjoy the stories about the countryside written by T.G. Evens, a man who called himself Romany and who lived in a caravan with his dog and his young friends Muriel and Doris. He could relate to the stories as the descriptions of the wild animals and birds referred to were known to him.

Amy was surprisingly pleased at Jimmy's progress, stating that Rick's interest in children was one of the reasons she loved him. He seemed able to become friends with anyone of any age and from any background. She had taught for a while but meeting Rick and making plans to marry had persuaded her to give up her career, not without some relief. She knew she wasn't a natural teacher, not like Rick would have been. She was too impatient and, she admitted to herself, too critical. 'I can't help the way I am,' she often told Rick proudly, expecting praise. 'I strive for perfection and expect others to do the same.'

'Perfection is different when you're only ten years old.'

As well as reading, Rick introduced Jimmy to chess, explaining every move throughout the games at first then playing without comment as Jimmy became familiar with the moves. As he had guessed, Jimmy was very bright but had suffered from a lack of encouragement and self-confidence. Jimmy tried to tell his father about his improved reading skills and his introduction to the fascinating game of chess, but Walter didn't do anything but nod, his eyes glued to the newly acquired television or his newspaper.

Netta tried to show interest but her eyes glazed as he explained about kings, queens, bishops, knights, rooks and pawns. Jimmy didn't mind. His new friends were interested in him and Gwilym offered him a game – if Valmai could find his chess set.

Although Amy was happy to spend a little time with Jimmy and approved of Rick's efforts to encourage the boy, she was still very prickly with most of the neighbours. Sally Travis, she ignored. Accepting Milly Sewell's opinion that she was one of the criminal class made her decide not to give even a polite 'good morning', as that might be misconstrued as a friendly gesture.

Determined not to give up on the albeit slight chance of Gwilym starting to work, Valmai withdrew their savings and bought a shed. The workmen who delivered it also erected it, electricity and water was laid on and that Saturday morning in August, Gwilym went to inspect it.

'It isn't finished yet,' Valmai told him. 'On Monday there's a surprise coming.'

'Not more expense?' he said softly. 'We've spent so much, and so far there's only the building. There's the inside to set up before I can do anything, places for tools and a bench for me to work on.'

'No more expense, I promise. I've spent the last penny I intend to spend. Now it's up to you to make money. Of course you might like to take our wonderful friends for a pint in the Dragon. They've earned it. Ages since you've been there.'

He looked at her sorrowfully. 'Not yet.'

'Then we'll get a few drinks and they can come here. Right?'

Eric had been to see the builders that were clearing the remains of the furniture factory ready for building houses and explained what he needed. Help was promised for Monday morning.

'If only Rhys would come home, everything would be perfect,' Valmai sighed as she closed her eyes and imagined Gwilym settle himself against the bench in the new shed.

In Bristol, Rhys was picking up the latest brown envelope from Sally and felt that his guilt and shame must be visible on his face. He walked out of the café as eyes followed him, convinced they all knew how badly he was treating someone who loved him, someone who didn't deserve to be stuck with someone as dishonest as himself.

*

Someone else was thinking of Rhys that day. It was more than a month since the date she had expected Rhys to come home, face the police and tell everyone they were to be married. She had written to him, trying not to beg, but asking when he expected to appear. The situation had to be resolved soon.

Although she hadn't been to the doctor to get it confirmed, Sally knew she was again expecting a child. Four months, during which she had fought against morning sickness and lethargy, had passed and soon her condition would be clear for everyone to see and she knew she could ignore it no longer. Rhys must come home. Once she had spoken to him, then she'd go and start the procedures for the baby's care. How she would manage, that was a very different thing. They wouldn't have much money at first, and how could she work and cope with two small children? How would she feed them? She had to persuade him to stay, face the police and answer any questions. There hadn't been any talk about his guilt apart from people like Milly Sewell, and the Waterstones – who had altered details slightly, just enough to build rumours about Rhys's involvement, rumours that had made Rhys run away, afraid he would lose the chance of training as a teacher if accusations by the police resulted in an arrest.

It was Tuesday, the day she went to the butcher's, and Milly was certain to be there. Would she guess? Would she be the first to point out to others that the unmarried mother was expecting again and with no sign of a husband?

Fortunately she was delayed and the shop was empty when she went to buy her midweek order. That simple reprieve made the day just a little happier.

Gwilym heard the sound of activity at the end of the garden and cautiously peeped out through the curtains. Six of the men he had once worked beside were struggling to fit the bench into the shed. The door had been taken off and lay on the path alongside the gate, also removed to allow them to deliver the bench. Gwilym opened the door and, hiding his legs beneath the blanket, waved. He felt ashamed. These men had lost their jobs, too. One suffered from arthritis, another had poor sight, but they had found work. Over tea and pasties he learned about others. Ted and Arthur Jones had gone to Australia. Peter Powell was in London, Maldwyn Porter had been killed in a fight in Liverpool aboard a ship. Then there was Walter, idling his time away being supported by Netta – who had found another job as soon as the closure had been announced. He should have done the same after the accident, not hidden here and allowed his wife to feed him. Guilt was a severe pain but it didn't force him to go outside and join them. He'd left it too late. 'I'll make tea,' he called. 'Come when you're ready.'

Valmai came down to pick up a bag of tools she had put ready. 'Come on, Gwilym, you can face your friends, surely? They need to know where you want things placed. They need your help.'

'I am helping. I'm making the tea,' he muttered, wheeling himself back inside the kitchen.

Patching up the old shed hadn't resulted in a beautiful building and by comparison with the new one it looked even worse. But to Valmai both sheds looked beautiful. By the evening everything was in place.

As soon as the men had gone, Gwilym went up to see what they had done and he felt as weepy as a child. The bench was perfect and the lathe, bought by Valmai as part of the surprise, had been set up exactly where it was most convenient. On the bench was a drawing pad and an assortment of pencils. Hesitantly at first, he picked up the pencil and began to draw. An ark, filled with couples of animals, and Noah and his family. Valmai crept up and watched for a few minutes, then with fingers tightly crossed she went back to the kitchen.

Rhys alighted from the train at the station a few miles from Tre Melin. He didn't want to be seen by someone who knew him, although this time he would visit his parents. It would have to be after dark, which, as it was August, would be quite late. He went first to the mill and deposited his rucksack there. The sun had shone all day and the evening was so light it seemed set to go on and on, as though darkness would never come. He sat in the ruined mill, staring out at the trees grown so tall since he had played there as a child.

A movement caught his eye and he stiffened and prepared to get away. He didn't recognize the boy, and as he concentrated on him, he realized he was talking to someone in a low voice. Rhys climbed up into the loft and hoped they wouldn't come in. His belongings were there; there had been no time to move them.

'See,' he heard the boy say, 'on that paddle wheel? That was where the ducks raised their young. Gone now they have but perhaps they'll come again next year.'

Rhys could now see the man with the boy but didn't recognize him either. He'd been away two years. People come and go, he thought – perhaps they were new neighbours.

'Want to go inside?' the boy asked.

'I think it's getting a bit late, Jimmy.'

'Jimmy Prosser,' Rhys murmured. Taller and thinner in the face, but I recognize him now. The man's a stranger, though.

'Tell you what,' the man said. 'We'll come back tomorrow. Your father will he wondering where you are.'

'No, he won't, Rick,' Jimmy said. 'He's never bothered as long as I'm out of his hair.' Rhys saw a slight flash of white teeth as the boy grinned. 'Get out of my hair, that's what he says, and him as bald as a coot!' The sound of their laughter faded as they moved away.

Rhys followed them but turned across the fields towards School Lane before they reached the houses. The curtains were open in the room Sally rented. He couldn't go in. Darting between bushes that offered cover, he picked up the pebble that was their sign and placed it in the middle of the porch. Risking a knock at the door, he ran back into the protection of the trees. There he waited until the door opened and Sally picked up the pebble, looked around for a few seconds then went back inside, leaving the door open. The curtains were drawn and moments later he was inside and holding Sally in his arms.

Chapter Three

RHYS WAS AFRAID to stay with Sally very long, but after their emotional reunion they talked about their future plans. Sally had been longing to tell him the news about a new baby, but she held back. She was waiting for him to tell her he was coming home, their long separation was at an end. Then she would tell him. Everyone would know about their secret love, about her support for him. She was a little surprised that he hadn't noticed her thickening waist but presumed he would remark on it as soon as she told him about the baby.

'I'm so ashamed of the way I've left you to deal with Sadie and the gossip,' he said, holding her close. 'I know you agreed – in fact it was your idea for me to get my qualification before risking talking to the police – but I still feel guilty.'

'Two years out of a lifetime isn't much when the rest of our lives will be so perfect.'

'I'll never forget what you're doing, my darling Sally. I only hope it does have a satisfactory ending. There have been no more burglaries, and that, together with the fact I ran away, could make persuading the police I'm innocent very difficult.'

'Looking back, was it the right thing to do? There has been no contact from the police. I'm sure they'd have found you if they'd really wanted to talk to you. A few miles wouldn't deter them, would it?' He didn't reply and she asked, 'Why did you leave? What convinced you that the police would accuse you? More than two years have passed and now I can't remember what happened to make you run away.'

Rhys had never told her of the threat hanging over him from the plot set by David Gorse. He changed the subject with a brief silence and a shrug, and her heart raced at his refusal to discuss it. She waited in silence, hoping he would explain, but when he spoke again it was about their daughter, asking about the latest developments. Then he asked casually, 'See much of David Gorse these days? Did he find another job after the factory closed?'

'No, he just hangs around, being kept by his doting mother, and complaining a lot about how life is unfair.'

'He was sweet on you once. And he's always hated me.'

'He calls often and tries to become a friend, but I've always suspected he helped to spread the rumours. Many were easily convinced that you were a thief even though they disliked the man.' She tried again to make him talk about the reasons he left but again he was evasive.

'Don't let's talk about stuff like that. The few hours we have together are so valuable, darling Sally. I miss you so much when I'm away, I can't think of anything but being here, close to you.' He kissed her but there was something restrained about it. He wasn't acting as the words implied; his mind was elsewhere.

She began to have fearful doubts. Too many questions without answers, no date even hinted at for his return, no news about applying for a job. What wasn't he telling her?

Rhys's thoughts were on David. He had often wondered whether David's attraction to the shy, quiet Sally had been the reason for creating incriminating evidence then not using it. He'd had a few anxious moments after leaving, wondering whether Sally had been tempted by the presence of David's admiration and the absence of his. Thank goodness his trust had been justified. Sally had already been pregnant when he'd left although he hadn't known until later, at which point Sally had agreed to continue without him, support him and keep his whereabouts a secret. The thought of David bringing up his daughter was the stuff nightmares are made of.

'Darling,' he said with a sigh, 'I have to go.'

'Just another hour?' she pleaded. She was filled with increasing alarm. Something was wrong.

'No, I hate having to leave but this time I must see Mam and Dad. They've survived all this time on occasional postcards to remind them I'm still alive. It's time to trust them with our secret.'

Your secret, she thought, not mine. She stood still for a long moment when, after a prolonged goodbye, he slipped silently out of the house.

Sally was left with the feeling that their meeting was unsatisfactory, unfinished. She usually felt a glow of happiness when he had stayed for a few hours. Stolen hours, secret loving hours, and she daydreamed happily for days after his visits; of how soon they would be together, sharing their secret love. Secret love, how romantic it sounded. Yet this time she was filled with deep disappointment. If his exams were finished, why hadn't he told her he was coming home to face the accusations and get their relationship on a firm base?

She walked to the door, opened it and looked out. She wanted to run after him, stand beside him as he told his parents the truth but she couldn't leave Sadie. She tried to calm herself, she mustn't get impatient after all this time. He was probably already planning their reunion and intending a wonderful surprise. She slid into her lonely bed and tried to relive the short time he had been with her, remembering how he had looked down at their sleeping daughter with such love and pride. It would be all right and very soon the empty years, the accusations, the sneering remarks would be nothing more than unimportant memories. She slipped into sleep, imagining his expression of joy when he learned about their second child.

Rhys moved slowly and carefully through the gardens, taking the long way round to keep out of sight for longer, cutting through the corner of the woods that led down to the old mill; a scene of his many fights with David Gorse. Feeling his way, avoiding anything that would give away his presence, his shadow an occasional companion, he heard nothing to indicate the presence of another soul. It was reminiscent of the games he used to play as a small boy, he mused, unaware then of how useful it would be to move silently all these years later.

Jimmy Prosser saw him and watched as he made his way towards Valmai and Gwilym's house. He had been on the way to the mill and wondered whether the man had been sleeping there and whether it was he who had lost the mine worker's token some months ago. Putting down the cakes and fruit he'd brought for a lonely midnight meal, he followed, excited at the impromptu game. Although they had been neighbours until a few years ago, Jimmy didn't recognize him, partly because he wouldn't expect to see him there.

Rhys's eyes became accustomed to the poor light, and as he neared the houses, the faint glow from the streetlamps at first made the darkness more intense, then the extra light added to his ability to see his way. He cut into a path leading from Mill Road to the old mill and quickly became aware of someone following him and he made a circle and came up behind Jimmy. He was relieved to see it was a young boy, although he didn't recognize him in the shadowy semi-darkness. He stood perfectly still until the boy had moved away, using his ears to ensure he hadn't turned off the path to do the same as he had done and come up behind him.

Puzzled by the man's disappearance, Jimmy shrugged and went back for his midnight picnic, disappointed that he wouldn't have company. Even David Gorse, whom he sometimes met and who ate more than his share, was better than no one.

Rhys knocked softly on his parents' door. He heard his mother say, 'That'll be Netta, run out of milk or something. Come in, Netta,' then as the living room door opened she leapt to her feet. 'Rhys!'

Gwilym almost rose to his feet as well, forgetting in that moment of utter disbelief that he had been wheelchair-bound for over two years. He sat back and held out both arms. Rhys held them both, emotion making speech impossible.

'Mam, Dad, I'm so sorry for what I've put you through.'

'Why?' Gwilym said, the words choked and guttural. 'That's what we want to know. Why did you leave?' He couldn't ask whether his son had been guilty of the thefts of which he'd been accused but the words were there, wanting to be said.

'Guilty or not we're your parents and we'd have supported you. Surely you know that?'

Valmai was less inhibited. 'Did you do all those burglaries?'

Rhys led his mother to the couch where they sat close to Gwilym in his chair. He reached for their hands and said, 'No, Mam, I didn't, but there's some evidence that says I did. I can't explain, but I can tell you that if I'd stayed the evidence would have been handed to the police together with a story to convince them and I'd have been arrested. I had to get away. Sally willingly agreed to help me, but other things occurred and – nothing that can't be sorted. Very soon everything will be all right and I can come back.' He smiled as he spoke; it sounded so easy he almost convinced himself. Then the image of David's sneering face filled his mind and he felt that hope draining away. Perhaps his only chance was to stay away, take Sally and Sadie with him and begin a new life far away from his parents and the town that he'd always called home.

'And Sally?' Valmai asked, a frown creasing her brow, glancing at Gwilym.

Gwilym shifted in his chair. 'I know Sadie's your daughter, Rhys. That's the part I find most difficult to understand.'

'You knew?' Valmai gasped. 'I've been so careful not to say a word.'

'I might be housebound but it's my leg that's missing, not my brain,' he said, and smiled at her to avoid sounding critical. 'I guessed as soon as the news of her baby reached us but didn't say anything in case you were disapproving of the girl, then after weeks passed and you said nothing it seemed best to remain silent.'

Valmai laughed then. 'Talk about secrets! What a family, eh?'

Gwilym wasn't laughing. 'Well?' he said, staring at his son. 'What justification d'you give for leaving Sally to face everything on her own? The birth of a baby, the comments of vicious women like Milly Sewell? Was that necessary too? Denying that the baby's yours, are you?'

'Dad, we've stayed in touch. I've visited them when I dared. I couldn't risk coming here, I'm sorry. But you're right about her having to face the birth and the gossip on her own. Believe me, it wasn't something I wanted to do but she insisted. She knew that if there had been even a hint of trouble with the police I might have lost my freedom. Sally is a remarkable young woman and I'll never forget her loyalty and bravery. She is a wonderful person and I'm very lucky to have her love.'

'And Sally, does she have yours?' Gwilym asked softly. 'Or is she just useful?'

'The most important things in my life are Sally and Sadie and everything else comes a poor second.' He eased himself away from them and stood up. 'Now I have to go. It gets light around five and I have to be well away from here by then.' He paused and added, 'Sorry to sound dramatic, but please don't mention my visit, or that

I've been living in Bristol. Just in case the police are given the misleading evidence. For one thing I don't want Sally to be hassled.'

Valmai was tearful after he left, hurt by the revelation that Sally had known how to get in touch and had seen him, while they hadn't received more than a few misleading postcards. As though guessing her thoughts, Gwilym said, 'We're too close to a lot of houses. Sally lives down in School Lane. Besides, we have friends and might have been tempted to tell someone out of pride, rather than have everyone think he'd forgotten us.'

'And now? We're trusted with his secret after more than two years so what's changed?'

'We know a part of the reason. And inviting Sally and Sadie to visit won't add to the faded gossip, will it?'

A week later Sally brought her little girl to tea. Young Jimmy from next door came in and surprised them by getting on the floor with a couple of books Valmai had bought and entertaining the little girl. He didn't read well and Valmai quietly helped when he stumbled over words.

Some gossip resulted from the visit, mainly encouraged, unsurprisingly, by Milly Sewell but as there was little to add, it quickly died. In late September it began again. Sally's pregnancy was becoming impossible to hide.

Milly was walking past and as usual she gave Sally a searching look then asked, 'All right, are you? You and your poor little fatherless child?'

Sally ignored her but Milly's sharp eyes noticed something Rhys had not. 'You're never expecting again! Don't deny it. I can see from your face that I'm right! Haven't you got any shame? Pity help that poor little girl being brought up by a mother who takes men to her bed without a thought for anyone else.'

Sally began to protest, longing to explain, but she knew she couldn't. Her promise to Rhys must be kept. Instead she hotly denied it and dared Milly to repeat her lies. Milly watched as Sally, red-faced and distressed, hurried away. 'Mrs Falconer first, I think,' she muttered.

Amy and Rick were still appearing at the Waterstones' house during the evenings and on Sundays. The house was beginning to look ready for residents again after the upheavals and Jimmy began to be a regular visitor. He helped with some of the chores and was rewarded by a few hours of their attention. Not being a capable reader had made Rick believe he had some problems but his ability with the game of chess changed his mind. He was a quick learner and after a dozen lessons, going through the game explaining his moves, Rick found him a capable player. One Sunday at the end of September, he was presented with his own chess set. 'Perhaps you can teach your father,' Amy suggested.

Jimmy only laughed, but when he went home, proud of his new ability, he did show the figures to his father, explaining what they were and the moves they could make. That night he heard his parents quarrelling.

He stepped out on to the landing and heard the gruff voice of his father. 'Turning the boy's head!' he was shouting. 'Giving him games he can't play. Chess isn't for the likes of us and it's stupid to think he can learn.'

'Glad you should be that someone's taking an interest. That's more than you've ever done, Walter Prosser! You never wanted him.'

'You're right there. I didn't! The boy's useless. Gets on my nerves.'

Jimmy slapped his hands over his ears and hid under the covers. Why did his father hate him so much? What was wrong with chess? When he woke the following morning he looked for the beautiful chess pieces and board and found them thrown into the ash bin.

Aware that her new baby was soon to be a new chapter in the local gossip, Sally left Sadie with Mrs Glover and went to tell Valmai and Gwilym. Thanks to Milly, Valmai already knew. Gwilym was angry, not with Sally but with his son.

You'll have to come here and be looked after by us,' Valmai said, but Sally shook her head.

'I've coped for more than two years and I want to leave things as they are,' she said. 'I agreed to this and I made up my mind that I'd deal with everything that happened without involving anyone else.'

'We aren't just everyone else, Sally, love. We're Sadie's grandparents and I don't mind who knows it.'

'I do.' Sally smiled to make the words sound less harsh. 'It was my decision to help him and I want to see it through till the end. It can't be any worse than the last time and I don't want you involved in the gossip. When the explanations come there'll be a few red faces around here.'

Valmai couldn't see why. An unmarried mother of two – how could anyone be less critical once Rhys admitted to being the father? He'd left Sally to deal with it alone. Hardly a praiseworthy act. She said nothing more. Sally needed help and help she would get.

Sally went back to her two rooms after picking up Sadie from Mrs Glover, smiling happily. Any day now she would hear from Rhys and this awful period in her life would end. She felt strong and capable, restless with unspent energy. Mrs Falconer was out and to surprise her she swept the yard then hosed it, the water rising in the air to amuse her daughter, catching the sun and falling like diamonds. Sadie shrieked with delight and Sally took off her shoes and socks and let her paddle in the resulting stream. Then she took off her own shoes and holding hands they danced through the sparkling water. Hugging her daughter after drying her and dressing her in warm socks, Sally felt surprisingly happy. Soon, everything would be all right.

Giving Sadie a few toy building bricks to occupy her she started preparing their meal. She was singing when she heard Mrs Falconer come in. 'Cup of tea?' she called and was surprised when, in a subdued voice, her landlady declined. Then she heard the lower voice of Mr Falconer and guessed that his presence had been the reason for the refusal. She was surprised when Mrs Falconer didn't knock and pop her head around the door. They talked often and it was unusual for there not to be some kind of greeting.

It was after she had put Sadie to bed that a knock on the door heralded the appearance of Mrs Falconer and when she opened the door she was startled to see her husband was with her, both looking uneasy. Sally's immediate thought was that they had guessed about the new pregnancy and she wished she had spoken to them sooner. But surely that couldn't be the reason for the serious faces? 'Is something wrong?' she asked.

'I'm afraid so,' Mr Falconer said.

'I'm sorry, dear,' added his wife. 'I should have told you before this.'

Mr Falconer gave a nervous cough and said, 'We have to ask you to leave.'

'What? But why? What have I done?'

As though she hadn't spoken he went on, 'One illegitimate child was difficult for us, but you're expecting again and, well, with no husband and no boyfriend, it's no good, Sally. People gossip and I – we can't have this any longer.'

'I'm sorry, dear,' Mrs Falconer repeated. 'It's the gossip, you see.'

'Who told you? Milly, I presume.'

'She could never resist a bit of gossip. Sorry, my dear.'

'I'll start looking first thing tomorrow. Thank you for your kindness. I've been so happy living here with you. But you're right, this unfortunate situation is more than I can expect you to cope with. I'll move as soon as I find a place.' She was stunned by the interview and too numb to cry.

Washing her face, she put on a little makeup and asked if Mrs Falconer would stay with Sadie for an hour while she went to see someone who might help. She never went out in the evenings except in the summer when she took Sadie with her and Mrs Falconer was surprised, and ashamed, so she willingly agreed.

Sally was intending to go and see Eric to ask if there were any rooms to rent in the awful boarding house in which he lived but instead she walked towards the old mill. This wasn't the time for conversation or planning her next move; she needed to be on her own to accept what had happened, let the shock of it shower over her and gradually subside.

It wasn't quite dark and the woods held no fear for her as she stepped out along the narrow path towards the mill. If birds sang or small animals shuffled around in the undergrowth she was unaware. She was in a cocoon of misery, unable to think of anything but that the last thread of normality was being snapped. That she had no one to blame but herself, her carelessness when Rhys came for those few wonderful hours, made it harder to bear. Why had she been so careless? Why wasn't he here?

She stopped and listened when she reached the clearing where the abandoned building stood. The only sound was the low murmur of the stream bypassing the enormous wheel to which it had given life, now leaving it without movement except for the weeds covering the paddles that slowly waved when coaxed by the wind. She went up stone steps and into the first room where the fearsome-looking cog wheels were still in place, then climbed up the wooden stairs, dangerous in places but still giving access to the room where flour sacks were once filled.

The shock had stilled her brain and although she tried, no logical thoughts seeped in and she sat and looked into nothingness as the darkness came more complete. After an hour she became aware of being chilled; she was wearing a thin dress and hadn't stopped to collect a coat. Rousing herself, she made her way cautiously down the wooden stairs. No decisions had been made except her determination not to accept help from Rhys's parents. This was her problem and she would solve it.

She was walking back towards School Lane when she heard someone call. She turned and allowed the man to catch up. It was Rick Perry, whom she had briefly met.

'You're out late, Miss Travis,' he said. 'And not suitably dressed for this cool evening. You should look after yourself more.'

To her consternation she began to cry. Rick said nothing; he just put an arm around her shoulders and held her until the sobs had ceased.

'Good heavens, you're so cold! Here, take my coat.' Without protest she allowed him to slip his jacket around her, felt the warmth of it soothe her. She had always refused to discuss her situation but now she said, 'I have to leave the rooms I've rented since before Sadie was born and I don't know what to do.'

'It can't be that difficult to find a place to live. I'll ask around if you like. I haven't actually moved in yet but I'm already getting to know the local people.'

'Thank you,' she whispered, 'but I'll be all right. I'll ask at the place where Eric lives. You know Eric?'

'I know Eric and I know the place where he lives and you can't possibly live there.' he said firmly.

'I doubt whether I'll have much choice.'

'Did the landlady tell you why she wants you to leave?'

Taking a deep breath, wondering why she was talking about this to a comparative stranger, she replied, 'I'm going to have another baby and I think it's embarrassing for Mr Falconer.'

'More reason for you not to consider living at that place where Eric lives,' he said firmly. 'You'll need somewhere far better than that for the new baby, little Sadie and yourself.' She said nothing and he was silent for a while, his arms still around her shoulders, aware of the comfortable sensation of holding her and sharing his warmth. Then he asked softly, 'And the father? Can't he help?

'Soon,' she replied. 'He'll be back soon.'

Back from where? he wondered, but he dared not ask anything further. He knew this young unhappy woman would need help and if he pressed too far too soon he wouldn't be the one she approached. He knew with certainty that he wanted to be the one she turned to. 'Come on, I'll walk you back home,' he said. 'You need a hot drink and a good night's sleep.' He left her after a brief word with Mrs Falconer.

When Rick reached the house where he lived with his parents, Amy was there. 'Darling, where have you been?' she asked, concern clouding her wide blue eyes. 'We've been worried.'

'Worried?' He laughed. 'I'm a bit old for kidnap and too wise to fall into a ditch. I've been wandering through the woods beyond the house, exploring the area. It got late and I was listening to the sounds of the night.'

Amy hugged him. 'Such a daydreamer, isn't he, Mrs Perry? I don't know what I'll do with him.'

Her words, spoken in an almost childish manner, irritated him. Then he was ashamed. He had been out late and she must have been waiting, expecting him to come home straight after work. 'Sorry, love. I should have let you know where I was going.'

'I did need to see you,' she replied, a little edgily. 'Mummy has chosen the material for your suit and selected the style, but you really have to go and see the tailor and let him take your measurements. Time is moving on,' she added playfully to soften the sharp tone she had used.

'I can't arrange anything this week. I've asked Eric to help me clear the rubble from the bottom of the garden ready to set out the vegetable plot. The builders piled it up just where I asked them not to. I'll dig a deep trench to put the kitchen waste in throughout the winter, then fill it up in the spring ready for the runner beans.'

'Don't do that, darling. I thought I told you, I explained to them that the rubble was needed there to build a platform on which the pond will sit.'

'We'll sink a pond, surely?'

She laughed. 'No, of course not, silly. We don't want wild things crawling in, do we?' She turned to Rick's parents for them to join in the laughter. 'It will be raised with a wall around it so we can sit there and watch the fish.'

Rick felt a grey disappointment hovering around his eyes. The garden was to have been his area and slowly but deliberately, all the decisions had been taken away. The house and the garden, everything about this wedding and home-making, would have been chosen by Amy and her mother. Even the material and style of his suit. He glanced at his father and saw that he was staring at him, a quizzical expression on his kindly face.

'Come on, Amy, I'll walk you home.' Abruptly he reached for her coat, folded and neatly placed on the back of a chair, and offered it up for her to slip on. She waved a little girl's goodbye with an opening and closing fist and he led her to the door. Outside, she turned into his arms and kissed him. 'I've been longing to do that since the moment you walked in,' she whispered.

'Me too,' he said, but he was lying. Something had changed and it was more than irritation about having his plans for the garden over-ruled. Tomorrow he would go at lunchtime and see the tailor, where he would make a few decisions of his own.

Valmai heard about Sally's search for somewhere to live and she went around to ask again if she would move in with her and Gwilym. 'Just till you find something suitable,' she explained. 'I know you wouldn't want to live with us permanently.' She was disappointed when Sally shook her head.

'I'll come and see you both often,' Sally promised. 'But I have to manage on my own. It's a promise I made to myself.'

'There's no shame in accepting help.'

'Specially when it's so kindly meant,' Sally agreed, patting Valmai's hand affectionately. 'Thank you and thank Mr Martin for me, but I need to cope on my own.'

'If you're sure.' She sighed. 'Have you asked around yet? There are always a few people looking for a decent lodger.'

'Not really. There's a room vacant where Eric lives if I'm desperate.' She laughed at the shock registering on Valmai's face.

'No, don't worry, I couldn't live there. I'd rather camp in the old mill!' She wondered anxiously whether she might have to change her mind. Thanks to Milly's wicked tongue, many thought of her as an immoral woman, not the kind of person who could be described as a decent lodger.

Valmai went home feeling unsettled. What was the matter with Rhys? He had left that young woman to cope with everything that had happened and she couldn't do a thing to help her. Surely he'd come home now a second baby was on the way. Then she wondered whether he had been told, or whether Sally's determination to cope alone had prevented her telling him.

As she reached the back gate she heard the sound of hammer on chisel and her heart lifted. At least Gwilym was beginning to accept his situation and was starting to work again. She went in to see the row of unfinished animals on a shelf near where he was working. The basic shapes were done and the small models would be finished by hand and painted before he would offer any for sale. Some were already complete and she admired them before going in to prepare their meal. 'Sorry I'm late, I called to see Sally. Will a sandwich do?'

Jimmy went to school and sat through a few lessons but his mind was not on the teacher's voice or the book they were to have studied. He was thinking about the woods and the fox he had seen the previous evening. At lunchtime he went home with no intention of going back to the classroom. His mother was out and she had left a few sandwiches and a packet of crisps. He put them in his school bag with a few more slices of bread and some cake, then made himself some toast. Tonight he'd picnic in the mill. Leaving food there every night had encouraged the fox to visit and he looked forward to the day when the animal would accept his presence and not run away from him.

Since it had fallen into disuse, the old mill had been a popular meeting place for children, walkers and lovers. It was close to a path leading to the next village, Frog Moor, so it was in regular use during the day when the weather allowed. As September moved on and autumn made its presence felt, Jimmy saw fewer people and hardly any during the hours of darkness. He had been told about the fights that had taken place there between Rhys and David Gorse when they were young, and visualized some of his own, with himself acting the part of a small man against a giant. He dosed and dreamed and woke, alarmed at how late it was.

He was walking home along the rather overgrown path when he was suddenly pushed from behind. He shouted in alarm as he fell heavily on to his face. He listened but there wasn't a sound apart from his sobs. He stood up and, glancing back into the darkness, hurried towards home. Hearing someone approaching, he slid into the hedge at the side of the path and was relieved to see the familiar figure of Eric.

'Someone pushed me over,' Jimmy said, brave now he wasn't alone.

'I saw someone running across the field. I couldn't see who it was, could you?'

'Pushed from behind, I was! I didn't see a thing!'

'Come on, boy, I'll walk back with you. I was on my way to see a farmer beyond Frog Moor – he's promised me a couple of rabbits.'

'Live ones?' Jimmy said hopefully.

'No, for the pot, I'm afraid.'

'Just as well. Dad wouldn't let me keep them.'

At the edge of the wood, David Gorse was standing as though waiting for them to appear. 'Someone ran out of the wood a while ago and almost knocked me down.'

'And me,' Jimmy said proudly.

'The thing is, I'm sure it was Rhys Martin. I wonder why he's hiding in the woods.'

'No, it definitely wasn't Rhys,' Eric said firmly. 'I saw him too and he wasn't tall enough. More your height. Now, come on, young Jimmy, and get yourself home – it's almost morning.'

'It was Rhys,' David insisted.

'No, it was not. The height was wrong and also the way he ran. Rhys was an athlete and moved like a well-oiled machine. The man who pushed Jimmy ran as though he had had a rat up his trousers!'

Jimmy laughed.

Sally had gone to the sale and bought a few small items of furniture and one large one. An armchair which no one wanted had been sold at a very low price and she had been unable to resist. Now, with no home, where could she keep it all? Some of the smaller items were found a space in what Valmai called, her 'mongrel of a shed', with its oddly uneven walls and the unsightly extension at the back. There was no access to the extension from inside; it was simply a cupboard added on, distorting the shape ever more than before. A bunion, Gwilym called it, but he was glad of it as it gave him places to store things, giving him more space inside the workshop. He gave no explanation for his need for extra room. Valmai didn't ask.

Sally had failed to find a suitable place to live and in desperation she accepted a room in the boarding house where Eric lived. It was on the ground floor and consisted of a single room with use of the kitchen and bathroom, As the other two ground floor rooms were unoccupied for the moment, she at least had sole use of these, for which she was grateful.

She sent a message to Rhys in one of the usual brown envelopes and began to move her few possessions. Jimmy was passing on his way home from the shops, with a loaf of bread of which he had nibbled the corner, and he saw her struggling with a small table. Seeing her difficulties, he ran to tell Rick, who was clearing a small area of the garden to plant some rose bushes. Together they went to help.

The following day, when she arrived with her daughter in a pushchair and a few carrier bags holding the last of her food store, Rick and Jimmy were sitting on the steps.

'Eric's lit a fire,' Jimmy reported. 'And we've got a picnic, made by my mam and Mrs Martin. Come on,' he encouraged, reached for Sadie's hand, 'I'm starvin'.'

Seeing a bright fire helped lessen the shabbiness of the room and she determined to get more paint and brighten the walls as soon as she could. They ate the food Valmai and Netta had sent and for a while the room was cheerful and she felt an optimism she had lost. It didn't last.

It was when they had all gone, leaving her to sort out the best places for her own things, that the loneliness hit her. In the silence, with Sadie asleep in her cot and the door closed, she was completely on her own, locked away from a disapproving world. That it had been her own choice didn't help. She stared at the back of the door where marks showed where a dartboard had been hung and well used, and she longed for Rhys to walk through it. His exams were over, the results learnt, so why hadn't he said something about when he was coming to join them? What about a job? Was that what he was waiting for? A place in a school in Bristol maybe. Was that why he hadn't told her? Afraid she wouldn't want to move from Tre Melin?

She wrote another letter with a secret message only he could interpret – a silly idea to prevent anyone reading it should the letter be opened by someone other than Rhys. The secret messages that had been such fun were now nothing more than a stupid and childish game. After all these years and months, it was time to end it and face the world. If there had been a fear of suspicion, it must surely have faded. With a second child on the way he had to realize she was more important than an unconfirmed threat. She knew that having to move into this terrible place was the reason for her resentment, although she doubted if she would have been tolerant for much longer, even if she'd stayed with Mrs Falconer.

Tearing up the letter she wrote another, this time in plain words telling of her pregnancy and the awful room. She placed it on the table ready to post the following day. A visit to the bank worried her. She suddenly realized that if Rhys decided not to return to her, she would have difficulty affording a decent place to live.

Valmai called to see the room and she was saddened to think that her son had reduced this lovely young woman to such a situation. She tried again to persuade Sally to move in with her and Gwilym but Sally refused.

With a growing feeling of unease, Sally didn't want to look too settled, too comfortable, when Rhys saw her. If he saw her in this awful place, surely he'd come home? Seeing her and Sadie comfortable and cared for, he'd have an excuse to delay his return. Obviously he was in no hurry, she thought sadly.

Valmai frequently brought soups and stews and a few cakes and, if Sally was out, she'd leave them with Eric, or near her door. For these Sally was grateful. The kitchen she was able to use didn't entice her to want to cook. Mrs Falconer also called and brought flowers, which were also welcome, adding a little cheer to the dull room.

Eric was walking along the streets, killing time before going home and locking himself in his room with only a radio for company, when he saw a pile of rubbish put out for the refuse collectors. There was a large planter there, which, if it was scrubbed, would make an attractive addition to Rick and Amy's garden. He knocked on the door and politely asked if he could take it. Permission given, he struggled with it along Mill Street as darkness was falling. Unfortunately he was seen by Milly Sewell, who immediately called the police.

Eric knocked on the door of Waterstones' house as he saw a light there and gave the planter to Rick. Amy stood behind him, frowning.

'It's all right, I know it needs a scrub and I'll do it for you tomorrow,' Eric promised, as Rick rubbed his hands over the sculpted surface in obvious pleasure. Before Eric had left, PC Harvey arrived and asked where he had bought it.

'Thrown out for the rubbish, it was,' Eric said.

Amy screamed and insisted he took it away. 'Bringing stolen goods to my house! How dare you?' she shouted.

Calmly, Eric gave the name and address of the place where he had found it and went with the constable to interview the woman, who agreed with Eric's story.

'Please, will you go and tell Amy and Rick that it wasn't stolen?' he asked. 'Amy's all right but she's easily convinced I'm either a dirty tramp or a criminal.' Laughing, the constable agreed.

Eric was slowly repairing the fence in Valmai and Gwilym's garden. He used some of the remnants of the old shed and he had been given some wood left from the summer house Amy had had built in the garden of the Waterstones' house. Rick confided to Eric that he would like to give him the whole thing! The garden had been planned down to the last inch and Amy had only accepted the rosebed because Rick had craftily told her they were his gift to her.

Eric was with Gwilym one day when Netta called in.

'You'll never guess,' she said, when Valmai had joined them. 'My Walter has actually got a job! Never thought it would happen, did you? Since the factory closed down he's refused everything that's been offered. But yesterday he was offered a job and accepted. What d'you think of that, eh?'

In answer to a barrage of questions, she told them that a large house had been sold and someone was needed to decorate it. 'Right through, mind, every room. It'll keep him busy for months, and there's no one living there, so he won't feel he's clock watching.'

They all cheered and hoped the work wouldn't tire him too much, a comment Netta took literally, unaware of the grins passing between them. They all knew how enthusiastic Walter was and counted his proposed employment in days rather than months.

Each day, after posting the now daily letters to Rhys, Sally watched for the postman. A week passed during which she cleaned and painted the overcrowded room, then another. She shouldn't have started to improve it; the worse it looked the more chance of Rhys facing up to his promise. His time was up and now it was her turn. She was still determined not to complain. The decision had to come from him.

Seeing the round pebble halfway up the steps a couple of weeks later, at the beginning of October, her heart leaped. Rhys was here! He'd received her letters and was coming to put everything right at last and she'd see him in a few hours.

She settled Sadie into her cot, unlocked the door and waited. It was past eleven o'clock when he came and at once she welcomed him lovingly. He stepped back and stared at her.

'You're pregnant! Why didn't you tell me?' he asked. His reaction was far from what she had hoped. She sat down and asked him why he hadn't replied to her letters.

'I haven't been to the café for a while. I didn't think you'd write so soon after seeing me. I – I didn't think you'd have news like this.'

'I didn't think I'd be writing such news in a letter posted to a café in Bristol after more than two years have passed. What's happening, Rhys? Tell me.'

'I'm thrilled, really, I couldn't be more excited, love, but it's making things a little bit awkward.'

'In what way?' she asked, her heart thumping with anxiety. 'Your two years are over, and you must have a place in a school. Everything you wanted. Now we can be together at last and the critics can find someone else to fuel their gossip.'

'I haven't told you this – I've been trying to find a way around it, but I need another year.'

'Another year?'

'A school year. Once I have taught for a year I'm a fully qualified teacher and – it's only until next July,' he added. 'The school year, not twelve months.'

'Our baby will be born in January.' She looked around the dreary room. 'Can you really want your daughter or son to be born here?'

'Well, no, of course not, and that's why I've arranged something much better for you.'

'We're coming to Bristol?' Hope surged then fell again as he shook his head. 'I want you to move in with Mam and Dad.'

'I've already been asked and I refused. We agreed to deal with this whole thing ourselves.'

'But we didn't plan on two children.' His voice was sharp and she gasped with shock. 'You must see that it changes everything.' He spoke again in that harsh, unrecognized voice, his eyes avoiding meeting hers.

'You don't want this baby.'

'Of course I do. But it's so badly timed.'

'I can hardly ask it to wait until you're ready, can I?'

'Aren't there ways of – you know.'

'An abortion? It's far too late, and besides, at the moment, Rhys, I think I want this baby more than I want you.'

The rest of his brief visit was strained. Neither of them knew what to say. They were different sides of a very high fence.

Chapter Four

WHEN RHYS WAS leaving, Sally didn't go with him to the door and wait for that final kiss; she sat and stared at the closing door of her shabby room and wondered if she would ever feel again the love they had shared for so long. Her loyalty had been misplaced. He wasn't the strong partner she had thought him. He would have asked her to abandon this child if it hadn't been too late and he hadn't even attempted to hide his disappointment.

She heard Sadie rouse and stretch in her sleep and she stood up and tucked the covers around her more securely, bending to kiss the child's head. She was on her own with Sadie and the new baby and for their sakes she had to accept help. Tomorrow she would talk to Valmai and Gwilym. Until things became clearer, she would stay with them and the new baby would be born into a comfortable home. After that, well, she still had enough of the money left by her parents to make a start somewhere else.

Into the stunned silence, Rhys had explained that he would be working as many hours as he could and would manage with only a little help just to start. He'd have to find fresh accommodation and books, paper and art materials. Once he'd acquired all those, he'd cope. 'Just this final hurdle,' he told her, 'and I'll be back and everything will be all right. For the four of us,' he added.

Sally had hardly heard a word. All she could think of was that she, Sadie and this new baby weren't worth changing his plans for. Weren't important enough. She doubted if they were even included in his future plans. Once he'd achieved his aim, he might disappear from their lives completely.

Dawn broke on a dark, gloomy morning before she slept. Her

mind was going round and round, confused thoughts of a magical solution, tangling with the harsh reality, touching on vague plans and the dream of Rhys coming back and promising to stay, vying with the more likely outcome of Rhys staying with the life he'd been living for more than two years, with strangers, people she would never know. The confusion of hopes and dismay was still with her when Sadie woke her, calling, 'Mummy? Mummy?'

That's what I am, she thought. First and last I am Sadie's mummy. Sadie and the new baby, they are my life. Everything else comes a poor second.

Valmai welcomed her and Sadie with delight, which increased as Sally asked if she and Sadie might move in, just for a while, until the baby was born and she had found them all a proper home. She opened the door wide and called, 'Gwilym? Look who's here! And they're coming to stay!'

Sally looked towards the shed and saw, through the window, the head of Gwilym, and a hand waving in welcome.

'Making a surprise present, he is,' Valmai explained. 'Won't let me see it. Not that I mind. I'm so relieved to have him showing an interest in the tools again. He can keep as many secrets as he likes.'

Not as big as the secrets kept by your son, Sally thought bitterly.

'I'll just put the kettle on and make some tea then we'll go up to see him. He won't come down while there's anyone here,' she added quietly. 'I still can't persuade him to be seen in that chair of his. Stubborn, he is. I tell him he's got to face the world sometime but will he listen?'

'Perhaps I'm the one to persuade him. Look at me, a second child and no sign of a husband. There's gossip in plenty and at least the talk about him will be kindly. Mrs Sewell never misses a chance to hint that I'm not suitable company for decent people.'

'Leave Milly Sewell to me. I'll put her straight.'

'No, please. Rhys doesn't want anyone to know. Not yet.' She was still held by unreasonable support for Rhys, even though he'd treated her so badly.

'I thought he'd finished his two years and was coming home?'

'So did I,' Sally murmured.

'Can you tell me what's happened?'

'Everything is too confused at the moment.'

'When you're ready to talk, I'm here. Now let's get this tea and Gwilym can show you your surprise.'

When she saw the beautifully carved baby cradle Gwilym had made, Sally burst into tears.

Stories spread easily in the houses around Mill Road and School Lane and David heard of Sally's intention to move in with Rhys's parents before a day had passed. Would Rhys call on Sally before the move? He kept watch on the back of the house for three nights, patiently scanning the porch for movement. His eyes were well accustomed to the night and he knew that the appearance of Rhys and the opening of the door would not be missed. He sat against a tree, almost invisible to the casual glance, hooded by an old ex-army coat against the chill. On his knees there was a camera. In his eyes there was excitement.

Valmai had proudly shown Sally the room she had prepared for her and Sadie. It had quickly been made, ready for them to move out of the awful boarding house the following weekend. She had written a brief note to tell Rhys what was happening and hearing the letter, formal and without any of the usual loving messages, dropping into the post-box, was like saying goodbye.

On her last evening she saw the round pebble was in the middle of the porch and her heart dropped. What could she say to him? The room was cluttered with boxes filled with her possessions and only Sadie's cot was clear of muddle. The little girl was sleeping soundly and Sally had almost decided not to answer Rhys's knock, but when the second gentle tap came she rose, took a deep breath and opened the door.

As Rhys stepped forward, the light shining out from the open door, someone called and he turned. At that moment there was the flash and a brief whirring sound, followed by a repeat.

'Someone took my photograph!' he said angrily. He left Sally and ran in the direction of the sound. Footsteps ahead of him led him across the road through fields towards the mill. He stopped before reaching the building and listened but there wasn't a sound apart from the peaceful murmur of the stream, and he turned back.

He was cautious as he approached the shabby boarding house and when he eventually reached the door it was locked. This time, Sally didn't answer his call.

The following day, stories went around the houses of a series of burglaries. Most of the pieces stolen were small, easily transported china and silver items. In three cases money was taken and this amounted in total to ninety-six pounds. When the police called on Valmai and Gwilym, they were told there was evidence that Rhys had been in the area on the night the crimes took place.

Sally was interviewed and she could tell them more or less honestly that she hadn't spoken to Rhys that night. Less truthfully, she told them she hadn't seen him since he had run away more than two years before.

'Yes, he disappeared at the time of previous robberies, didn't he?'

'A coincidence,' she said at once. She knew the photograph, which was probably the evidence to which they referred, had been a trick. Rhys had let her down, treated her like an idiot, but she couldn't believe he was a thief. Or could she? a small voice in her heart questioned. How well did she really know him? The photograph might have been a trick but perhaps the camera had been held by a victim of one of the robberies and not David Gorse, who had been her instant suspicion. Rhys had never fully explained why he had run away when the police had wanted to speak to him before and he wasn't here to answer their questions now.

Whether they believed her or not didn't matter. Guilty or innocent, he was out of her life. Once she had given birth and found herself a proper place to stay, she would say goodbye to Valmai and Gwilym too, much as she appreciated their kindness. She had been used and lied to, and made to look a fool. Enough of all that; she was on her own and she knew she'd cope.

The police knocked on doors asking questions and at each house they asked whether anyone had seen Rhys Martin. Walter Prosser was most disparaging, referring to Rhys as a dishonest and dishonourable man. 'Everyone knows he got that poor girl into trouble then ran out on her,' he said.

'Working, are you, Mr Prosser?' the police officer asked casually as he was leaving. 'No, but the wife is and I'm no thief! I was determined to redecorate that big house but I had to give up, didn't I? It's my back – suffered with it for years – but at least I try, not like some.'

'Admirable, you are,' he was told, the sarcasm wasted on him.

At Valmai and Gwilym's house they stayed a very long time, repeating their questions in different words, approaching their queries from different angles, trying to trick them into making a mistake. Both were upset at the disappearance of their son and the police finally left, promising to call again if they had more questions.

Constable Harvey called later and said, 'If there's anything you want to tell me, remember I'll help in any way I can. Rhys and I were at school together. I won't find it easy to believe him guilty of these robberies.'

Gwilym thanked him.

'Why did he disappear if he was innocent?' Constable Harvey asked. 'Does someone hold some kind of evidence against him? Have you any idea what it can be?'

'None,' Valmai said. 'D'you think we wouldn't say if we knew?' The policeman waited, staring at them both for a long moment, then went on his way. If they were lying, they were very convincing.

The enquiries went on and the police officers called several times more but there didn't appear to be any progress in the case.

Amy and Rick were washing windows when Amy saw Eric walking past the house. She looked at Rick, who nodded encouragingly. 'Would you like to come in for a cup of tea?' she called in her rather prim voice and Eric turned and looked at her in surprise. Rick waved, beckoning him in.

Eric walked towards them, eyeing Amy nervously. She wasn't going to tell him off again, was she?

'I owe you an apology,' Amy said, reaching for Rick's arm. 'Bringing that lovely planter was a very kind thought. I'm very sorry I – um – misunderstood.'

Eric smiled and shook his head. 'You weren't to know, but I can assure you that I never steal. Never take anything that isn't mine or kindly offered to me.'

'I won't make that mistake again. I really am sorry, Mr Thomas.'

'Eric will do.'

'Right then. Now, a cup of tea and one of Mummy's scones?'

As Amy was making tea, Eric began scrubbing the planter and he stayed talking to them for a while after the scones were demolished. He and Rick finished cleaning the pot while Amy was busy inside the house.

'Ever been married. Eric?' Rick asked as they rubbed at the pot, revealing its elegant design.

'Oh, yes. I have a daughter.' He took out a rather battered photograph of a girl aged about twelve. 'Julia she's called but I haven't seen her for years. She'll be twenty-four at Christmas.'

'What happened?'

'My wife took her away, you see. She'd got herself in a spot of bother. Debts she couldn't clear. She liked pretty things, see, and loved wandering around the shops.'

'She left you with the debts?' Rick asked softly.

'I'd sold the house and had just managed to clear the last one, although it meant I had to sell the last of my possessions, then the factory closed. I was left with no money, a small pension and no home.'

Afraid to ask more Rick said, 'Closing that factory ruined quite a few lives, didn't it? Walter hasn't worked since, or David. Several families had to move away in the search for employment.'

'Walter didn't miss a day when the factory was there, but once he was made redundant he quickly gave up looking for something similar, and was afraid of trying something new, so he settled into the bad-tempered misery he now is. He and Netta are always quarrelling.'

'And he's making young Jimmy's life a misery.'

'Netta worked in the factory too, in the wages office, and she got a job straight away. Pity, he might have made more effort if she hadn't.'

Rick grinned. 'Mind, he does have a bad back!'

'You learn quick. You haven't been here long but you've got most of us sussed!'

'He gave up on the decorating job. Nervous exhaustion, he told me. The job was too big, too daunting, for someone with his sensibilities.'

'Aw. Poor dab!'

*

Rhys stayed away from his usual haunts, aware that the photograph would be clear enough for him to be recognized. He searched the newspapers waiting with dread for the rest of it to come out. David had his fingerprints on stolen property and this might be the chance he'd been waiting for to hand them to the police. Thankfully, not even Sally knew exactly where he could be found and even though they had parted on bad terms, due to his shock and stupidity, she wouldn't help them find him. Still, better to change his address, just in case.

David surprised Sally by becoming a regular visitor to the Martins' house. He usually stayed in the shed with Gwilym, and according to Gwilym he was helping with ideas as well as some of the stages of the models being made. He also brought gifts of flowers to Valmai, and sweets and an occasional toy for Sadie.

Although Sally had never been deeply fond of the man, she had been going out with him occasionally before Rhys began to show an interest and now she wondered if Rhys's attraction to her had been nothing more on his part than stupid revenge, due to David's interest. It was so easy, she mused, to dislike someone having heard one side of a story. The person whose story you hear first is usually the one you believe. Rhys's dislike of David Gorse had coloured her opinion of him, she realized that. Recently she had seen more of David and found him increasingly easy to talk to and he never once mentioned his stupid feud with Rhys that had begun at school.

From what she had gathered from Rhys, it had been little more than childish rivalry. David had copied some of Rhys's work then told the teacher the reverse was true and Rhys had been punished for cheating. That deliberate set-up had been an angry response from David because Rhys had spoilt one of his drawings and, from such trivial beginnings, the dislike had grown.

Sally was thinking of Rhys, trying to retain her anger, trying to hate him, but she couldn't. She remembered some of the times they had spent together and knew she was wrong. She and Rhys *had* been deeply in love and she *had* been right to trust him enough to give him support for two years and a large amount of her money. But where was he now? The baby was due in a couple of months, she had no home and she needed him badly. Surely he wouldn't let her down?

October 1960 was a cold month even though the sun shone weakly and the skies sometimes looked like summer. Sally continued to work although her cleaning jobs had been changed to less strenuous ones. Valmai had often offered to look after Sadie for Sally to have some free time but Sally refused. Her intention was to leave, go right away and start again, and she didn't think it fair for Rhys's parents to become too fond of the little girl. One Sunday afternoon, however, when her back ached and she was restless but couldn't relax, she accepted.

She wrapped her swollen form in a loose coat borrowed from Valmai and set off through the woodland path towards the mill. Someone called and she turned to see Rick waving to her. She waited as he ran towards her.

'Going for a walk? Where's little Sadie?' he asked.

'Mrs Martin is looking after her for an hour so I can get some fresh air.'

'Mind if I come? Unless you want to be on your own?'

'As long as you don't walk too fast. I'm a bit slow these days.'

'Suits me. I'm a bit slow myself. My muscles are complaining because I've been digging a patch of the garden that I hope to call my own. Amy isn't keen on a vegetable garden, insists they're untidy, so I've got less and less space as she and her mother find ways of filling the plot with other things.'

'I'd love to grow and eat freshly picked food. Vegetables and a few chickens to provide eggs – I've dreamed of that since I was a child. My parents did those things, you see, and although they died when I was very young I still remember feeding the chickens and helping pull carrots, pick peas and marvelling at them. Putting a fork in the ground and potatoes appearing as though by magic is one of my strongest memories.'

'Perhaps you can help change Amy's mind,' he said with a smile. 'Although I don't think so. It's two against one these days as her mother advises her on practically everything.'

'I don't suppose many marriages are equal. Everyone has to learn to compromise.'

'What about you, when will you marry? I presume there's a handsome young man somewhere waiting for the moment when everything is just right.'

'It never is right. He asked me to support him for two years while he studied to become a teacher. The two years are up and instead of coming home and facing everything as he promised, he asked for another year.'

'But the baby? How does he expect you to manage?'

'He's just sorry it's too late for an abortion,' she said bitterly.

He could see tears threatening and he put an arm around her and handed her a clean handkerchief. 'It must have been a shock and he simply spoke his first fearful reaction out loud, that's all. Most of us can leave it unsaid until we've had time to recover. I'm good at that. I need to be with a strong-minded mother-in-law-to-be. Come on, let's sit in the old mill for a while.'

'I always come here when things are wrong these days, yet it used to be the place to come when something wonderful happened.'

'What sort of things?'

'Exam results, getting my first job, promotion, you know the sort of thing. Then meeting Rhys and realizing he was the most important person in my life and I in his.'

'I'm sure you still are,' he said. 'This nonsense about him being the man breaking into houses and stealing, it's a story invented by the real thief, conveniently made easier to believe by Rhys's absence.'

'I don't even know where to find him,' she said, wiping her tears away with his handkerchief.

'Any clues?'

'He's just completed a teacher-training course in Bristol and there's an address where I used to write where he collected the letters. But that's no longer valid. So many changes, so many lies.'

'Amy and her mother are going to Cardiff all day on Saturday to choose her going-away outfit.' He laughed. 'I hope it clashes with mine. Would you believe that mother-in-law-to-be chose the material and the style of my suit? In a rare brave moment I went in and changed it all. I hope they're suitably shocked. Amy's mother had picked a dark navy and a very formal style that I would never wear. I changed it for something more sporty, much to the tailor's concern. But I insisted and asked him not to tell Mrs Seaton-Jones. It's light grey with a hint of green.'

He took the handkerchief and wiped her cheeks gently. 'I don't know if this will help, but I have a few days' holiday due and as Amy will be away all day, I could take a day off and if we went to Bristol early, you me and Sadie, we'd have hours to search for him. The college would be a good place to start. What about it? Shall we try? It would be a day out for you and Sadie if nothing else.'

Sally shook her head and patted her swollen body. 'How can you spend a day with me in this state and with a two-year-old. What would people think?'

'That I was a lucky man?'

She frowned, and was about to refuse, her usual reaction to offers of help, but he seemed so anxious for her to agree she smiled. 'Thank you, I'd love a day out and if we do find Rhys, I'm in the mood to get a few things straight.'

The first shock was when they went to the address to which Sally had been writing and sending money. It was a small café.

'Sorry, love,' the proprietor said, 'but I've no idea where you'll find Rhys. Comes in from time to time and has a meal, then picks up any letters that have come for him.' The man gestured with his head to a shelf where she could see a neat pile of brown envelopes. They were all addressed to Rhys and all in her writing. He hadn't picked up his mail for weeks.

The college was closed but the secretary was there until one o'clock and offered to help. She went through various lists and files but came back shaking her head. 'I'm sorry, but there's no one of that name registered here at present.'

'Sorry, I should have told you, he finished the two years last July so he'll be on last year's list,' Sally apologized.

Again the young woman searched through lists and files, then she left the room. It was ten minutes before she returned and again she was shaking her head. 'The only reference I can find is a student of that name registering two years ago then failing to complete more than three months. I have no idea where he is now. I'm very sorry.'

White-faced, her eyes wide with disbelief, Sally thanked her and walked out, holding Sadie's hand, Rick following. They went back to the café.

'Now what do we do?'

'There must be an explanation. There are other colleges – we just have to find them.' Rick tried to sound positive, as though what they had learned had been only a slight glitch in their search. 'Come on, Sadie, time to find you and your mother something to eat. Not here though.' He wanted to get her away from the sight of those ignored letters. He picked the little girl up and guided them to a restaurant.

'Where can we ask?' Sally wondered, as she tried to eat the food in front of her. 'We can hardly go to the police. If they're looking for him he wouldn't thank us for that.'

Rick wasn't thinking about what Rhys needed. 'Look, there isn't much more we can do here. Saturday was a stupid day to chose, I don't know what I was thinking of. All the offices are closed. I'll start making a few enquiries from home. Carefully, not causing any curiosity, and together we'll work out what to do.'

'Why should you bother? It's my problem.'

'It was, but after you trusted me with the situation, it's mine too. I don't think you confide in many people. Now, there's a nice park somewhere near and I think Sadie deserves some of our time, don't you?'

There was a shop selling toys near the park and he bought a coloured ball. Sally sat on a bench, aware of aching in every bone, while he and Sadie played a complicated game of football which involved Rick falling over quite a lot. It was a good way to end their visit, with laughter and silly games, and despite the unanswered questions and the discovery of Rhys's deceit, Sally was surprisingly happy as they travelled home.

It wasn't until she went to her room, after offering Valmai and Gwilym an edited version of their day out, that reality set in and she began to wonder where Rhys was and what had happened to all the money she had sent to him.

Another sleepless night followed during which she wondered how much – if anything – she should tell Rhys's parents. Perhaps it would be better to wait until she had at least some of the answers.

One decision she did make was not to send any more money until Rhys had told her the truth. The second was to withdraw some of her money for her own use and cut down on the hours she was working.

The woods and the old mill had always been a favourite place and when the weather allowed she would take Sadie in her pushchair and they would walk down and sit listening to the birds, feeding them to encourage them to come closer, and the sound of the water was always soothing. Today, after learning of Rhys's deceit, the water sounded angry and they didn't stay. Instead they walked on to the next village where, it being Sunday, the shops were closed and the only people about were either going to church or visiting family.

Cars emptied and family groups piled into houses, calling excitedly, in contrast to the more solemn groups heading for the ancient building from where the sound of organ music came. A car stopped near her, a door of a cottage opened and an elderly couple stepped out and were quickly surrounded by lively children as their parents unloaded the car. She felt invisible, as though, not having a family to visit, she had no importance.

'At least you'll have a brother or a sister,' she said to Sadie as they turned to return home. 'You'll have someone who belongs, who'll always be there.' She gave Sadie a small biscuit, aware of her own hunger, and thought of the dinner Valmai and Gwilym had promised. A kindness to a person in need. Nothing more. They wouldn't be her family, not now. Rhys had ruined that dream. She had believed for a long time that they'd be her and Sadie's family but now she was an intruder in their house even though Sadie was their grandchild. Sadie might be a part of their family but she was excluded. She would never marry Rhys. She was on her own, as she had been for most of her life.

Rick had enjoyed his day out with Sally and her little daughter but he knew he had to tell Amy what had happened. If one of the Milly Sewells of this world had seen them and given her a slightly exaggerated report, she might be upset. He waited until they were at the house, where he was painting and Amy was measuring for curtains and deciding on the cupboards she would need in the empty room that would be their kitchen. Stopping for a cup of coffee from a flask he said. 'I went to Bristol last Saturday while you and your mother were looking for clothes.'

'Bristol? Why did you go there?'

'I went with Sally Travis and Sadie. Sally hasn't heard from the man she's planning to marry and I took her there hoping she could find out what was happening.'

'And did you? Find out what had happened to this mystery man? If he exists.'

'He exists all right but he's in a spot of trouble and is lying low. But no, we didn't find him. At least the little girl enjoyed a day out.'

'Lovely, Nick, darling. But I hope you won't do that again.'

'Why not? Sally is in trouble and I tried to help, without success, as it happened.'

'Didn't you think that you might have succeeded in making me look a fool? If someone had seen you together, you with a pregnant woman and a small child, what would they have thought? How could you do that to me?'

'Do what? I drove them to Bristol, spent a few hours there and brought them home. I enjoyed it. Sadie is a happy child. I hope when we have children they'll be as contented and as easy to enjoy as Sadie.'

'Children? I don't think so. I can't imagine being a mother and dealing with a child day in day out for years and years. No, you don't need practice to play with children. I don't want any.' She put down her cup and stood up. 'I don't even know whether I want you at this moment. What were you thinking of? Going out for the day with a woman who's obviously expecting a child. You didn't think of the embarrassment it would cause me, did you? And as for a mysterious man who will one day marry her, I don't believe that for a moment. She's got herself in trouble. Twice. The story of the secretive man is an attempt to cover up her disgraceful behaviour.'

'No, Amy. I won't think that badly of her. She's genuinely hurt by this man who promised her everything. She's been helping him and now he seems to have let her down. Please, don't add to the gossip. She doesn't deserve it.'

'You're too gullible. Everyone knows there's no man. I doubt if this one has the same father as the last one.'

Rick didn't try to argue any more; it wouldn't have done any good. He stood and reached out for her. 'Amy, love, you're wrong about her, but I shouldn't have tried to help. I just didn't think. It certainly didn't occur to me that you'd be hurt or embarrassed. I can see now how it might have looked, especially as there's no obvious man in her life and people are quick to gossip. I should have thought. But I didn't. Hearing Sally's story, I impulsively offered help. I'm so sorry.'

Eating humble pie wasn't difficult. Their wedding wasn't far off and she was working hard to make their home ready in time. He had been thoughtless. He put aside the jobs they had planned and took her home, where her mother explained all she had done towards planning the buffet lunch. He hugged her and smiled encouragingly even though it was hard to keep his mind on what was being said.

Jimmy struggled with school. It wasn't that he couldn't do the work but looking out of the window made him restless. He wanted to be outside. He'd had a row that morning from his father, after the teacher had called to discuss his frequent absences. Then at lunchtime he'd walked into yet another argument between his parents.

'Don't be so hard on the boy,' Netta was saying. 'He's only ten.'

'Time he learned to behave. He's out for hours at a time, only comes in when he's hungry. And he spends too much time with that couple moving into the Waterstones' place. Giving him ideas they are.'

'Better than any he can learn from you!' Netta shouted.

Jimmy darted in, grabbed some food and ran out again. He had started cleaning off the paddles of the waterwheel at the mill. It was stained with green slime where it occasionally touched the water and there was even greener moss on the higher places. After he'd eaten his lonely meal, he rubbed it with a stone and then a blunt knife and slowly the wood was clear and to his relief was surprisingly sound. There was no purpose to the task but it was very satisfying to see the wood revived, brought back to life. He sat and dreamed of one day starting the wheel turning, seeing the water cascading below the ancient wheel and pressing against each paddle until the weight sent it on its way.

Rick helped him with homework whenever he could and although he was often absent from school once lunchtime was over, he kept up with the class-work, often with information they hadn't covered in class, which mystified the teachers, unaware of the help he was being given and the books he was able to borrow.

He was at the mill one chilly November day, scrubbing away and clearing the resulting mess of moss and weeds into a pile within the wood. He had found an abandoned trenching tool and with this he was digging out the silted-up leat. He imagined how it would look with the stream running and the great wheel turning and spent hours working towards his dream. He had a cold and insisted his mother wrote a note to excuse him from attending school. He had food, and a vacuum flask of cocoa as well as a couple of apples given to him by Valmai.

He was just finishing his meal when he heard footsteps. People rarely stayed now summer was gone. Any footsteps he heard would hurry past, but these footsteps stopped. He looked warily out and recognized Sally and saw that she was crying. He didn't know what to do so he stayed perfectly still and waited for her to move on. But she didn't.

Sally had still not heard anything from Rhys. Rick had tried to find him, ringing up various schools and colleges and had even driven to Bristol a second time, this time taking Amy with him. No one had heard of him. He even took a photograph in case he was using a different name. He was nowhere to be found.

Where was he? Sally wondered. What was he doing? More worryingly, who was he with? There had to be someone else. His shock at realizing she was expecting a second child had been more than a brief reaction. He more or less admitted wishing there was time to arrange an abortion. There had to be someone else. It was the only explanation. Sadie was out with Valmai, who was taking her to the shops promising to buy her a new doll to go in a doll's bed Gwilym had made her.

Restless and deeply unhappy, she walked with her arms under her coat, around her unborn child as though protecting it from the troubles that faced the three of them. Her back ached and she had a few niggling pains that she presumed were what some called false labour. A sudden fast and growing pain made her gasp. It eased and she relaxed. It was two months before the baby was due and she presumed it was only the weight that was causing the backache. She leaned slightly back to ease the discomfort. Another sharp pain alarmed her. She was utterly lonely. When the baby was born, she'd face life as the unmarried mother of two. Yet she didn't feel any regrets about the pregnancy. As soon as she had guessed she was expecting this baby, she felt a joyful excitement. Now, at this moment, she had doubts. How would she manage?

The sharp pain came again and she began to feel very afraid. They were nothing in themselves but were reminders of the brief time she had left to make plans and start to prepare for life with two children.

She wanted to turn back to the Martins' house but decided to rest in the mill. Foolishly she half hoped to find Rhys there, where they had met so many times, until he'd run away and everything had gone wrong.

She stood for a while, her hand on her lower back to ease the discomfort, just looking at the wheel, and to distract her thoughts from her predicament she imagined it working to provide bread for the local inhabitants of the villages many years before. She forced herself to think about the lives of the villagers at that time, trying to take her mind away from the present with its seemingly impossible problems.

She noticed that some of the moss had been cleared and wondered whether Jimmy was responsible, unaware of his presence just yards away from her. She knew he spent time here. Reaching over, she pushed at the green moss and with a finger began to work it free. The water smelt unpleasant as Jimmy's disturbance had brought rotting leaves to the surface. Picking up a piece of slate from among the stones, she concentrated on clearing a small area, choosing to start on a different paddle from the partially cleared one. It became important to clear one of the paddles and she leaned across to continue, when she slipped.

It hadn't been a careless move, she told herself as she scrabbled for a hand hold. The pain had been sudden, sharp and taken her unaware. She hadn't fallen far, just about two feet, and once the pain had again receded she tried to get back up. Stay calm, she told herself as the pain came again. It's nothing but a warning, plenty of time and I'm not far from the Martins' house. Then she thought of walking along the path and the distance seemed too great. A pain engulfed her, staying too long and with increasing intensity, and she cried out loud. She had to walk back; she couldn't stay here.

She tried again to get back up and this time she stopped pretending. Early or not, she was in the first stages of labour. Panic filled her, perspiration burst out on her forehead. All attempts to stay calm were forgotten in the urgent need to get back to where there were houses and people who would help.

In the room at the top of the mill, Jimmy listened and wished he could run away. Then he felt a sneeze coming on and he covered his face with his jacket. Sally heard the muffled sound and called.

'Is anyone there? Can you come and help me, please?'

Jimmy stayed perfectly still.

'Please, help me. I'm stuck and I need to get home.'

Slowly Jimmy peered out over one of the broken walls. Recognizing Sally, he came down. 'What are you doing down there, miss?'

A pain caused her to grimace and when it had passed she smiled and said, 'Being stupid, Jimmy. Will you go and bring help? Just knock on someone's door if you can't find Mrs Martin, will you? Please, Jimmy, I need a doctor, and fast. I think my baby is about to be born.'

That was enough. He ran. He'd heard about babies, about how they came with a lot of moaning and groaning and a lot of blood and he didn't want any of that! He ran down the path but when he reached the road he saw Rick Perry and ducked down behind a wall. He was nice enough but he'd ask why he wasn't in school and wouldn't believe his excuse of having a nasty cold.

He ran to his house but his mother wasn't there and his father was sleeping and he didn't dare wake him and talk about babies being born in the old mill. He ran next door but Gwilym couldn't help. 'Go to the phone box as fast as you can, Jimmy. Dial 999 and ask for a doctor and an ambulance. Quick! Sally's in real trouble!'

His legs began to feel like wet string as he dashed back to the road. 'I'm only ten!' he wailed as he ran. Then he saw David Gorse. He wouldn't worry about him missing school.

'Sally Travis is at the mill,' he said. 'Moaning a lot. Having a baby she says and needs a doctor.'

'At the mill? You aren't lying, are you, Jimmy?'

'Honest! She asked me to run and tell someone and get a doctor fast. Moaning she is and that red in the face you'd think she'll burst.'

'What on earth is she doing there?'

'I just told you, she's having a—' He didn't finish the sentence. David pushed him out of the way and ran into a house and demanded to use their phone.

Jimmy didn't know what to do. He didn't want to go home but he certainly didn't want to go back to the mill. He went to tell Valmai Martin but she was still out. To his relief he saw his mother coming, so he told her instead, crying like a baby, afraid something would go wrong and he'd get the blame. 'I'm only ten!' he wailed again after telling her, between sobs, what had happened.

Netta gathered a few things from the house, kicked Walter awake and told him where she was going and ran out towards the mill.

Somehow, Sally had struggled back up from the edge of the stagnant water around the wheel and prepared her coat for a bed. The rest was a blur of pain and fear and then the terrible and wonderful sensation of birth. She was trembling and shivering with shock and felt the urge to push again, before being aware of the afterbirth coming away. She wrapped the tiny baby in a cardigan she had taken off in readiness and before she could do anything else help arrived. David saw to his amazement that she lay there, propped against a tree, nursing a small infant.

'Sally? You've had your baby out here? All alone?'

'That's my life, David. I am all alone, with Sadie and now Samuel to look after.'

'Samuel?' He took off his coat and wrapped it around them both then sat beside Sally and held her. She was feeling sick, her eyes were swollen with tears and she was still trembling uncontrollably.

'Samuel. My father's name.' She moved slightly to make sure the baby was covered with the cardigan she had removed. 'I'm so afraid he'll be damaged. I didn't know what to do. Isn't that ridiculous? He isn't the first; I should have known exactly what to do. I'm so afraid I haven't done the right things.'

David leaned over and looked at the tiny face and felt a warm, protective feeling overwhelm him. 'He's so perfect. I've never seen such a young baby before. I didn't expect him to be so – so perfect.'

Sally was weary and past tears. She sat staring down at her child as they waited just a few minutes more for the doctor to arrive. Netta Prosser came first, carrying a couple of blankets. After a few words she ran back to hurry the doctor. 'I'll telephone again in case he didn't get the message,' she promised. She met the doctor on the path and at once scolded him for being so idle. 'Hurry, man, there's a newborn baby back there,' she shouted as she ran after him back to the mill.

'An ambulance is on its way. Now please keep your voice down – we don't want the mother panicking. Stay out of the way so I can examine my patient in peace.' The doctor and David wrapped her in the blankets then she was carried in a stretcher the ambulance crew had brought, everyone talking soothingly to her, assuring her that everything would be all right. Netta offered to carry the baby but Sally wouldn't let him go. Netta ran then, to tell Valmai. David went with Sally in the ambulance and sat in the waiting room until there was news. Jimmy had locked himself in his room and drawn the curtains.

Sally complained tearfully as the baby was taken from her, but the nurse assured her it was only for a few tests to make sure the unconventional birth hadn't caused him harm.

Half an hour later the nurse returned with a doctor.

'I'm afraid your baby is in need of extra care, Mrs Travis,' the doctor began.

'Where is he? I want to see him,' she sobbed.

'He's rather ill – a shock birth, you see – but believe me we'll do everything we can,' the nurse promised.

An hour later David was told that the infant had died.

'Samuel,' he said sharply. 'His name was Samuel.' He stared at the doctor. 'Why?'

'He was tiny, and he needed immediate help and by the time we got there it was too late, I'm afraid.'

'But he was perfect.'

'Oh yes. He was a beautiful boy.'

'Can I see her?'

'For a moment, but she needs sleep.'

David felt so emotional he didn't think his voice would work. Sally was in a side ward and he went over and touched her shoulder.

'He's gone,' she whispered.

David leaned over and kissed her cheek. 'And I'm so pleased I met him,' he whispered. 'Samuel is so beautiful.'

She reached out a hand and he held it until she slept.

Chapter Five

WHEN SALLY WOKE after a brief and very disturbed sleep, there were several people waiting to see her. The nurse told her that David was in the waiting room having been there all night, anxiously waiting to be told that she was going to be all right. 'But first, Miss Travis, the police want to talk to you and then there's the childcare workers.'

Hardly taking in the nurse's comments, her first words were to ask about Sadie.

'Mr and Mrs Martin are looking after her and she's fine,' one of the policemen told her. 'Now if you're up to answering a few questions, Mrs – Miss Travis?'

'I want to see Sadie. I need my daughter.' Her mind was full of confusion. She felt a terrible ache in her arms; they were empty and she had painful need to hold the baby she had lost. She was unable to concentrate on what was being said. All she could think about was the baby, and the urgent need to see Sadie, hold her, make sure she was safe.

'Miss Travis?'

'Can't it wait? I want to know that Sadie is all right. Can't I see Mrs Martin?'

'This won't take a moment and then we can leave you in peace.'

Peace, Sally thought, was a luxury she would never know again. Samuel had died and it was her fault. How could she have been so negligent of him?

One of the nurses brought a cup of tea and sat with her as she became calmer and able to talk. The childcare people asked very few questions. They asked about her situation but seemed more anxious to reassure her that she wasn't to blame herself.

'You were perfectly all right when you left to go for the walk?' one of them asked. 'No pains?'

'Only backache but that wasn't uncommon in the past few weeks.' She covered her face with her hands. 'Why did I go out and walk so far? I should have known.'

'With two months to go you couldn't have known. None of this is your fault, please believe that.'

The doctor asked about her health during the pregnancy and she mentioned that Samuel hadn't moved as much as Sadie, but she'd presumed he was a calm, gentle child. Again tears welled up in her eyes. Seeing that she was shivering, trembling with shock and misery, the nurse said, 'Now get some rest, my dear. You can see Mrs Martin very soon. We'll come too and look after Sadie while you talk to her.'

Then, after much protest from the nurses, David came in. She was so relieved to see him. After the professional people, he was someone who might understand.

'Sally, I'm so sorry. You must be devastated. Samuel was so beautiful, wasn't he?' He held her trembling shoulders while she cried then said, 'I've never seen a baby so young and his face will stay in my memory for always.' He didn't say anything more, just held her, felt her trembling ease and her sobs abate.

'Not too long, Mr Gorse,' a nurse called and regretfully, a few minutes later, he left. Sally slept again and when she woke Mrs Martin was sitting beside her bed. After a few comforting words and assuring Sally that Sadie was safe and happy, Valmai said, 'I'll never forgive Rhys for this. He should have been with you, looking after you.'

'I promised to help him through his training and believed he'd come home to us once he had finished the two years and everything would be all right. That thought kept me going through the difficulties, the jibes of the Milly Sewells of this town and being on my own through it all. Now I know he was lying. He let me down.'

'Come back to us as soon as the doctors are satisfied you're well enough, dear. I love having you and Sadie living in our house. Every day is brighter with your little girl there.'

Sally shook her head. She didn't know what she would do after this but going back to Rhys's parents was not a possibility. Living with them after all that had happened would appear to be condoning what Rhys had done, make her look even more of a foolish victim. She needed to be on her own, cope alone as she always had ever since her parents had died. Trusting Rhys had been a mistake; she had been a romantic idiot. She could trust no one but herself.

'Time to leave, Mrs Martin. We mustn't let our patient get over-tired, must we?' the cheerful voice of the nurse called and, after a kiss on Sally's pale cheek, Valmai left.

Valmai was dreadfully upset and ashamed of her son. 'How could he have left that poor dear girl to cope alone?' she asked Netta when she reached home.

They stood near to Gwilym's workshop and although she tried to avoid actually putting some of the blame on Gwilym, she was angry enough to hope he heard and was ashamed of his weakness. 'If Gwilym had gone to the phone as soon as Jimmy told him what was happening,' she said, 'the outcome might have been different. Minutes later and Sally could have lost her life too. Minutes sooner and poor little Samuel might have been saved.' In a lower voice she added, 'Surely in such an emergency Gwilym could have got to the phone and made sure help was on its way. They might not have taken young Jimmy seriously.'

In the workshop, Gwilym listened and felt sick with guilt. When Valmai came in he acted as though he hadn't heard. Soon. He must do something positive very soon. The thought of Sally being left there with a newly born child was a shadow that would never leave him.

Rick was upset, aware that if he'd been the one Jimmy had met he could have been there when Sally so desperately needed help. He didn't know how but he was convinced that he would have been able to do more than David and made sure Sally and the baby had been safe.

'What makes you think you'd have done more than this David Gorse?' Amy asked. 'You have no training for anything medical.'

'I just know that I'd have helped her, acted more quickly. It's so sad, a little baby carried all those months and born in such circum-stances then to die only hours later.'

'It's probably for the best,' she said. 'She couldn't have coped.'

'How can losing a baby be for the best?' Rick said angrily. 'She wanted this baby and she'd have done everything necessary to care for him.'

'The child would probably be taken into care. What life is that?'

'Of course he wouldn't! Can't you feel any sympathy for a mother losing a child? You must be able to imagine how you'd feel if it happened to us.'

'Oh, it wouldn't happen to us, darling. I wouldn't make a mistake like that.'

'How can you know? Sally would probably have said the same. She wasn't careless or negligent. Circumstances she could never have foreseen put her in danger. It could have happened to anyone.'

'Not me, darling. Not to people like us.'

Rick's distress at the death of the baby increased after Amy's glib response but he said nothing more. Amy's life had been safe and secure, her parents hadn't allowed anything to upset her or cause her a moment's worry. How could she understand? He addressed a letter to Rhys, writing down everything that had happened, graphically describing the situation in which his son had been born, and drove to Bristol. His anger made him careless and he knew his driving was a danger to himself and others, but he couldn't calm himself. The man was a fool to neglect Sally the way he had and someone had to tell him so.

He handed the letter to the café owner where the others still awaited Rhys's collection. 'No sign of Rhys Martin then?' he said to the café owner. 'Will you put this with the others, please?' The man threw Rick's letter carelessly on to the cluttered shelf and went back to his customers. Later that evening, when the café closed, he looked at the dates on the earliest envelopes, shrugged and threw the lot in with the rubbish.

Milly Sewell called to see Amy after seeing her in the garden and called across in her rather loud voice.

'Isn't it terrible about that woman having a baby out in the fields!' She walked closer. 'As if it wasn't enough to have two children without a husband in sight, she had to give birth to that poor little scrap in a field.'

'Good morning, Mrs Sewell,' Amy called, turning away, hoping to discourage her.

Milly hurried towards her. 'I had to tell Mrs Green about her disgraceful behaviour. Sally used to clean for her but now she knows what kind of person she is, she'll find someone else. D'you know of someone who'd work for her?'

Amy turned to face her, not liking what she saw. The woman was smiling, eyes glittering, obviously enjoying the story she had to tell. Although Amy was inclined to agree with what the woman was saying, she didn't like her, so she played devil's advocate and disagreed.

'Sally has been very unfortunate, being let down so badly. Can't blame her for trusting someone who purports to love her, can you?'

'Which one d'you mean, the father of Sadie or the father of the poor little scrap who died? How many other men has she been with? Terrible way to live, don't you think?'

Angry now, Amy said, 'One man. Just one, and he let her down.'

Milly had a good idea of the man in question so she said, 'Good of Valmai to offer Sally and Sadie a home, isn't it? Terrible shaming for a mother to have a son like that.'

'I don't know what happened, but I'm sure Rhys will be home soon to sort everything out and be a proper father to his little girl.'

Satisfied that her suspicions were confirmed, Milly went on her way. Outside the post office she made a phone call.

David came to the hospital again at visiting time and at once Sally asked for his help.

'Remember the house that Walter Prosser was going to clean and decorate?' she asked.

'The one that he was too idle to attempt? Yes. Greenways in Grove Lane.'

'Will you ask if the job is still available and whether I can live there while I do the work?'

'You can't. You aren't well enough.'

'Not this week, but if I can live there, I'll be able to start fairly soon. Once I'm out of here I need somewhere to live – and something to fill the hours. I can't stay with the Martins, I just can't. I want a place of my own. For one thing, I'd be afraid of Rhys coming home and I never want to see him again.'

She didn't see David's wide smile. At last, he thought, she was trusting him, being honest about Rhys Martin.

'I'll go to see the owner straight after leaving here,' he promised. 'But you aren't to think about working until you've recovered.' He reached over and held her hand. 'Sally, I'll help you in any way I can. If I can get the owner to agree, Mam and I will make sure the place is ready for you and Sadie.'

She smiled, the first smile for a long time, grateful for his concern.

A newspaper reporter came to the hospital later that day and the flash of a camera startled her. Other photographs were taken and to her further alarm the reporter had the story about Rhys Martin, the vanishing father. She denied that Rhys was the father of her child but they had talked to Milly Sewell and had all the facts and rumours they needed.

The piece appeared on the front page and included photographs of Rhys and herself. More worrying still, there was a reference to the burglaries that had taken place at the time he had left and again after he had been seen in the area. The wording was carefully chosen but there wasn't much room for doubt. The implications were clear: Rhys Martin was a suspect in the crimes and had run away, leaving his girlfriend to cope with childbirth alone. Twice.

A week later, when Sally was able to leave hospital, David came with his mother to escort her to her temporary home, Mrs Gorse fussing, making sure Sally knew how pleased she was to be able to help. David had arranged for her to go straight to Greenways, the house in need of decoration, having reached an agreement with the owner Matthew Miller, about her living there rent free and also the promise of a small lump sum when the work was completed.

She was apprehensive about living alone in a large, empty house with the worst of winter ahead of them but she didn't have much choice. She wondered if she'd be brave enough to use more than one room. Restricting her use to just a kitchen and one room for everything else was sensible, it would be cheaper to heat, and more like a home than rattling around in empty rooms with bare boards and hollow-sounding corridors. One room, she decided. As cosy as I can make it.

David and his mother had taken her possessions to Greenways, and they carried her few belongings from the hospital to where a taxi waited. An empty house was not a pleasant prospect and she was uneasy about it being a suitable home.

Recognizing her concerns, Mrs Gorse said cheerfully. 'Lovely it'll be. Plenty of room for Sadie to run about. The kitchen is clean and we've put a bed and Sadie's cot in one of the downstairs rooms.'

'We've put food in the pantry and there's coal in the bunker,' David added.

'Thank you both. I'll pay what I owe you as soon as I can get to the post office. David, I really don't know what I'd have done without your help.'

'You'd have managed,' David said with a smile. 'You're the managing type. Come on, Sadie will be waiting for us. She's with one of the nurses. She's quite excited about a ride in a taxi.'

Getting into the taxi, Sally hugged her daughter as though she would never let go.

Jimmy was kicking a ball around outside the house and he waved casually when she called to him, before running off.

'I must go and thank him as soon as I can get out,' Sally said. 'He was the one who ran for help.'

'And thankfully found me,' David said as he opened the door. Sadie ran in and Sally followed, giving a gasp of delight. Behind a sturdy fire guard a fire blazed a welcome. On a small table, within the circle of the warm glow, plates and cups and saucers. Mrs Gorse, a plump, smiling lady with a thick halo of hair and cheeks so red – Sally always likened her to a rosy apple – busied herself in the sparse kitchen and returned with a pot of tea and some cakes, assuring Sally that there were plenty more in the kitchen.

'We brought everything of yours from the Martins' place as well as some pieces we had spare,' she explained cheerfully.

'We aren't stopping long, just time for you to look around and see if there's anything we've forgotten,' David said. With an excited Sadie running ahead of them, Sally looked at the large, old, empty rooms sadly in need of decoration. This would keep her busy for quite a while, enough time for her to sort out something permanent. Half an hour later, David and his mother left, and she was in the empty house that was already less daunting because of the welcome they had arranged.

She decided to keep Sadie up until she herself was ready to sleep, which wouldn't be very long, she thought, stifling a yawn. A knock at the door surprised her.

'Rick! Come in. How did you know I was here?' Then she remembered. 'Jimmy has been watching for me, hasn't he?'

'He proudly insists he's involved, as he was the one who found you and got help. Sally, Amy and I are very sorry about the baby. David said he was beautiful.'

'His name was Sam,' she said softly. 'And yes, he was beautiful.'

'He always will be, won't he? Your memory will keep him with you and he'll always be beautiful.'

Tears pricked her eyes. 'Thank you for coming.'

'If there's anything you need, just ask,' he said as he turned to leave. 'Oh, and I brought you these. From Amy and me.' Reaching outside the door he handed her a large bunch of bright yellow chrysanthemums. 'To brighten a dark corner,' he said as he closed the door behind him.

The room chosen by David and his mother to use as a bedroom was smaller than the one in which they had placed the table and chairs, but it too had a fireplace and it was that one Sally decided on for their living-cum-bedroom-cum-everything. It looked out over the front garden which at present was a brown mess of overgrown and rotting grass. She wondered whether she and Sadie would stay there long enough to tame it and thought not. Just as soon as possible she wanted to get far away from this place.

Rhys had been her future but now he was nothing more than a miserable memory of the past, so it was with a shock that she saw him walking up the front path a week later. He was dressed in a duffel coat, the hood drawn around his face, but she knew it was him. To her utter disbelief she saw he was carrying flowers. Did he really think he could calm her pain and disappointment with flowers?

She picked up Sadie and ran up the stairs and watched from the window as he looked up at the house then approached the door. He knocked several times, glancing up in between and then walked around to the back of the house. Thankfully, she remembered the door was locked. She had a brief look at his face and was shocked. He looked ill. Was that the reason he was staying away from her? But no, he'd need her and his parents if that were the reason. It must have been a trick of the light.

He came back and knocked again on the door before pushing

something through the letterbox. Then he walked away, stopping to look back several times as though reluctant to accept defeat. She waited a long time before going back down the stairs.

There was a note on the floor and she picked it up and held it between finger and thumb as though it was contaminated. It was brief, just an apology and telling her of his grief at the loss of their son. He promised to explain everything if she could be patient for just a few more months. She was glad there was a fire burning and watched the flames destroy his words with some satisfaction.

Jimmy had ridden around outside the house several times but had cycled away each time she had called to him to come in. He felt a strong embarrassment having seen her about to give birth and later, as she sat against the tree nursing the newly born baby. He hadn't been back to the mill either, unable to cope with the fear of the place since that day, half believing it was haunted by the baby who had died. He had walked down the path twice but could go no further than halfway. Once during the night, he heard the call of a vixen and convinced himself it was the cries of the dead baby.

Two weeks after Sally had moved into the house, he packed some food while his parents were out and promised himself that this time he would go right to the mill and lay the fear of ghosts for ever. I'm almost eleven years old, he told himself, and I've been walking through the wood at night since I was eight.

He dressed, packed his bag with food and his torch and bottle of water, and he stood, with a blanket over his arm, listening impatiently to his parents downstairs, arguing as usual. The television was quiet. Why didn't they come to bed?

'Useless you are!' he heard his father shout. Useless was his favourite word, Jimmy thought with a sigh. 'You and that son of yours. I can't believe how useless you are. Why don't you get a decent dressing gown? Look at you, slovenly old thing, tatty slippers, it's all you ever wear in the house. Dress up smart for work though.'

'If you got a job and we didn't have to depend on my wages you might be justified in complaining!' his mother retaliated. There was the sound of furniture being dragged and he could picture the scene as though he were there. His father threatening, his mother defiant, although he had never known a blow to be struck.

It was half past eleven before he considered it safe to leave and he hurried from the house on tiptoes, his feet not making a sound. Once out on the road he moved fast, and his determination not to waver remained strong, but as he approached the mill his feet slowed and he began to listen for the sounds of the countryside at night with dread.

As he drew near to the mill he lost his nerve. He was aware of that atavistic fear of attack, that vulnerability, that cold sensation between his shoulder blades. He stood undecided for a moment and then twitched his nostrils. He thought he smelt smoke. Someone was there. Or had been. No one could be sleeping there at this time of year, surely? He stepped closer and as his nerve was about to break he heard someone coughing. Eric!

'Hi,' he called casually as he came in sight of a bright fire with Eric shrouded in blankets sitting beside it. 'I didn't expect to see anyone here in this weather. November isn't the time for picnicking, but I've brought some food. Supper tastes better out here. Fancy a jam sandwich?'

'Hello, young Jimmy, why aren't you in bed?'

'Couldn't sleep. I hoped to get a sight of the fox. Seen him, have you?'

As naturally as always, he sat beside Eric and they shared their food. Jimmy was careful not to eat too much, aware that Eric must be broke to have to sleep in the mill in the winter. 'Got kicked out again, did you?' he asked, muttering around a rather stale cake.

'No, this time it was my choice. Not a word, mind, but I wanted to buy a present for Sadie. She had to leave the Martins' house and I don't think there's much comfort in the place they're living in at present.'

'A present. That's nice,' Jimmy said.

When he walked back home leaving his blanket for Eric to use, the wood seemed as friendly as it had always been. The damp, warm scent of early winter was comforting and familiar, relaxing him. He stopped several times and listened to the quiet rustling as small creatures went about their foraging. An owl flew past and he marvelled at its almost silent flight, trying not to think of the small animals who would provide its supper. Back home he slept soundly, still half dressed, until his mother called him for school. If she wondered why his pyjamas were unused on the chair, she didn't bother to enquire.

Amy was at the nursery one morning when Sally was waiting to collect Sadie. 'I hope you are fully recovered, Sally,' she said. She looked uneasy.

'I have to be,' Sally told her. 'My grieving has to be in private. I had to put on the brave woman act for everyone, including Sadie, and I think it helped in a way. Mourning can go on for ever if you dwell on it and even the kindest people have had enough after a while.'

'Rick and I were very upset. When that Milly woman came around to tell me of your ordeal, I'm afraid I was angry with her and, well, I presumed she knew, about you and Rhys being – you know – and I said too much. I'm terribly sorry, but I think I was unwittingly responsible for that newspaper article.'

'Don't worry, it's a miracle it hadn't been guessed before this. It had to come out sometime. At least I had a bit of sympathy. Mrs Green had told me she didn't want me working for her any more and that was a shock – I depended on her and a couple more to pay for nursery for Sadie. After the article she asked me to go back.'

'I'm glad it wasn't all disaster. Look, here she comes!' She pointed to where Sadie was running to the door, a very messy model made from oddments in her hand.

'Thank you for being so understanding about my mistake,' Amy said as Sally hugged her daughter, getting paint over her face in the process. 'As soon as we're settled in, I'd love it if you could come and have tea with me one day.'

Sally thanked her and as she walked away she had the happy feeling that Amy might become a friend.

Sally and Sadie had been in the house for two weeks when Eric called. Jimmy was with him. He carried a large parcel which Sadie gleefully unwrapped, tearing at the paper in great excitement. Eric had bought her a very large teddy bear which the little girl at once placed on the floor and cuddled. Neither Eric nor Jimmy explained what he had done to get the money but she guessed he'd have had to give up something. She offered them food and hurriedly provided a steaming bowl of homemade soup followed by pancakes.

Sally certainly wasn't short of visitors although once her friends realized she was working on her cleaning jobs during the mornings and the decorating most evenings after Sadie was asleep, they timed their visits accordingly and kept them brief. The afternoons were for Sadie and friends.

Rhys called several times and although she knew he had seen her, she still didn't answer the door. On one occasion she had a good look at him and was further alarmed by the gauntness of his face. He looked so tired and again she wondered if illness had been the reason he had stayed away. TB maybe? Something he might be afraid of passing on to her or Sadie?

Valmai came often but she didn't ask her about her son. She didn't want to show any interest in the man who had let her down so badly.

She did ask David if he had heard news of him and he looked at her quizzically. 'Still care, do you?'

'I want nothing more to do with him,' she replied vehemently. 'But I saw him yesterday when he knocked at the door and I thought he looked ill.'

'Why don't you ask Mrs Martin?'

She shook her head. 'I don't want to show any interest. She has to accept that one day soon I'll leave here and she mustn't be given hope of a happy ending.'

'Where will you go? Not too far away, Sally. You know I don't want to lose touch with you and Sadie.'

She smiled. 'I don't think there's anyone who will grieve for very long when I go, not even you, David.'

'You're wrong. I don't want you to go. I've always liked you and now, seeing so much of you and Sadie, my feelings are stronger. You must know that.' He moved closer, his arm reaching for her as though they were about to kiss and she stepped away, not abruptly or very far, just enough to avoid his kiss.

Sally was surprised. Having loved Rhys for so long, it hadn't occurred to her that David could be anything more than the friend he'd always been. 'I'll always value your friendship,' she said warmly. 'You and your mother are very good friends and I won't find it easy to say goodbye to either of you.'

'I see,' he replied, sadly. Then after a moment he added, 'Don't be too ready to leave people who care about you. Did you know that

Eric slept at the old mill for a week so he could buy something for Sadie with his rent money?'

'Oh, no! What a dear, foolish man. He's too generous. Don't you often find that the people with the least give the most? I often take him some food but I'll do more, without him guessing that I know, of course.'

After David had gone she sat and thought about his words. Despite the unpleasant few who relished the gossip she caused, there were so many people here who had helped her, showed their concern. Even Amy had mellowed and sometimes called for a cup of tea and might soon be called a friend. And Valmai and Gwilym were Sadie's grandparents. Could she deprive them by taking Sadie away? She'd have to make sure David didn't get the wrong idea about her feelings for him but he was right, she was better to stay here among friends.

David ran as he left the house, embarrassed. Although Sally had been careful not to exaggerate her unwillingness to make that move into more than friendship, he felt foolish. Then he began to think about his situation. He was a highly skilled carpenter but he was unemployed and there were no prospects of any suitable work in the near future. Of course, that was why she had refused his attempt at showing his feelings. She was a mother and would need security. 'Fool that I am,' he muttered as he slowed to a walk. I have to get work, show her I can look after her and Sadie. Then she'll respond. I know she will. He smiled then as he imagined the look on Rhys's face when he learned of his daughter being brought up by David Gorse. One day perhaps even having his name.

He called at Greenways a few days later and offered to repair a built-in cupboard in the living room before Sally painted the woodwork. He took a bag of tools and set about the task, talking to Sally casually, determined he would get a job before attempting to show his feeling again. 'Make haste slowly', seemed a ridiculous expression but he understood it now. He was pleased with the repair and went to tell Gwilym, and promised to bring Sadie home from her visit to the Martins.

Gwilym was in his shed working on a headboard for a single bed. He had drawn the design of flowers and dragonflies and small fairy-like figures. About a third of it was already carved and it was beautiful.

'Gwilym, that is wonderful. Who's the lucky customer?'

'I'm making it for Sadie. Wherever they live, she'll need a bed.'

'You are an artist.'

'This is the work I love best.'

After admiring Gwilym's skill, watching the fascinating work-manship for a while, sadly aware he didn't have the ability to match Gwilym's steady and sure handling of the tools, David said, 'I've decided to try again to get a job. But I won't take just anything. I was a supervisor – I just couldn't go back to using the tools again.'

'You were quite good at what you did, but more suited to the administration side. Administration is a skill of its own. Forget carpentry, you could work for any business.'

'Are you saying I wasn't good enough with the tools? That was why I was promoted to supervisor?'

Gwilym stared at him with a frown. 'You messed up a few times, didn't you?'

'And Rhys? He was good, was he?'

'Not as good as Eric was in his time. Rhys faced it and decided to teach instead.' He smiled then. 'Go down and put the kettle on, will you? I expect Valmai will be back from the park with Sadie soon.' As usual, Gwilym waited until David wasn't looking before pushing himself down the path and in through the kitchen door.

David felt humiliated. No one had ever suggested he wasn't among the best at the factory. Although, thinking back to where he didn't want to go, he knew the work he had been given hadn't been projects needing the greatest skill. Old Eric better than me? Anger swelled and confidence returned as his thoughts turned to Sally, who preferred Rhys to himself. Rhys Martin, a cowardly man who had run away from her, leaving her to cope alone! How could she prefer a man like that? Obviously she wasn't as clever as she believed. But he'd convince her. How could he fail?

It was December and decorating Greenways was beginning to make the place look more homely although the bitterly cold weather was making the work harder. It had the not unpleasant smell of scrubbed wooden floors and new paint. But it was very cold. There were no curtains and no floor covering apart from a rug given to her by Mrs Falconer. A small electric fire burning in a bare, unfurnished room made very little difference to the temperature. The wooden floors, devoid of covering, meant the heat disappeared leaving nothing more than a glow which didn't make working any easier. The dark evening at least meant a coal fire, which helped keep the one room cosy. It also meant Sadie went to sleep early, allowing Sally to start painting straight after they had eaten.

Once each week, Sadie was met from nursery by Valmai and taken back to spend the afternoon with her and Gwilym. That meant Sally could spend the afternoon on the endless decorating. One day, when the wind howled around the house in a fury so she kept away from the windows and didn't see him approaching, Rhys came. She heard the knock and got up to answer the door expecting it to be one of her regular visitors. Wearing the hooded duffel coat, his thin face looked like that of a stranger at first. His eyes seemed too large, the nose and chin sharp, his face lacking its former roundness.

'Go away,' she said at once and tried to close the door.

He held it and stared at her. 'Sally, please. Just five minutes. Please, love. I want to explain.' Afraid then that her fears of an illness were true, she opened the door and walked ahead of him into the one room she and Sadie used.

'I'll make some tea,' she said, needing a moment or two to compose herself. She went into the kitchen, leaving him looking down into Sadie's empty cot. She couldn't see his expression and wondered rather cynically whether it would show affection and regret or if he was just imagining a sleeping child who might have belonged to a stranger.

She dawdled over making the tea and putting out some biscuits and when she carried them through he was sprawled in the solitary armchair, fast asleep.

She didn't know what to do. She couldn't wake him and tell him to go but he couldn't stay either. There was a knock at the door and she hurried to open it, hoping it was Mrs Martin, who would help persuade him to leave. It was David.

'Come in,' she said. 'You'll never guess who's here.'

'What's he doing here?' he demanded, taking hold of Rhys's arm and shaking it. 'Wake up, come on, you're leaving. Haven't you caused Sally enough trouble without this? More gossip to contend with? How much more will you put her through?'

Sluggishly, Rhys stood and at that moment, with Sally staring at him and David pulling on his arm, Rick walked in, his arms full of firewood. 'I thought you might be glad of – what's going on? Sorry, but the door was open, and—'

'Rhys is just leaving,' David said and he pushed Rhys from the room. Sally heard the sound of the door slamming with disappointment that was edged with pain. He looked so exhausted. She should have insisted he stayed at least until she had spoken to his mother.

'I'll just make sure he's gone,' David said and the door closed more softly behind him. Sally sank into the chair and Rick, seeing the tray, poured her some tea. He too left quite soon after, making her promise to lock the door and not open it to anyone.

'He looks so ill,' was all she said. Guessing who the stranger was, Rick didn't comment. Criticism could be misplaced if the expression in Sally's eyes was a guide and he didn't want to lose her friendship.

When she took Sadie to nursery the following morning there was talk about two burglaries and this time the police were definitely looking for Rhys Martin.

Sally was interviewed and the police made denial impossible as both David and Rick had seen Rhys in her room. 'He looked so tired,' she said. 'I don't think he was capable of anything as energetic as breaking into someone's house.'

'Burglars work at night. Being tired goes with the job, miss,' the sergeant replied sarcastically. Constable Harvey put a hand on her shoulder. 'Sorry I am, you and he being, well, fond of each other, but you have to face facts – whenever there've been robberies Rhys has been seen in the area. Between those times he vanishes.'

'But why would he bring attention to himself if he knows he's suspected? There are other places where he could break into houses. He isn't my favourite person any more but he isn't stupid! Someone could be using his occasional visits to cover their own activities!'

'We've thought of that, miss, but we have to interview him and make sure he isn't our man. If you see him, will you tell him that?'

'I won't be seeing him!'

'But if you do, you will explain how important it is for us to talk to him?'

Too tired to argue, she nodded wearily.

After the spate of visitors the house seemed larger and emptier than before. The shadows moved unnervingly around the walls and sounds she had previously ignored as the house settled for the night became more insistent. She picked up some of the wood Rick had brought and threw some on the slowly dying fire with a shovelful of small coals. She knew she wouldn't sleep and the living fire was a companion, of sorts.

At 5 a.m. she woke stiffly, having dozed in the armchair and, taking the electric fire Valmai had given her, went into the kitchen. This was the room she had chosen to be her next project but it was difficult being in use and so filled with clutter and it was only occasionally she managed to make some progress there. But surprisingly it was nearing completion. Dressed in an old dressing gown and furry boots, she began putting the second coat of paint on the walls, listening for a sound to tell her Sadie was waking.

At a quarter to nine she had finished the walls and fed, washed and dressed Sadie. Then she took her to the nursery before making her way to the first of her day's cleaning jobs. Not much of a life, she murmured as she kissed her daughter goodbye, but it won't be for long. Soon I'll work out our future, I'll find a place where you and I will he happy.

The work on Greenways might stretch to two more months, maybe longer if she could persuade the landlord to include the outside and the garden in the agreement and by then she would surely have come up with a plan.

She finished her cleaning jobs early. One lady was visiting her daughter in London and wouldn't need her, another only wanted some ironing done. She hurried back to Greenways with a little more than an hour before she needed to meet Sadie. Without waiting for even a cup of tea she carried the stepladder up the stairs and into the smallest bedroom. The ceiling needed at least two coats and if she were quick she might complete the first.

She lit the electric fire to take the chill from the room and put on the dressing gown that she used as an overall. Covering her head with an old scarf, she began. The work went well and she was singing as she brushed rhythmically with the wide brush, then she leaned over to hold the top of the door as she stretched to the final corner. The ladder tilted very slightly and she saw the paint tin begin to slide and reached for it. She wailed as she missed and saw the contents flow down on to the floor. In a panic, anxious to save as much mess as possible, her hand missed the door and she fell.

She was afraid to move for a moment or two, not certain how badly she was hurt. She felt nothing at first but as she began to move the pains began. Her hand was still holding the brush and her wrist hurt. Her shoulders too, and her neck seemed as though it would refuse to straighten. Slowly she stood up and threw the paint-covered dressing gown on to the floor. Thank goodness the tin had been almost empty and the floorboards were protected with several layers of newspapers.

Ignoring the aches that were increasing minute by minute, she scooped up the tin, brush and papers, wrapped them in the dressing gown and carried the lot out into the garden. Then she looked at herself. She was covered in paint. How on earth was she going to get herself cleaned in time to meet Sadie? A glance at the clock told her she had only a few minutes before having to leave.

She put the kettle on to clean herself and the floor of the bedroom, but while she waited for the first kettleful to heat, she agonizingly washed herself with cold. Thank goodness she hadn't been using gloss paint! She had to make sure the floor didn't show any sign of the disaster. Shivering uncontrollably, she dressed in as many clothes as she could reasonably wear and stood in hot water and sipped a cup of hot cocoa to warm herself. Then she jumped up and down, swinging her arms for the final few minutes before leaving to meet Sadie. Aware of the picture she'd have made a short time earlier, she began to laugh. At least she'd have a good story to tell Sadie.

Chapter Six

ON THE MORNING following the accident, Sally woke and was immediately aware of pain and discomfort. She had cut her face and had landed with her head against the skirting board and had obviously wrenched her neck. Beside that, her hand was bruised and her shoulder was also stiff and painful. Getting Sadie up, dressed and ready for nursery took longer than usual and she was reminded of what an amiable child she was, and tried to imagine how she would have coped with all that had happened, including the fall, if Sadie had been fractious or demanding. She hugged her and held her for longer than usual, telling the little girl how much she was loved. Reaction to the accident was mixed, most people laughing as Sally told the story to the mothers at nursery with that intention but when the news reached her, Valmai was concerned and went to Greenways at once.

'You must see a doctor,' she said. 'I'll come with you now, shall I? I can look after Sadie while you see him.'

'But I'm bruised, that's all,' Sally protested, trying to hide her painful hand, now a startlingly dark blue. 'Besides, I haven't cleaned all the paint off myself yet. I keep finding smears on my arms and in my hair. I can't be seen looking like this.'

'Tomorrow,' Valmai insisted. 'I'll meet you after you've taken Sadie to nursery. Right?'

'I can't tomorrow, I have work to do.'

'So have I, but this is important. Besides, you can't work. Just look at that hand. Nine o'clock, right? And look, I've brought some soup for your supper, save you bothering and I've sliced some bread.'

She knew Valmai was right; she did need to see a doctor to make sure the damage was nothing more than bruising. Whatever he advised she would have to carry on as usual. A few weeks of being unable to work and she would lose all her clients. So it was pointless really. She went to the surgery as soon as Sadie had been handed over to the assistant at the nursery. Valmai was waiting.

The hand and other injuries were examined and then the shoulder and arm were strapped and she was told she must rest. She thanked the doctor and the nurse who had applied the dressings to the cuts but as soon as she was outside, she shook her head. 'Rest? That's a joke. I have to keep my cleaning jobs, and if I don't continue with the decorating, Sadie and I will have to move out of Greenways.'

'You know there's a home with Gwilym and me for as long as you need one,' Valmai said, adding quickly, 'Don't worry, I know you and Rhys won't get back together and I don't blame you for that, I really don't. But we still want to help. Fond of you, we are, and full of admiration for the way you've conducted yourself through all this.'

'Thank you.' Sally hesitated then said, 'There is something you can help with, if you're sure you don't mind.'

'Anything.'

'I've been asked to do a full house-cleaning for Mrs Glover ready for when her visitors come next week but it will take a day at least and I can't really expect her to look after Sadie for the whole afternoon, much as she loves to see her. Would you meet Sadie from nursery and look after her until I've finished? There'll be two of us, and Mrs Glover also does what she can, so I hope to finish after one whole day and the following morning.'

'Glad to. I'll take her to the park – she loves that, even though it's so cold – and Gwilym will be pleased to spend some time with her. Just let me have some spare clothes in case she gets dirty and we'll have a lovely day.'

News of the accident and Sally's injuries spread and when David's mother told him, he was concerned and went to Greenways at once.

'You must do as the doctor said and rest,' he said.

'But I'm just a bit bruised, that's all,' Sally insisted, trying to hide her painful hand.

'At least let me help. I can light the fire for a start.' He moved the electric fire to one side and, ignoring her protests, he set about cleaning out the grate and getting the fire to blaze.

Rather unkindly, Sally wondered why he didn't show the same enthusiasm when looking for work. For more than two years he'd been unemployed. She couldn't imagine Rhys doing nothing for all that time. Then that train of thought stopped abruptly. As far as she knew that's exactly what Rhys had been doing. Nothing! No college, and certainly no job or he wouldn't have been using the money she had been sending regularly. What had he been doing? He must be in serious trouble but why couldn't he talk about it?

'I'll just go and fill the coal scuttle. I'll come tomorrow and do the same, shall I?' David's comment startled her out of her puzzled musings.

'Thank you, David, it does cheer the room, doesn't it?'

'And tomorrow, before you get home with Sadie?'

She searched her mind for an excuse then remembered she had a genuine one. 'Not tomorrow. Sadie is going to stay with Mr and Mrs Martin. I'll be out all day helping Mrs Glover. It's sooner than I expected but she's expecting visitors next week and wants it done straight away. Pity really. I'd hoped to get the front bedroom walls papered this week. I set everything out ready to start, but now it will have to wait.'

'Forget it for a while. I don't think you should be climbing stepladders until you've lost the bruises from the last time,' he said jokingly. 'The work will get done. Just be a bit patient.'

She was apprehensive when the day of the landlord's inspection came and spent as much time as she could spare making sure the place looked clean and tidy. Mr Davies was a man in his fifties formally dressed in a dark suit and a smart overcoat. His shoes shone with much polishing and he wore gloves. He said very little at first but seemed satisfied with what he saw.

'I've bought it for my parents,' he explained. 'My father is retiring in April and they'll move here.'

'I'll be finished and gone long before then,' she said.

'Fine, but if you still need a place, you can stay after the work is done. We can arrange for a small rent to help cover the expenses.' He glanced at the accounts and told her not to spend any of her own money when he noticed there were a few items not listed. 'I've opened an account at the local paint shop. Just get what you need and I'll deal with it.'

'Is there anything else you'd like me to do?'

'You've hurt your hand. Don't try to do anything until it's better. There's plenty of time.' He looked around the room where she spent most of her time and asked, 'What about Christmas? You don't seem to have made any preparations. No trimmings?'

She couldn't tell him that she hadn't given the festival a moment's thought. 'I don't want to risk marking the newly painted walls,' she told him.

'I'll come next week to put up the curtain rails. I'll bring a tree.'

'Thanks,' she murmured, wondering what she would use to decorate it.

Mrs Glover was one of Sally's favourite clients. She helped her with the work, making her feel more of a friend than a person employed to clean. Sally knew some of the work would be difficult with a bruised hand and shoulder but was determined to do the best she could to please the lady.

It was a tiring day, washing curtains and ironing them. Brushing walls and lifting carpets. Cleaning windows and the inside of cupboards and wardrobes. Washing light fittings and occasionally used china and glasses. Mattresses were moved and the old-fashioned springs dusted. Sally and the young woman hired for the day to help didn't stop, even drinking tea and eating sandwiches as they worked.

When Sally went to collect Sadie from the Martins at six o'clock she wondered how she'd continue to place one foot in front of the other. To her relief, Valmai had the table set for four and a casserole, sending out tempting smells, was ready to serve.

They stayed until eight o'clock then Valmai walked them home. She took her bicycle and gave Sadie a ride, so she'd be able to ride back. Sally wished it was she sitting on the bike and being pushed.

She got Sadie ready for bed and the little girl was almost asleep before she had kissed her goodnight, then she undressed and after the briefest of washes, fell into her own bed completely exhausted.

The plan was to finish the last of Mrs Glover's tasks the following morning and despite her aching body and throbbing hand and shoulder, she rose early. After the usual chores and before Sadie awoke, she went upstairs to look at the room she was due to wallpaper, to plan in her mind the best place to begin and check the length of the pattern on the paper and consider the waste a large pattern would mean. She wondered whether she'd ordered enough paper. When she opened the door she shouted in dismay. Someone had started the job. Two walls were papered but the sheets weren't straight. Staring in disbelief she could see that whoever had done it had used the door jamb as a guide instead of checking it was upright. So the paper had been hung at an angle. Very slight, but enough for her to know it wouldn't do. It would all have to come off and more paper bought. Who could have been so stupid? She used anger to avoid precipitate tears. Not Valmai, but who else had a key?

'Sally?' a voice called and at once she knew. David!

'I'm up here. I hope you didn't do this,' she said, fury making her voice tight in her throat. 'Someone has interfered and ruined this job and now I'll have to take it all down and start again. And buy more wallpaper – which I'll have to pay for.'

'What's wrong with it?' David ran up the stairs and looked at the walls. 'I matched the pattern as best I could. I thought you'd be pleased.'

'Mummy?' Sadie called and, pushing past him, Sally ran down the stairs and began talking to her daughter, ignoring David's comments, knowing that if she looked at him she'd scream in frustration. Why did nothing go right for her she wondered?

Valmai was waiting at the nursery to see if she was all right and her anger and despair burst from her and she told her what had happened. 'Please, don't offer to help,' Sally said as they parted. 'I can't stand the thought of someone else doing a poor job. I want the landlord to be pleased with everything I do and he'll be around again next week to check on my progress.'

'What was David thinking of? I'll help you to take the wallpaper off and then I think you should go away for a couple of days. You're worn out and you can't hide the fact that you're finding it painful to use that hand. You aren't in the right frame of mind to do anything at present. I've got a friend in Saundersfoot. Pretty little place. She'll have you there and won't charge much, it being out of season. Go, love, and relax for a couple of days. You'd benefit from a break. Just you and Sadie.'

Sally was about to argue. There wasn't time. She had to finish the room. She had to conserve her savings. There were a dozen reasons why she should refuse, but then, as she stared into Valmai's kindly face, she suddenly felt more calm and in control. In that moment she changed her mind about two things. One, she would go away for the weekend and two, she would never move far from Valmai and deprive her of her granddaughter. Whatever happened between herself and Rhys, Valmai didn't deserve such treatment.

'Thank you. You're right and I'll do that. Just me and Sadie, somewhere near the sea.'

She went on the train and found the cottage advertising bed and breakfast and Mrs Daniels offered to provide an evening meal. 'I don't usually, mind, but as I'm not busy and you're only staying for the weekend I'll let you come in for a bit of lunch too if you find the weather too much for little Sadie.'

With Sadie in her pushchair and wrapped cosily with fluffy blankets, Sally explored the small town. Many places were closed for the winter but the beach sheltered from the wind during those few days was a fascination for Sadie. They even managed to survive the cold weather long enough to build a sandcastle and gather some shells and pretty pebbles.

The contrast between beach and town was marked: the cold, empty sand and rocky coast and the bright, overheated, glittery shops in their brightest displays. Carols were sung by small groups of people collecting for charities and from out of some of the shops other seasonal music emerged and distorted their efforts. Yet still the approach of Christmas hadn't penetrated Sally's thoughts. Probably because she had never had a home where her parents had indulged themselves in all the excitement and gaiety of the celebration.

Her parents had died when she was young and her memories of the years before were vague. They hadn't been there to set traditions: large amounts of luxurious food, the stocking filling, the secrets, the mysterious and colourful parcels under the Christmas tree. Those things had always happened to other people and without a home of her own, no one with which to share the joy if it all, she didn't know how to begin.

She tried not to think of the empty house she presently called home and the mess of the wallpapering that would be waiting when she got back and the tension eased from her. She felt anger every time she thought of David and his stupid attempt at helping but pushed it away more and more easily as the hours passed. She felt calm, philosophical about the disasters that had befallen her and better able to cope. There was nothing that she couldn't deal with. Once her hand and shoulder were strong again, she would look for work, build a new career. She wasn't a failure, she had just trusted the wrong person, that's all. A human mistake, not a criminal or negligent act.

The good feeling lasted until she reached the railway station to begin the journey home. A young man she had noticed once or twice on the beach stood near the entrance and she smiled politely and he spoke to her, as a stranger might.

'Have you and your little girl enjoyed your break?'

'Yes, thank you.'

'Mrs Daniels is my aunt and she told me you were here to rest after an accident.'

'Hardly an accident,' she said with a smile. 'I slipped when I was painting a wall. Just bruises, nothing dramatic. Getting covered in paint was the worst thing.'

'I'm Geraint.' He held out a hand and she shook it.

'I'm Sally and this is—' She smiled and waited for her daughter to speak.

'My name is Sadie Travis,' she provided.

'Hello, Sadie.'

He bent down and talked to the little girl until the train arrived, then helped her into a carriage and sat near them. He didn't force his attentions on them, just an occasional remark, and once or twice picking up a book or a toy Sadie dropped. Then when they reached the station and the train squealed to a stop he helped her down with the pushchair and her small case while she held Sadie's hand. She thanked him and they went out of the station together and bumped right into Milly Sewell.

She said nothing when she saw the young man pick Sadie up and fit her into the pushchair, she just waited until Sally looked at her. Then she raised an eyebrow and muttered to her friend, 'Another mysterious father, d'you suppose?' Sally heard the words as Milly intended her to and she hurried away without a goodbye to the friendly young man. Humiliated and aware that the restful interlude was well and truly over, she almost ran back to Greenways, her shoulder agonizingly painful as she dragged the suitcase and pushed her daughter's pushchair. She was in a place where critics were determined to think the worst of her and home meant hours of hard work and little comfort. Something would have to change.

The fire was alight when she opened the living-room door and the warmth was a wonderful welcome. For a while at least she could wallow in the pleasure of the knowledge that not everyone was as unpleasant as Milly Sewell; the town held more people who were kind than were unpleasant.

Valmai had left food and a note on the table to welcome her home and that helped too. But it wasn't until Sadie was asleep that she could face walking up to look at the disaster in the bedroom. She took a deep breath, convinced it would look even worse than the first time and switched on the light. The room was completely decorated. The wallpaper perfectly hung, a matching lampshade added, and even in the poor light she could see that the windows had been cleaned of paint splashes. The floor had been thoroughly scrubbed and the room smelled refreshingly of pine soap.

Who could have done this? Certainly not David. Could Valmai have made such a good job of it? There was no one else. It was too late to find out tonight. Once Sadie was asleep she couldn't go anywhere, so she settled beside the glowing fire and thought about the good friends who must have somehow arranged this wonderful surprise. Tomorrow she would find them and thank them.

Her Monday jobs kept her busy until lunchtime and after collecting Sadie she went to the butchers to buy sausages and in the doorway as she turned to leave was Milly Sewell.

'Nice time with your new friend, was it? Saundersfoot's a bit cold for me in December but if you've got love to keep you warm I don't suppose it matters what time of the year, does it?'

'Sadie and I were on our own and—'

'Sorry, Mrs Sewell, but I'm closing for an hour,' the butcher interrupted. 'I *might* serve you if you come back later, if there's anything left.' The butcher ushered the woman out of the shop but continued to serve others who were waiting. 'And any such comments from any of you and you'll be banned, the lot of you. Right?' He winked at Sally and continued to serve a very subdued queue.

Sally didn't go back home. She knew Valmai finished around lunchtime and went to her house. Sadie ran excitedly towards the shed and Sally chased after her, arriving in time to see Gwilym, out of his chair, exercising his limbs. She stared, embarrassed at the man's expression of, what? Shame? Guilt? With the aid of sticks he walked back to the bench to hide his disability.

'Hello, I hope you don't mind us calling. We want to ask Mrs Martin about the miracle of the ruined bedroom.' She spoke light-heartedly as though she had not witnessed his movements. Sadie climbed into his lap and began talking about sandcastles and train rides.

The sound of a bicycle bell announced Valmai's arrival and Gwilym said, 'Not a word to Valmai. She'd be keeping on, pushing me to get out and I can't, see. I just can't.'

'One day something will happen and you'll have to,' was all Sally said, before turning to greet his wife.

To Sally's surprise she learned that Eric and Rick had papered the room and Valmai had cleaned it.

'I thought I must be dreaming when I went to assess the damage and found the room finished, and perfectly done too. How can I thank you all?'

'No need. What are friends for? Now, what about a bite to eat before I have to go back to work. I bet you're starving, aren't you, Sadie?'

With Sadie helping by throwing assorted cutlery on the table and setting the table in her own inimitable style, and Sally putting out plates of sandwiches quickly made by Valmai, they ate a pleasant lunch before Valmai set off for work pushing her bicycle with Sally and a chattering Sadie walking beside her.

Waiting for her at the gate was someone she didn't recognize at first – a smartly dressed young woman in a fur-trimmed coat and a fur hat. When she turned to face them she saw the sharp-featured face within the furry frame, of Amy, Rick's fiancée. She wasn't smiling. Oh dear, Sally thought. She looks as though something has upset her and it's probably me. And I thought we were becoming friends!

'Amy? This is a nice surprise. Will you come in?'

'I can't stay long. I just wanted to ask you not to expect my fiancé to help you out of any more of your so frequent problems.' Her voice was shrill. Her face showed disapproval and she ignored Sadie completely. 'He has quite enough to do with the wedding imminent and getting our home ready in time.'

'I quite understand, I really do, but I don't ask him for any. He's just a very kind-hearted man and I'm grateful for his help. But if we both have a word with him and remind him how inappropriate it is, I'm sure he'll ignore my "frequent problems" and concentrate on yours.' She ushered the woman inside and lit the electric fire. 'Stay and have a cup of tea. I'd love to hear about all your plans for the wedding and your future home. It's such an exciting time, isn't it?'

'No, I won't accept tea. We aren't exactly friends, and I'd be glad if you'd avoid both of us in future.'

'Have you been talking to Milly Sewell by any chance?'

'Well, yes, I have.'

Sally gave Sadie a few toy building bricks and said firmly, 'Please sit down, Miss Jones. I think you should at least listen to my side of the story, don't you?'

'It's Seaton-Jones, actually.'

With a smile, Sally said, 'All right, Miss Seaton-Jones-Actually! Firstly I am not promiscuous. My fiancé, Rhys Martin, ran away when he was afraid the police were about to question him about some robberies. He wanted to train as a teacher and knew if a criminal record was attached to his name he wouldn't be accepted. So I have been sending money to him each month and in July he had completed two years and presumably qualified. Only he didn't come home, and when I went to look for him I found out that he hadn't been to college and certainly hadn't qualified. What he was doing with my money I have no idea. And why he ran away yet insisted he was innocent, well, that's another mystery.' She went on, over Amy's attempt to speak, 'Sadie and I have enjoyed a couple of days in Saundersfoot, just the two of us until another kind young man helped us off the train, and—'

'Really, this is nothing to do with me.' Amy moved towards the door.

'No? Yet you were happy to listen to Milly's gossip, Miss Seaton-Jones-Actually,' she retorted sharply.

Then Amy smiled. 'Call me Amy,' she said.

'And there's another thing,' Sally went on and when Amy looked startled, she added, 'I have decided to invite a few friends to lunch on Sunday. People I owe a big thank you to. I'd like it if you and Rick would join us. Trays on laps, I'm afraid, but as you see, this place isn't exactly well furnished.'

'We usually go to Mummy's on Sundays, but, yes, thank you, we'll both look forward to that.'

When Sally showed her the work already done on the house she was impressed. Particularly the troublesome bedroom. 'I didn't dream that Rick could do anything like this. Mummy arranged for a decorating firm to do the work on our home.'

'I don't know, but I imagine Eric was the guiding hand. He's such a lovely man, a particularly fine craftsman too. It was just bad luck he lost his job at the age when it's difficult to start again. His wife took all his savings and left him in serious debt a few years ago, leaving Eric with nothing. And now he never hears from her or his daughter.'

'Eric?'

'Yes, he's the one you called the tramp.'

Amy looked ashamed. And when she had gone Sally felt guilty. How could she have been so rude to the woman? She hoped she and Rick would still come on Sunday.

A cold wind was rising with the end of the day, and she wrapped Sadie up in her warmest coat and a thick scarf and went to put an invitation through Eric's door and another through Valmai's without interrupting Gwilym. Perhaps she had better make amends and do the same for David. He might have ruined the wallpapering but he had tried to help and he had done many kindnesses before. She felt happy with her day. She was badly shocked by Milly's remarks but it had resulted in a Sunday lunch party to plan and at least a slight thawing of her acquaintanceship with Amy Seaton-Jones. She was excited at the prospect of welcoming friends to the house for the first time.

The following morning the invitation to David was sticking out of her letterbox with the invitation scored through and the words 'No thanks!' added.

She had obviously offended him and she determined to make amends. After collecting Sadie from nursery she went to where David lived with his mother. Mrs Gorse opened the door and greeted her with a smile.

'Sally! Come in, come in, dear. Lovely to see you and this pretty little girl. Let's see if I can find a chocolate.' Taking Sadie's hand, she led them into the living room.

The house was dark and filled with clutter and the windowsills were so covered with ornaments and greenery that hardly any light entered. The living room was cosy with a fire burning brightly, sending patterns of brightness over the dark walls.

'It's David I've called to see,' Sally explained, as Mrs Gorse searched among several tins for some chocolate.

After giving Sadie the promised chocolate, she said, 'David's asleep. Keeps strange hours, he does, wandering around all hours of the night unable to sleep, then dozes for much of the day. Ever since the factory closed and he couldn't find another job. I keep asking him to see the doctor – he needs help adjusting his sleep pattern – but will he listen?'

'I owe him an apology. As a surprise, he very kindly helped me with some decorating and I – well – it wasn't as good as I'd hoped and I was rude to him. He was only trying to help.'

Mrs Gorse frowned. 'Are you sure it was my David? He's wonderful at wallpapering and the like. Look at this room – did it on his own, he did. Made the shelves and that glass-fronted cupboard. Clever with things like that, he is.'

Sally looked more closely at the small amount of wallpaper still visible among the confusion of pictures and shelves covered with ornaments. She prepared for the worst but in fact the papering was neat and perfectly matched. If he had done this, then why had he made such a mess of the bedroom?

'I must have got it wrong, Mrs Gorse. It must have been someone else who messed up the bedroom. Will you tell him I'm very sorry and I would really like him to come to lunch on Sunday?'

'Sundays we always eat together – he's always up and dressed ready for lunch on Sundays – but I'm sure he'll accept if I assure him I won't mind.'

'Thank you. You're very kind.' She hesitated then said, 'I'd be more than happy if you come as well.'

She hurried from the house, not wanting to see David and have to grovel. There hadn't been a mistake. David had told her the work was his. Yet it was impossible for him to have made such a disaster of the bedroom and yet be capable of doing a perfectly acceptable job in his mother's living room. What was going on?

On Sunday, Sally woke very early and with Sadie still peacefully sleeping, she began her preparations for lunch. She had some qualms having invited so many into a house that looked more like an abandoned building than a home, but once both fires were alight and the place was warm she knew people wouldn't be disappointed. There were some early daffodils in the shops and she filled a few vases and added some branches with leaf buds and some ivy trails. The rooms looked as good as she could make them.

David and his mother were the first to arrive and she stifled a sigh. Too early could be as difficult as people who were always late, she mused, as she took their coats. She still had a lot to do. Mrs Gorse followed her into the kitchen. David didn't say a word or even look at her.

As it happened she was glad they were there half an hour before anyone else as Mrs Gorse had brought flowers to add to the displays and also some cakes and mince pies. 'Handy they'll be to offer with a cup of tea before your guests leave,' she said, unpacking them on to plates, which she had also brought.

Sally planned to use two rooms and with the extra flowers and foliage the place looked surprisingly festive. The bustle of people arriving filled the silence and the ill will emanating from David was lost in an atmosphere that was friendly and lively.

She happened to be looking at David when Rick walked in with Amy and was startled to see his expression change to dislike. Oh dear, she thought. I'd better keep those two apart. She sat the new arrivals down beside Eric and was relieved to see Amy talking to the man, stiffly at first but thawing as minutes passed. David had disappeared. Valmai sat on a sofa with a chatting Sadie on her lap.

As the food was consumed and cups of tea were replenished, the group rearranged itself and the conversations grew louder, interspersed with laughter. Sally looked around and smiled. It had been a success despite the lack of a formal setting. They consumed more of Mrs Gorse's mince pies and the conversations became low and easy. She saw David get up and at almost the same time, Rick also rose and left the room. He came back with a coal scuttle to add fuel to the fire and David snatched the tongs from him and muttered, 'Thank you but I'll do this.'

'As you wish.' Rick said, and turning to look at Sally he shrugged as though puzzled.

The slight action changed the mood. Amy stood and reached for her handbag, preparing to leave, and others followed suit. Within ten minutes everyone except David, his mother and Valmai had gone. Wordlessly Valmai stood Sadie on her feet and came to hug Sally. Then she went into the kitchen with a few dishes, where Mrs Gorse was starting to wash up. Sadly, wondering what had gone wrong, Sally followed.

'It's been a lovely day, thank you, Sally,' Mrs Gorse said. 'Strange isn't it that when someone leaves it's like a signal for all the rest to do the same.'

'I had hoped they'd stay to finish the cakes you brought,' Sally replied.

'Never mind, they'll keep for a day or so.'

When everyone had gone Sally sat and hugged Sadie and wondered what it was about David that he managed to spoil things. Alone he was a kind, thoughtful man but when anyone else was present he ruined the occasion with a hint of – jealousy? But why? There was nothing between them that could cause such a destructive feeling.

She went for a walk to the park and in the fading light she saw David watching the house. He didn't acknowledge her and turned a corner before she could speak. She gave an involuntary shiver. Was he a friend, or an enemy? That was a dramatic thought and she walked faster as though to run away from it, but it remained. She had the feeling that with David Gorse, she had to be either friend or enemy; with him there was no middle ground. The thought played on her mind as she drifted into sleep and caused troubled dreams.

The landlord came back and fixed curtain rails in all the rooms and as he was leaving he brought in a very large Christmas tree.

'Thank you.' she said politely, wondering what she would find to fill it. He went to the car again and came back with an assortment of tinsel. 'This will make a start,' he said as though reading her thoughts.

In fact the tree was fun to decorate. Sally made stars which Sadie helped to colour and place among the branches and hair ribbons were used too, much to Sadie's amusement.

Amy called while the work was in progress and advised uselessly on the position of some of the better of Sadie's efforts. Sally smiled in relief that at least one problem had been eased. Amy was certainly more friendly.

'I hope you don't mind, Sally, but Rick and I have talked over this problem of yours. He told me about your not knowing where Rhys is living. I have to go to Bristol to buy some special material and I wondered if you and Sadie would like to come? I can leave you in the area you need to search and pick you up later.' Once they had decided on the most suitable day for them both, Sally agreed.

The journey was pleasant and they talked mostly about the forthcoming wedding. As they drew closer to their destination, Sally went quiet, afraid of what she would learn. Amy went to deal with her business, having arranged a meeting place for later, and Sally took Sadie in her pushchair to the café.

It was with some trepidation that she approached the place to which she had posted her letters and the monthly sum of money. The man behind the counter was not the same as before. He was young and obviously new as he had difficulty finding what was needed when Sally asked for cheese on toast.

'I'm just filling in for my uncle,' he explained, having found the cheese in a second fridge.

'You wouldn't know anything about the man who used to collect his post here, would you?' Sally asked, with little hope. To her surprise the young man looked away as though embarrassed.

'I don't know anything about post, Mrs. Now, cheese on toast, a pot of tea and orange juice for the little girl. Will that be all?'

Since she had asked her question he hadn't looked at her. Softly she asked, 'Can't you tell me where to find him? I really need to talk to him. Please?'

'Sorry, Mrs, I don't know him.'

'Does he live near here? At least tell me in which direction to look. I don't wish him any harm. I just need to see him.'

Lowering his head, the young man said, 'I didn't tell you, all right? But if you watch at the school gates when the children leave you might see him.' Paying for the food which she didn't stop to eat, she thanked him and left.

After buying a couple of currant buns to compensate for missing their lunch, she played with Sadie for a while then found the school. She stood in sight of the gates and prepared to wait. Thankfully, Sadie had fallen asleep.

Her heart was racing as mothers began to arrive, some with pushchairs, some rattling car keys, some loaded with cheerfully patterned bags of Christmas shopping. Of Rhys there was no sign. She moved further along the road and stood once again watching the arrivals. Then the doors opened and the children ran out, searching the group at the gate then running to hug their mothers. Then she saw Rhys.

She moved towards him, about to speak, words racing through her mind as she tried to decide on the best thing to say to him. Then a girl aged about seven approached him and he picked her up and hugged her before moving away from the diminishing crowd. Her mind in complete confusion, Sally followed him.

He didn't go far, just walked around a corner and up some steps leading to the front of a neat terraced house. As he and the little girl reached the door it opened and a smartly dressed woman came out, smiled at Rhys and kissed him on the cheek. Sally could hear them laughing as she stood, undecided, a few houses away. Then Rhys went inside.

She continued to stand watching the door, wondering whether to knock or walk away. If she did knock, what could she say to him? She gasped as the door reopened and he came out and ran lightly down the steps, turning to wave as he reached the pavement. She remained frozen to the ground wondering which way he would turn. He was whistling as he turned towards her and he was staring down at a piece of paper in his hand. She said, 'Hello, Rhys.'

'Sally!'

'You haven't forgotten my name. That's nice. And your daughter? D'you remember her?'

'This isn't what you think.'

'You mean this isn't you living with someone else, meeting their daughter from school? That is a shopping list in your hand, isn't it? Very domestic, meeting the daughter, shopping for your evening meal.'

'It isn't like that. I can explain, but not yet. Please, Sally, you've been so patient, just a few more weeks and I'll tell you everything.'

She shook her head. 'You've just run out of time.' She turned and hurried away, pride and anger preventing tears, and went back to where Amy had arranged to meet her and take her home.

When Amy asked if she had learned anything, she replied, 'Yes. I've learnt that it's time to restart my life. That's a good lesson to learn, don't you think?'

The mystery of what Rhys had been doing all this time deepened, but later that day another mystery was cleared up. She went to the post office. Walter was standing nearby and he called to her, 'I hear you didn't think much of my wallpapering, then,' he said.

'What d'you mean? Your wallpapering? You can't mean the work in Greenways, David Gorse did that.'

'No, it was me. Paid me to do it he did. Trouble is, my back isn't up to it. I couldn't get it finished in time.'

'Just as well. There was enough of a mess to put right as it was!'

A bad back was just an excuse for laziness. Someone had once told her that a lazy man is the worst. Even a drunkard would work even if only for his drink. The thought brought her thoughts back to Rhys. What was he if not lazy? There was no evidence of him doing anything for all the months he'd been away.

Christmas came and went and at least Sadie enjoyed the thrills and even Sally got caught up in the excitement. It had been Valmai who carefully asked her if she realized it was the day before Christmas Eve and asked if she'd done anything towards Sadie's stocking. The misery of finding out about Rhys's dishonesty had left her in a daze into which Christmas hadn't entered. All the plans and excitements were for other people, not for her and Sadie.

The memory of her second child wouldn't leave her at this time, the loss of Samuel overlaying every happy thought. She hadn't the right to enjoy the family celebration. Then she watched her daughter's face as she stood near the school children singing carols near the shops and with a shock reminded herself that Sadie was the important one. Sadie was her wonderful daughter, the most precious gift. She was alive and deserved all she could give her. Samuel would remain in her heart as a sad and beautiful memory.

Leaving Sadie with the kindly Mrs Glover, she had dashed into town and bought a few toys and colouring pencils as well as wrapping paper and gifts for Valmai and Gwilym.

Next year she'd do better. She and Sadie would have a proper home and they'd prepare properly and have the very best Christmas ever. She firmly built a picture of the two of them, just Sadie and herself sitting beside a tree very like the one in their room, but properly decorated with a fairy, some coloured lights and lots of glitter. They didn't need anyone else. 'Just you and me,' she whispered to her sleeping child. 'That's all I want. No one else.'

Chapter Seven

SALLY HADN'T TOLD Valmai and Gwilym about her visit to Bristol and seeing Rhys with the woman and the child. She was hurt and humiliated and needed time to nurse her wounded pride before revealing the truth to them. Partly it was her own realization that she had been foolish to just walk away. She should have sat on the steps and waited until he returned then demanded an explanation.

She also realized she had been foolish by not making a note of the address. It was as though she had been searching for an excuse to go there again, and, without telling anyone, not even Amy, she went by train to Bristol.

She dressed with care, choosing Sadie's newest clothes, and set off with the pushchair and all that was necessary for the day, determined to stay until she had faced Rhys, and the woman he was obviously living with, and learn the truth.

There was no reply to her knock on the door and after waiting a few minutes she asked a neighbour if she knew where they could be found.

'They've gone away. A little holiday I believe.'

'All of them? The man as well as the woman and the little girl?'

'Yes. Little Erica was so excited at going to stay with her grand-mother.'

There was no point in staying. Dejectedly she walked away and after a snack in a café near the railway station, they went home. Now she had to tell Valmai and Gwilym what she had learned. She would leave any further contact to them. Rhys was no longer anything to do with her or Sadie.

She hesitated about talking to Rhys's parents. She kept putting it off and when she had finally made up her mind to face them with it, Amy asked if she would like to go to Cardiff sales to buy bedding and towels for the new home, and she gladly accepted the reprieve.

They had a successful spending spree and Sally managed to forget for a while the pain of losing Rhys and enjoy the atmosphere of busy shoppers searching for bargains.

She said very little on the way home. Amy asked a few questions but quickly realized that her companion was not in the mood to discuss what had so obviously upset her. Instead she talked to the little girl, pointing out things she thought might interest her but after a while Sadie fell asleep and the journey continued in silence. 'Would you like to stop and have a cup of tea?' Sally asked eventually, aware of her rudeness in ignoring Amy, who had so kindly given her a lift. 'I'm sorry I've been so quiet but I have a lot to think about. That's no excuse for my rudeness though. A cup of tea and I'll tell you a little of what has happened.'

Smiling, Amy shook her head. 'There's no need for any explanations, but if you want to talk, can we talk about my wedding dress? It's beautiful but I think the train might be a bit too much for little hands to manage.'

They stopped in a small village where a row of shops boasted a café that advertised homemade scones. Sally carried Sadie and Amy went to find a table. Amy pulled a face when they saw the place was filled with men, whom she guessed were delivery men from their clothes and overalls. The tables were covered with plastic cloths and the steamy atmosphere didn't auger well for a tasty snack. But Sally was already sitting down and she reluctantly followed.

In her loud, imperious voice she asked for scones and tea and a drink for Sadie. A huge red-haired man dressed in overalls with a clean, open-necked shirt showing at his beefy neck, scraped back his chair and stood up. Sally stared in alarm. Then the man smiled, showing perfect white teeth and said, 'I'm afraid you have to go to the counter to order and pay, miss.'

'What? How ridiculous!'

'Tell me what you want and I'll ask them, shall I?'

'Thank you.' He went to whisper something to the woman behind the counter, who came, with an amused look in her eyes, took her order then held out her hand for the money.

The scones were very good and there was a generous amount of jam and cream. Sadie ate all of hers with Amy's help and, when they stood to leave, to Sally's surprise Amy went to the counter and thanked the woman for a delicious snack. She also thanked the man who had helped her to order.

Amy was laughing as they went back to the car. 'Shout loud enough and someone will help, even if it's simply to shut you up,' she said as she unlocked the car.

Sally's mood was lifted by the brief incident and she chattered to Amy for the rest of the journey while Sadie slept. They were almost home when the car began to make strange sounds. It spluttered, moved, slowed down and finally stopped.

'I can't believe this,' Amy gasped. 'I'm out of petrol! How can that be? I always fill up each month and I rarely need to bother between times.' She looked up and down the road. 'No phone box, of course. Typical!'

A lorry rumbled into view on the same side of the road and, seeing Amy standing beside her car, he stopped. 'Blimey, miss, you do seem to find trouble, don't you?' It was the red-haired giant from the café.

He parked his vehicle and strode over. After discussing the problem he said, 'There's a garage not far ahead. Stay here and I'll take a can and bring some petrol back.' He reached into the cab and brought out a two-gallon can and, waving it, he strode off and was soon out of sight.

Sally slid the sleeping child on to the back seat and stood outside with Amy. They heard a car approaching and stepped back between the lorry and the car. The car driver slowed and seemed about to stop and offer help but then he put his foot down, the tyres squealing as he drove quickly away.

'Did you see who that was?' Amy asked.

'I thought it was David Gorse, but it couldn't have been him. He doesn't have a car.'

'I didn't see the driver but I'm sure the car belongs to the hairdresser. Christine, she calls herself although her name is Margaret. How very odd.'

'Perhaps we were both wrong,' Sally replied doubtfully.

'I'm sure about the car – it has a stupid curtain in the side window. Dangerous. According to Rick, anything that impedes the driver's view is a silly idea. I don't go to her of course. My hairdresser is Olivier's, in Cardiff.'

'Very expensive.'

'If you settle for second best that's what you always have!' She looked at Sally thoughtfully. 'Like cleaning floors when you could do something more interesting – and better paid.'

The lorry driver returned with the petrol for which Amy paid him, and a bar of chocolate, 'For the little girl when she wakes,' he said, handing the treat to Amy.

'She isn't mine!' Amy protested, horrified, and Sally took the chocolate and thanked him.

It had been a tiring day and once Sadie was settled into bed, Sally sat for a long time wondering about Rhys and why he had failed her. She tried to think about her future which was all up to her; she was on her own and had to face it. Amy's words about accepting second best wouldn't leave her mind and at 1 a.m., when she was still sitting beside an electric fire in the silent house, she came to a decision.

Before Rhys and Sadie, she had lived in a smart flat in a pleasant area and had earned enough to live comfortably. Surely there was no reason why she couldn't go back to what she did best? She had been a buyer of fashionable clothes and accessories for a chain of stores in South Wales and beyond. The job had taken her to many other towns as exhibitions and clothes shows had led her to find new and exciting additions to her ranges. Nothing had changed apart from her own attitude. She smiled then as she remembered another of Amy's rules for life. Speak loudly and with confidence if you want to be noticed.

Wide awake, she reached for the newspaper and began thumbing down the vacancies column. There were very few vacancies in the fashion business apart from sales ladies and she knew that, as Amy had advised, she needed to avoid accepting second-rate choices and aim high. She was still buzzing with excitement an hour later but eventually slept. When the morning alarm woke her, her mind was filled with ideas.

Firstly she had to talk to Valmai and Gwilym. They were entitled to know what she had learned even though her news was disturbing. Leaving Sadie at the nursery, she went to a phone box to rearrange her calls and at eleven o'clock went to find Valmai. She was due home after an early start so she waited. Gwilym was sitting in his usual place near the workbench, with his legs tucked out of sight.

'I've seen Rhys,' she said, as soon as Valmai arrived. 'He appears to be living with a woman, and there's a child, a girl about six or seven years old.' The words had burst from her and now she stopped and waited for their reaction.

'Oh, no,' Gwilym murmured.

'I'm afraid it's true.'

White faced, Valmai was staring at her as though she were a stranger. 'Tell us exactly what happened. Where is he?'

'In Bristol. I asked around at the café where letters were sent and was told he might be at the school. I saw him there, meeting a little girl. I followed him to a house and as he reached the front door it opened and a woman came out to greet him. She was smiling and they hugged and she kissed his cheek. He followed her inside and I stood there wondering what to do and he came out again, with the woman, who handed him a piece of paper which I presumed was a shopping list.'

'Then you spoke to him?'

'He was so shocked to see me. He spluttered in a confused way and promised to explain, said it wasn't what it seemed, but I ran away. I couldn't stand there in sight of the house he shared with someone else and listen to more lies.'

'Tell us the address. I'll go and find out exactly what's going on.'

'If you wish, but it's no longer anything to do with me.' She handed Valmai a note bearing the address. 'I think the little girl's called Erica but I don't know the woman's name. Mrs Rhys Martin perhaps?' she added bitterly.

She walked with Valmai to where she worked but refused to discuss it further. Two years and more she had given him, years in which he had taken her money and lied about why he needed it. The request for more time was just more lies. It had to end here and now.

She worked particularly hard that day and the days that followed, using physical exhaustion to stop herself thinking about Rhys's lies and her own gullibility. Instead she thought about how she could change her life around. There were still a couple of hundred pounds in her savings and that would be for a new flat and a new life. But first she had to convince an employer that she was still capable of doing the job she had abandoned more than two years ago. That wouldn't be easy.

Over the following weeks, between her various jobs and working on finishing the decorating at Greenways, she applied for several positions, giving details of her previous work and explaining that she had given up for a while to look after her daughter. She carefully said nothing about her non-marital status. Three weeks later, in early March, she had still not found anything suitable and it was almost time to leave Greenways. She'd had the offer of two jobs but not what she wanted and what she was trained to do so, remembering Amy's words about accepting second best, she had decided to be strong and wait for the right one.

The decorating was finished and that meant there was little time left to find accommodation. Without a better paid job she would be moving into the awful boarding house where Eric lived. Surely she deserved a bit of luck? Then she met Amy again.

'Only two weeks for your wedding, isn't it?' she called as Amy stopped her car and lowered the window to speak to her.

'Yes, and everything is frantic. The house isn't finished, and Rick and I have argued about stupid things and I wish we'd married last year like he wanted to. A quiet wedding, no fuss.'

'I've just finished for the day. I have to meet Sadie then I'm making tea if you have time?' Sally suggested.

'You aren't still cleaning, are you?'

'I have tried to find something better but no luck I'm afraid. The trouble is I'll have to leave Greenways soon. The work there is almost finished.'

'Jump in. We'll meet Sadie then you can make me that cup of tea. I think we both need one.'

She stopped at the bakers and came back with a box of cream cakes, then they collected an excited Sadie with her arms full of the paintings she had done that day, and went back to Greenways.

While the kettle boiled Amy looked around the house, admiring the neat and clean rooms. 'I'm impressed,' she said. 'The place is transformed.'

'It's been hard but I'm very pleased with the result. It's earned me money and kept a roof over our heads.'

'But now it's time to move on.'

Sally shrugged. 'But where? And how? I have to consider Sadie in everything I do. She has to be happy and safe.'

'Will Rhys's parents help?'

'Gladly, but I don't want them to be involved. I have to keep away from Rhys and that means his parents too. I will let them see her as often as they want – she is their granddaughter, after all – but only when I'm sure Rhys won't be around.'

'Did you try to find work in the fashion industry?'

'I applied for several positions but I didn't get through the interview.'

'What did you wear?'

'A suit I bought two years ago. Expensive, but not at its best.'

'Your clothes are probably a mess. Out of date, well worn, shoes and tights not matching – you have to look the part, Sally, and if that means spending some money then that's what you have to do. Speculate to accumulate.'

'I need all the money I have left to get us a home.'

'Splash out and look the part of a successful fashion expert. I'll come with you and help you choose some decent clothes. After all, I've always been able to afford the best, as you could once.'

'Until the Rhys era!'

The following day Amy was waiting for her, bobbing with excitement when she went to meet Sadie. They drove home with Amy obviously bursting to tell her something. 'I won't tell you until you've made tea and sorted little Sadie out,' she teased.

With Sadie settled with her midday snack and the three of them sitting down beside the electric fire – Sally too curious and impatient to start lighting the coals – Amy said, 'You have an interview in ten days' time!'

'What? But how did that happen?' Sally gasped.

'My parents owned a large fashion house and after Daddy died, Mummy has kept in touch and she spoke to a few people and, there you are, an interview. Give it your best, Sally, and the job will be yours.' She handed her a pile of fashion magazines. 'Here's your homework. Look and absorb,' she said to a delighted Sally.

The following day, with Valmai having promised to meet Sadie from nursery, Sally and Amy went into Cardiff. They looked in all the better dress shops and Amy encouraged Sally to examine everything on display, try on several and discuss with the assistants what the summer styles and fabric were. She spoke to managers too, and a few buyers, discussing the fashion world as though she was well aware of the current trends and the prospective colours for autumn. She learned a lot and used her knowledge to learn more. In one department store she spoke to a senior buyer who told her she was due to retired. A word with the manager followed.

She had a flair for choosing the right accessories and bought scarves and hair ornaments as well as shoes and handbags. Amy said she was proud of her and knew she would be successful. 'You shed your unhappy put-upon self as soon as we walked into the first shop,' she told her.

They returned home exhausted and carrying two outfits plus the rest, and some jewellery. The jewellery was Amy's but she wanted Sally to borrow it for her interviews, of which there were now two.

Going to clean for Mrs Glover the following day was unreal. She had dreamed of going back to her previous career so strongly the real life was the dream, the new life the reality. She told the friendly lady what she was hoping to achieve and Mrs Glover gave her a pair of pure silk stockings. 'I know nylons are all the thing now, but real silk has a softness that caresses you and makes you feel so good you can achieve anything.'

Eric was waiting for her when she and Sadie reached home that day and he came in and began to light the fire while she prepared their usual light lunch. 'You'll stay, won't you, Eric?'

'I'm sure you're busy,' he said.

'Sit down and enjoy the fire you've lit,' she said, but he went first to the coal store to fill her scuttle and chopped sticks and brought them in to dry.

'I have two interviews in about ten days,' she told him.

'Good luck, it's about time things started to get better for you. You have to leave this place soon, I suppose, now the work is done.' He hesitated and she stared, smiled, encouraged him to speak. 'I have the best room in the boarding house at the moment,' he said, 'and if you're thinking of moving in – just until you get a proper place – I've arranged to move to the top room which is the only one vacant, and let you have mine. Better for Sadie, being on the ground floor.'

'Thank you, Eric. You're such a lovely man. But I wouldn't have you climbing all those stairs because of me. I'll manage fine. Who knows, if this interview becomes an offer I might be able to move into a flat. And you, dear Eric, will be our first visitor.'

She crossed her fingers superstitiously and reminded herself that the chances of well-paid work was little more than a dream and the dreary boarding house was likely to be her home for months to come.

She went to tell Valmai and Gwilym the times of her interview as they would be involved by looking after Sadie. Shouts were heard coming from next door, the voices of Netta and Walter raised in anger. She found Jimmy in with Gwilym, the radio turned up loud to muffle the distressing sounds of his parents' quarrel.

'Go on in, Valmai's in the kitchen,' Gwilym said. 'Come on Jimmy, we've got some freshly made pasties, just for you.'

Covering his ears, Jimmy ran inside.

Valmai willingly agreed to look after Sadie on the days of the interviews and Sally felt both relieved and guilty for making use of them while being determined never to let Rhys come near her daughter again. Jimmy walked back with them pushing Sadie's chair while the little girl walked beside him holding his hand and chatting happily.

Amy and Rick called that evening, carrying flowers and a book containing all the various lists of things to do for the wedding. 'Can you listen while I go through these arrangements for the last time? I know it's boring but I'm so afraid I'll forget something and turn the whole thing into a farce,' Amy said light-heartedly. 'Rick is going to see Gwilym about making an arch for the garden. We'll plant roses and honeysuckle. Rick's idea, but Mummy agrees.'

'For once,' Rick added, with a wink for Amy.

When they were on their own, with Sadie asleep, Amy said, 'How are you feeling, about the first interview?'

'Guilty about the money we spent, that's my strongest emotion. What if I don't get either? I'll be stuck with clothes I can't wear and not enough money to pay rent on a decent flat. Eric came earlier and he offered to move from his downstairs room so Sadie and I can have the best in the house.'

'Sweet of him, even if he's no better than a tramp!' Amy smiled ruefully. 'I was mistaken about him and several others, wasn't I?'

'We are all guilty of making snap judgements. I didn't like David Gorse but he helped me when the baby was born and he was kind and thoughtful. I presumed he was lazy and not to be trusted just from listening to others.'

'That's one person I haven't changed my mind about,' Amy said sharply. 'Smarmy – that's an old-fashioned word but it's how I'd describe him. Unpleasant to some and showing a different face to others.' She laughed then. 'When do you leave here?'

'At the end of April. I can't complain. The man has been very generous.'

'Plenty of time to find a place to live. Once you get this job everything will settle in no time at all.'

Sally wished she could believe her.

When Rick returned he came back to the door after Amy was seated in the car. 'Sally, I need someone to clean the house now the workmen have finished. It mustn't be you, but I wonder if you know someone who would do a good job. You know how fussy Amy is.'

'Leave it with me. I know just the person. But she's shy, so if you leave her money and give her the key, she'll work in the evenings. A week should see it done.'

'What's her name?'

'Frankie. I can really recommend her.'

The following week, while Valmai sat with Sadie, Sally scrubbed the house. Once she saw Amy at the gate and panicked but Amy obviously thought better of it and walked on. Rick had kept his word and no one came to interrupt her. The money was left for her in advance and at the end of the eight days it took to finish, there was an added bonus.

Sally could hardly move and the following day she stayed in bed on Valmai's firm instruction while Valmai took Sadie to nursery and then back to her home in Mill Road.

Sally was still very stiff and sore but after one day of being spoilt by Valmai she returned to her usual jobs. Monday was only three days away, the deciding moment when she knew that if she failed to get one of the jobs for which she was being interviewed she would have to accept facts and look for something less than the dream.

On Monday morning she rose early, bathed in the sunshine-yellow bathroom and laid out her new clothes. It was daunting, this sudden change from cleaning lady to fashion expert and she panicked and wondered why she had even considered being able to carry it off. She looked at her hands, neglected and with nails so short they almost looked bitten. With Sadie still sleeping, she filed them and applied some pale varnish. As she sat there waiting for them to dry, a letter came through the door. Puzzled, she picked it up to find a card from Amy and Rick, wishing her luck. She placed it on the hall table, telling herself that she would do her best and her best was very good. As a sort of mantra she repeatedly murmured to herself that 'Second best will not do'.

Later, with hair arranged and wearing her new clothes she went out to meet Amy, who was going to drive her to the first appointment. A last glance at the card cheered her and added a smile to her lovely face.

The questions were varied, mostly to test her knowledge of the business and others about herself and her ambition. Some were about Sadie, the interviewer wanting to know what arrangements she had made for childcare and if the little girl became ill. 'Reliability is paramount,' she was reminded. 'You will have to be prepared to travel at very short notice sometimes.'

'My daughter is a healthy child but if she were seriously ill she would be my priority.' She looked at the interviewer anxiously but he smiled and said, 'That's how it should be, Mrs Travis.' She didn't correct him about her marital status.

The second interview was similar in content but this time, instead of sitting in a chair facing someone across a desk, she was shown around the premises and asked her opinion on the layout and contents of the stockrooms. She decided to be bold and offered opinions on some areas that could be improved. Even in the office she pointed out, trying to hide her nervousness at her audacity, that the typists' desks should be moved as they were blocking the way to a cupboard that was in constant use. She added that blinds were more businesslike than the flowery curtains hanging at present and – trying not to smile – pointed out the need to tell the cleaners to move furniture occasionally and make a particular note of corners.

All the time, the interviewer made notes and at the end of the thirty minutes Sally was exhausted. She still waited for the one question she dreaded, why her left hand bore no wedding ring.

One more question, Mrs Travis.' Sally braced herself, determined to tell the truth even if it meant losing the job. 'Will you come to the staffroom and have a cup of tea with me? I bought some cakes specially.' Relaxing then and talking easily, she was surprised to be told that if she wanted it, the job was hers.

When she told the landlord of Greenways that she would be moving out as soon as she could find a place, she was prepared to move into the boarding house for six weeks, when she would have her first monthly cheque. Valmai wouldn't hear of it.

'Stay here, please, Sally. We won't interfere with anything you want to do. The bedroom will be your own private place and I'll only look after Sadie when you want me to.' How could she refuse?

She moved most of her things that day and left the rest to be collected by a storage firm. Then she made sure everything was clean for the new tenants. She left flowers for them and a card hoping they would be happy in their new home. Then headed back to the single room in the Martins' house, a place she did not want to be.

Jimmy continued to spend a lot of time out of the house. If his parents noticed, they said nothing. If they were aware of the days he missed school they didn't comment on that either. With Rick and Eric's encouragement he attended more regularly but sometimes the warmth of the sun, or the excitement of a gusty wind, or just the scent on the air made him head for the woods instead of the school-room. He frowned as he wondered how long it would take for his parents to miss him if he ran away from home and found a happier place to stay. Weeks, probably, he thought miserably.

The fields and woods were his playground, and he learned where to find many of the smaller animals and reptiles, like adders, which he watched nervously as though expecting them to leap up at him, although Eric assured them they would move away as soon as they became aware of his presence. He liked the lizards he occasionally saw darting about on warm banks, and the slow worms that looked as though they were made from metal when the sun shone on them. Sometimes he would catch them and draw them then let them go. His notebook was filled with these drawings and on occasions he showed them to his teacher, who admired this work but reminded him that his other subjects were in need of attention.

He smiled as he tucked the notebook away, having drawn a clump of reeds growing in the stream. Then he walked back to the mill, found his spade and settled to work on the foul-smelling silt around the waterwheel. He had talked to Eric about it and learned that, if he wanted to get the sluice gate to open and free the water, so it ran under the wheel through the leat, that would take a lot of work, freeing the rusted metal. Time to work on the mill was something he had in plenty. Home was a place to avoid.

A few people still gathered each day at the site of the factory where walls were now towering far higher than the original building. The carpenters were fixing the roof struts and soon the place would be weatherproof, allowing the men to work inside. The factory had vanished, and the men who watched its demise wandered off to talk some more about the good old days, when they had work. Eric no longer went to watch the progress but he would sit in a café when he had the money for a snack, and listen to the others talking about the 'wonderful' days when they had worked there, forgetting how they had moaned about the job and wished for something better.

The wedding of Amy and Rick was only days away when disaster struck. Amy's mother was taken ill and rushed to hospital. In panic, Amy came to Sally and together they wrote notes to all the guests explaining the cancellation. The booking for the hall, the florist and the car hire firm were informed, and Amy was sitting beside Sally's fire looking dejected when Rick came home from work and joined them.

'Darling, its terrible news, but we'll rebook as soon as your mother is well enough.'

'The honeymoon in Paris will have to be cancelled too. I was looking forward to that so much,' Amy said.

'Why cancel? You can still go, can't you? No one will know and you'd lose money on the bookings if you don't.'

'Sally! We couldn't! What a suggestion!' Amy covered her face with her hands.

'We could book an extra room,' Rick said. 'Or not, as you wish.'

'Oh, I don't want to continue with this conversation. What would my mother think?'

But they went. With her mother now convalescing in Bournemouth with a cousin, they were seen off by Sally and Sadie as they travelled by train from Cardiff, looking as happy as two lovers should. Sally waved until the last carriage was out of sight.

May brought its display of flowers in the hedgerows. The daffodils planted years before by schoolchildren were long gone but had been replaced with the lacy white borders of cow parsley. Blossoms transformed the trees and the scent of early wallflowers filled the air as Sally walked along Mill Road towards the fields. Sadie was pushing the picnic in her pushchair, stopping occasionally to put fingers together as she sang, 'Incie Wincie Spider'.

They walked through the fields towards the old mill. It was Sunday and the following day she and Sadie were moving out of Greenways. Any furniture she wanted to keep was being stored. Much of what she had needed for their brief sojourn had been discarded. A new flat and new beginning meant nothing dragging her back to the old life.

'It's only you and me from now on, Sadie, just you and me.'

Sadie began to feel tired and Sally lifted her into the pushchair where she immediately fell asleep. The woods on either side of the path were filled with birdsong and the chuckling of the stream and she stood for a while and listened. It was then, in the peace of the Sunday morning, that she heard crying. Deep, heartrending sobs. As quietly as she could, she crept forward until she could see the stream where the great wheel now stood, a silent witness. Jimmy was lying on the narrow bank, curled up with his hands covering his face.

Leaving the pushchair on the path Sally crept closer and moved carefully down until she stood beside him. She knelt and called his name. His head jerked up and he made a move but she held him. 'Jimmy, don't go. What's wrong? I might be able to help.'

'Go away. I hate you!'

'That's a shame. I rather like you,' Sally replied. 'I think you're clever, very knowledgeable about the countryside, and very handsome, and one day we'll all be able to boast that we once knew you.'

'What d'you mean?'

'Some people become famous or at least very important and then everyone who had known them will boast about it. You neglect schoolwork, I know that, and that's a pity. Learning is more difficult later without the base of schoolwork.' Seeing him relaxing and the tears drying, she then asked softly, 'But school isn't the problem, is it? Can you tell me about it?'

'Mam and Dad are always fighting. I hate living at home and wish I could run away.'

Please don't do that, Jimmy. Whatever you do, stay at home. It's bound to get better. Just bide your time. A couple more years, then, once you have a job, you'll be able to plan your escape.'

'Escape?' He gave a small smile. 'That's a funny word to use.'

'Better than running away, specially when it's too soon.'

'I haven't any aunties like some of my mates.'

'Nor I. I have Sadie now but my childhood was a lonely one.'

'Lonely's better than a mam and dad who fight all the time.'

'We've brought a picnic, plenty for three, will you set the cloth and blanket out for me?'

After eating a generous share of the food, he began to talk. 'Every day when I go home from school, or the woods,' he added with a grin, 'and the house is quiet I know at least one of them is out. As soon as Dad comes in it starts. He doesn't like what Mam's cooked, or the television programme is rubbish. I'm rubbish.' Tears threatened again and Sally didn't try to stop them; she just put an arm on his shoulders and waited for them to subside.

Sadie sat playing with some farm animals and a cart she had chosen to bring, looking up at Jimmy sometimes and smiling at her mother as though she understood the need to be quiet.

They walked home together and Jimmy went with her to see Gwilym before going home. She left them in the workshop, talking about cricket, and went to join Valmai.

'I'm worried about him myself,' Valmai said when Sally explained why Jimmy was with them. 'Things seem to be getting worse between Netta and Walter. He's always been aggressive but she seemed able to cope – she just ignored his jibes and waited until he calmed down. Now she retaliates and that isn't going to cure the problem.'

'Poor Jimmy, he's getting more and more abuse from his father. Constantly being told he's stupid and useless, and a boy of Jimmy's age can't cope with that.'

'That's probably why Netta has started answering back. Starting on the boy was probably more than she was prepared to take.'

In the workshop Jimmy watched as Gwilym modelled a small-sized cricket bat, the hands holding the tools sure and patient.

'Who's that for, Mr Martin?'

'Someone ordered it for a grandson's birthday.'

'You used to play cricket, didn't you? Can you teach me? They play at school but I never get chosen, see.'

'I used to play and I used to coach the youngsters too but those days are gone.'

'Why? You don't need legs to coach, only a bit of know-how. It's the know-how that's important, according to the teacher. He hates me, the teacher. That's why I'm never chosen.'

'No one hates you, Jimmy. Don't say such things.'

'Everyone does. I'd better go. Mam'll be home.'

'Of course, she'll be worrying about you.'

'No, she won't! But I'd better get home or I'll miss my tea. Ta-ra. Remember about the cricket when you have time, Mr Martin. It'd be good to show that teacher I can bowl a ball and break the wicket and hit a six. Real good that'd be!'

Gwilym put down the bat he was working on and sighed. If only he had faced things straight away, things would be very different. Stubbornness was as damaging as the loss of a leg. Too late now. He took a piece of paper from a drawer and began to sketch a plan of a cricket field. He became more and more absorbed in the task and Valmai called twice before he heard.

If only the factory hadn't closed. If only he and Eric hadn't been out riding their bikes that day. If only … The saddest words in the English language.

Sadie greeted him joyfully as he wheeled himself along the path. He lifted her, giving her a ride up the ramp and into the house, something that had already become a regular treat.

Sally slept fitfully that night. She was tense as she wondered how she would fare on her first day in the new job and how she would find someone suitable to care for Sadie. Besides those anxieties, thoughts of Jimmy entered her mind repeatedly and half-awake dreams were filled with worries about his safety.

Roll on next week, she murmured, she rearranged the pillows and tried once more to relax. By then I'll know whether or not I can do the job and a week might see an end to Walter and Netta's situation, although even in her weary, half-asleep state she knew that was wishful thinking. Walter had retired from the workforce and without him getting a job nothing could change.

Gwilym was sleepless that night. He was thinking of Jimmy too. He kept seeing the young boy's face, tinged with hope at the prospect of succeeding at school when everyone expected him to fail. It wasn't much to ask, just a few hours of his time, but the thought of going out in that hateful wheelchair and people seeing him helpless where he had once been so strong, was a powerful barrier. Even going out after dark had been denied him. What time of night was safe from the chance of meeting someone? Besides, that wouldn't help Jimmy. Cricket wasn't a game for the hours of darkness. Perhaps one day he'd face going just as far as the park and giving the boy a few pointers. But not now, not yet. Perhaps when Rhys came home.

Having given himself a long-term excuse to do nothing, his conscience was eased and he slept.

Amy and Rick returned home after their unofficial honeymoon and from the look on their faces Sally knew they had enjoyed the occasion.

'Knowing it was secret and unconventional added to the fun and even if Mummy finds out now it would be too late to spoil it,' Amy told her. She asked about the new job but was too excited to take in anything Sally told her.

A couple of weeks later the wedding was rearranged, a smaller version of the original and Amy asked Sally to help plan it. They sat in the Waterstones' house where everything was ready and waiting for them. 'Oh, this isn't as important any more, Sally. Paris was wonderful and I don't regret a thing, but the wedding will be an anti-climax now.' she said, then laughed. 'As if we care!'

Sally felt sadness and regret clouding her face. That was how she had felt too, until everything went so terribly wrong. Then she hugged her friend, wished her every happiness, and meant it.

Chapter Eight

WITH ONLY TWO weeks before she started her new job, Sally concentrated on finding suitable childcare for Sadie. She was settled in the nursery full-time and Valmai helped when she could but there was likely to be a shortfall and she needed to be prepared. A regular daily carer was essential. With the likelihood of moving away from Valmai and Gwilym when she found a suitable flat, she needed a person to look after her now, Therefore avoiding the lack of continuity to her routine. Sally knew she needed to be relaxed about Sadie's welfare in order to concentrate on the new job. If she failed, she might not have a second chance to revive a career she enjoyed. The thought of cleaning other people's houses again made her groan.

It was not as easy as she had expected. Several women came but none were suitable. She asked everyone she knew and Valmai did the same and eventually it was through Jimmy's mother that she found someone.

'Mrs Taylor hasn't any children left at home,' Netta explained. 'Jimmy's friend lives next door and she asked me about the job.'

'Do you know anything about her?'

Netta shrugged.

'Is she qualified?' Sally asked, and again Netta only shrugged.

She was suddenly filled with fear at the thought of leaving her precious child with a stranger. All the staff at the nursery were well known to her and to start again, leaving her in the sole care of this Mrs Taylor, was a serious concern. Until then the new job, the possibility of a new flat, none of it had been real. Now faced with this situation, her immediate impulse was to telephone and tell them she no longer wanted the job.

'Will you come with me when I interview her?' she asked Valmai, who instantly agreed.

'I wish I didn't have to work,' Valmai said. 'I'd love to have been your childminder, but with Gwilym earning little more than pocket money I don't have a choice.'

Sally didn't tell her she wasn't inclined to ask, for fear of Rhys turning up. Instead she said, 'There'll always be times when I'll be glad of your help.'

Mrs Gwen Taylor was in her fifties and she went at once to Sadie and spoke to her.

'Hello, Sadie, my name is Mrs Taylor, can you say that? Taylor?' She held the child's hand and talked to her about what was in the room and opened boxes and cupboards to reveal various toys. Sitting on the floor with her, Mrs Taylor discussed the dolls and pushchair, immediately involving Sadie with giving dolls and teddies rides. Sally and Valmai shared approving glances. Mrs Taylor was expensive but it was worth it to know Sadie was in such good hands.

As a trial, Sadie went to stay with Gwen Taylor for an afternoon and when she went to meet her, Sally was pleased to see her running out, smiling happily. 'Would you like to go again?' she asked.

'Nursery's best,' Sadie informed her seriously but she didn't hesitate overmuch when the trial was repeated the following day.

With three days to go before she was to begin working at the fashion house, 'Style', there was a hint that all was not well. Sally went earlier than arranged to collect Sadie and found the little girl dressed in her outdoor clothes and standing at the back door just outside the kitchen.

'Oh, she's ready to leave. Marvellous. But how did you know I would be early?' she asked, as she picked up Sadie, who clung to her very tightly.

'I always believe in fresh air and my little darling has been out in the garden while I tried to teach her to catch a ball,' Gwen explained, patting Sadie's head. 'She's getting quite good too, for a little girl who isn't quite three. Birthday soon, isn't it? And my favourite little three-year-old is going to have a party. Cake, balloons, everything. We've been practising party games today, all ready for the big occasion, haven't we, Sadie?'

Sadie was a bit subdued that evening but Sally presumed it was tiredness. If she played outside and did all the things Mrs Taylor told her, then that was understandable.

Sunday was filled with treats but Sadie was clingy and lacking her usual enthusiasm. They went to the mill in the afternoon, then Sally made a tasty meal. Sadie ate less than usual and fell asleep on her lap.

'Must be the new experiences tiring her out, and more activities than at nursery,' Valmai said.

'She isn't enjoying being with this Mrs Taylor,' Gwilym said. 'Our little Sadie isn't happy.'

'She'll soon get used to it.' Sally didn't sound very sure. Starting work again after so long was wonderful, but only if Sadie wasn't suffering for it.

Her first few days in her new position were exhausting as Sally tried to absorb everything that went on. She needed to know the finance allowed for each new season and who the regular agencies were from whom they bought. They visited two during the first week and she knew she would use neither of them again. Being offered old stock at a discount was not how she envisaged her new role. Finding others meant extra long days and Sadie was always happily playing at Mrs Taylor's when she arrived to collect her.

On Sadie's third birthday there was no real party planned, just the family plus Jimmy and a couple of children Sadie knew from when she had attended nursery. At least she'd have a party at Mrs Taylor's, she consoled herself, and I'll do better next year. She made certain she was there to collect her daughter herself and although there was evidence of a party with balloons and a partly eaten cake on the table, there were no signs of any guests. Gwen's voice was excessively jolly and Sadie didn't respond; she just clung to her mother in a very unusual way. Sadie had always been a confident child and Sally was worried as she went back to Mill Road.

She prepared their meal and encouraged Sadie to talk about her day. 'Do you like going into the garden to play ball with Gwen?' was one of the questions she asked.

'Not Gwen. Only Sadie,' Sadie replied solemnly. 'No ball, I played with cat.'

'A real cat?'

'The cat in the flowers,' was the casual reply.

After they had eaten, instead of putting Sadie to bed, Jimmy came and Sally was glad. She needed to talk to Valmai and while he played with Sadie and her new toys, she told Valmai that all was not well with the arrangement with Gwen Taylor.

Jimmy stayed a while longer, reluctant to go home, and Valmai whispered to Sally that only his father was there and he would wait until his mother came home. He usually had a difficult time when only Walter was there, taking the blame for everything wrong in his father's life and there was plenty – some real, most imagined. He had painted a card for Sadie with cats and rabbits on it and once she saw it, Sadie refused to put it down and carried it for the rest of the evening.

While Jimmy amused the little girl, Sally explained more fully her doubts about the care Gwen was providing and Valmai promised to call in and see what was happening, during her afternoon break on the following day.

That night Sally's sleep was troubled. She had been wrong to take the job. It was too soon to leave Sadie in the care of someone else. She was wide awake at midnight and went down to get a drink. She was quiet, not wanting to wake the others, and when she opened the door of the living room she was surprised to see Gwilym standing at the window, leaning on his sticks. As she watched he moved across the room and back again, several times, then sat in his usual chair and seemed to settle for sleep. Silently, hardly daring to breathe, she went back to her bed.

Before returning to the hotel for her evening session next day, Valmai went to telephone Sally to report what she had seen.

'I went round to the back garden without knocking on the door and there was your Sadie in the garden, wrapped up but shivering with the cold. The "cat" she played with was a concrete statue in among the dead flowers. No toys, not even a ball in sight. Sadie hadn't seen me so I crept away and came to tell you what I'd seen.'

Phoning to tell her boss she'd be a couple of hours late, Valmai waited for Sally and together went back to Gwen Taylor to find Sadie sipping a glass of milk and with biscuits in her hand. The room was immaculate, everything polished and nothing out of place. Sadie looked very subdued and didn't get up when they walked in. Sally picked her up and asked, 'What have you been doing today, darling?'

'Talking to Cat. I've got a biscuit,' she added, holding one up in a hand that was red with cold.

Sally pressed her head against her neck and her cheeks were like ice. 'Why is she so cold?' Sally asked. 'She's been outside too long.'

'I can't get her in, the little love. She likes playing ball and riding the little bike. With me holding her to keep her safe, of course.'

'I called earlier,' Valmai said. 'She was standing out there on her own, the door was closed and she was shivering with cold. There was no sign of you and certainly no toys to amuse herself.'

'Can I go home now, Mummy?' Sadie whispered.

'Well, yes, I do leave her for a moment or two,' Gwen said, ignoring the child's comment. 'I have to get our lunch, and clean the house. Mothers do the routine things even if they have half a dozen children, don't they? They don't need watching every minute.'

'They do when that's what you're being paid to do,' Sally said, turning towards the door. 'She won't be coming again.'

'About the money you owe—'

'Money?' Valmai snapped. 'You're lucky we aren't suing for cruelty!'

Although she was heavy, Sally carried Sadie back to Mill Road and didn't let her go until Valmai had made hot drinks.

'I'll have to forget any thought of full-time work until she's older. I'd never have a moment's peace wherever she was after this.'

'Don't think about it tonight. Tomorrow's another day and I have a few ideas,' Valmai said.

'There isn't an idea I can imagine that would solve this. I really thought Gwen Taylor was suitable, the way she went at once to talk to Sadie, became her friend. I'll phone first thing in the morning.'

'Two days, just give me two days.'

Valmai was thoughtful when she cycled to work for her evening shift. She was late and at once apologized to her boss. The meal was well underway and she checked the lists and began setting the tables to be ready for the guests and others who had booked for the evening. It was late when everything was finished and the last plate washed and in its place. Then she began to discuss how her hours could be changed to allow her to look after Sadie.

It was too late to talk to Sally that evening, finishing as she did at about eleven o'clock, but after her morning shift, she rang the office again. She had to stop Sally from handing in her notice. Sadie was with her.

'It's all fixed,' she announced when she answered. 'Sadie is going to nursery full-time and I'm changing my hours. I'll be free in the evenings until seven, by which time you'll be home.' She didn't tell Sally about the drop in her wages. She owed her a great deal after the way her son had let her down. 'My Gwilym is thrilled. Can't wait to see more of her. I'll pick her up from the nursery at four and she'll come to us until you're back. Now,' she added, as Sally began to make doubtful noises, 'doesn't that sound better than you giving up on a job you've hardly started?'

'Thank you, but I can't ask you to cut your hours for me.'

'Rubbish, glad I'll be to ease up a bit. So, will that be all right?'

'I'll be renting a flat as soon as I find one and I don't know where we'll be living.'

'Deal with that later. One thing at a time or we'll never get anything sorted. Now,' she said, quickly changing the subject, 'I bought a dozen balloons today, will that be enough for a party? After her disastrous birthday she deserves another party. A three-year-old has to invite all her friends. Sunday all right?'

Enquiries around the neighbours revealed that Sadie had been either shut in the kitchen or in the garden for most of the time she had been with Gwen Taylor and the more she learned the more anxious Sally became about the importance of her daughter's care. Valmai was the obvious – in fact the only – choice. A flat must be found, but it had to be somewhere in easy reach of Valmai.

The party took place in Valmai's overcrowded house and Sadie invited several friends from her nursery. All her cards were displayed, including one very large one from Rhys. In this instance, the less you care the bigger the card, Sally muttered when Sadie opened it.

Valmai helped with the food and Jimmy came and played with the children, feeling like a little boy enjoying a treat himself. Gwilym made small cat models for each girl and the occasion was one Sally felt sure would give everyone happy memories. She wondered where they would be on Sadie's next birthday and, in a weak moment, whether Rhys would be there. The thought was immediately stifled with anger. Sadie was his daughter but he had lost all rights to be involved in her life, by lying and cheating.

*

During those first weeks of her new appointment Sally had spent a lot of time following members of staff to acclimatize herself with the way the business was run. She made a few changes and in the middle of May, she arranged to go to Bristol on her own to visit a warehouse and to see a fashion show to view the autumn styles. The arrangements with Valmai meant Sadie was safe and happy, giving her a mind free to be able to think about the job and all it entailed.

Bristol was scary as she expected to bump into Rhys every time she turned a corner, but most of the time was spent in the hotel where the fashion show was taking place and the day went off without that unpleasant meeting happening. She drove home in the firm's car she had been given and greeted a happy Sadie soon after six o'clock.

She met up with Amy again, who was keen to hear about the new job and sympathized over the worries of Sadie's unfortunate child-care. 'So now all is well except you'll probably need some more decent outfits if you're going to go gallivanting around the country dealing with expensive clothes, eh?'

Amy was easily tempted by the idea of a mild spending spree and they talked enthusiastically about British and Paris fashions.

'The women of Paris have that special touch. Even a simple outfit is made to look elegant with a few additions or an adjustment to make the fit just perfect. It's attention to detail really. They always spend those important extra moments before being satisfied, even if it's only a brief visit to friends. You ought to persuade your boss that you need to go and see for yourself just how clever they are with clothes,' she added. 'I might be persuaded to go with you, once I tell Rick it's for research and you need my support.'

'Not quite yet!' Sally laughed. 'I'd better give it a week or so.'

The only disconcerting note during those days were the increasingly noisy arguments from next door. Valmai and Gwilym often invited young Jimmy in and with Gwilym he was making a model of a watermill, carefully supervised as he used some of the tools.

'The blade is sharp,' Gwilym told him before allowing him one of the knives. 'Don't push, that's how accidents happen. Just gently and patiently use its sharpness.'

They usually turned up the radio to disguise the voices as Netta and Walter argued.

'What's worrying,' Valmai told her, 'is the way Netta now retaliates. Once she more or less ignored his constant criticism and the way he banged furniture about. Now she retaliates and sometimes she screams in rage. Poor Jimmy can't cope. Walter bringing the boy into the arguments made Netta change. Everything got worse and Jimmy is in the middle of it. Poor lad.'

Early summer surprised them with some wonderfully sunny days and Sally wondered, not for the first time, what David was doing and why he hadn't been in touch for so long. She thought it might be because she was living with the Martins but he hadn't been seen for longer than that. She had called on his mother a couple of times but each time she had been told that he was either out, or sleeping. He was avoiding her and she wondered why, after his previous friendship.

Whenever time allowed and the weather was suitable, picnics were a regular feature of their week. They went either to the park or the mill, where they sometimes met Eric. They frequently invited Jimmy, who, she noticed, still spent a lot of time there and was continuing to clean the wooden paddles of the huge waterwheel and someone – most likely him, she surmised – was gradually deepening the stream where the wheel was locked with the silt, weeds and rubbish collected over many years.

She knew he dreaded going home. The quiet didn't offer any relief from his anxiety; he just waited for it start over again. One day he told her that Eric was ill.

'The doctor thinks he ought to be in hospital but Valmai – I mean Mrs Martin – has promised to look after him. It was that Amy who found him. That's a surprise, eh? Got the doctor she did and told Val – Mrs Martin and they've arranged help.'

'I'll call and see him tomorrow,' Sally promised. 'He's been very kind to me.'

'Mrs Martin would like to have him staying with her I think. Known him for years, she told my mam.'

'But she can't. Because of me,' Sally murmured.

The flat hunting wasn't easy, but she had to find something very soon. She had looked at all the vacant flats in the area and none were suitable. Then she went to see Eric.

He was sitting beside a mock coal fire in his small but clean and tidy room, wrapped in a dressing gown and with an assortment of fruit and drinks on a table nearby. She added the food and drinks she had brought and asked how he was feeling.

'Are you set on renting a flat?' he asked, after assuring her he was improving by the day. 'Would you consider a small house? Only there's one for rent in School Lane past the old mill. People have just moved out and the owner can't decide whether to rent it again or sell. If you had a word you might persuade him to rent to you.'

'I know it. I used to live in School Lane, remember. I'll certainly look at it.' When Eric told her the number, it was next door to Mr and Mrs Falconer, who had asked her to leave the rooms she had rented from them when she had been expecting Samuel. She remembered the couple in the now vacant house and Eric explained they had moved to be nearer to their son in Cardiff.

The house would be ideal. Two bedrooms and two living rooms, a bathroom and a large kitchen. The garden was too large, but she'd gradually tame it. But could she afford it? Living next door to Mr and Mrs Falconer, who had been so disapproving, wasn't an ideal situation but when she looked at the house and imagined having so much space she telephoned the owner at once and asked if he would consider renting it.

The man who stepped out of the car later that day made her gasp with surprise. It was the man she thought of as the red-haired giant, the kindly man who had helped when she and Amy had run out of petrol.

He kept smiling at her as she looked around the rooms, which were rather shabby, and when she asked again if he would consider renting to her, he nodded. 'I don't want you doing all the decorating, mind. I think you've done enough of that. I'll see to anything that needs doing. Right?'

'How did you know about that?' she asked.

'Old Eric. A friend of mine he is.' He held out a huge hand and said, 'Matthew Miller. I reckon my family must have owned the mill once, what d'you think?'

'I don't know. Why haven't I seen you before? I've lived here for more than two years.'

'I don't come often. My father calls for the rent. The house is actually his, but I see to things for him.'

She offered her hand again and said, 'I'm Sally Travis and—'

'Oh, I know all about you, Sally. I'm looking forward to seeing your daughter Sadie again.'

They discussed terms and when he asked if she needed anything done before moving in she shook her head. 'I need to get everything sorted fairly quickly. I have a new job you see, and—'

Again he interrupted her. 'I know, you work for "Style", and you need to get Sadie settled so you can concentrate on your career.'

She laughed then. 'All right, you tell me if you have any questions to which you *don't* know the answer.'

'When d'you want to move in?'

'This week!'

So it was settled. She was sad at leaving the Martins' home; they had been very kind and it was only the thought of Rhys returning home that made it imperative that she moved out. She had to cut that link. Within three days she and Sadie were installed in the modest little house in School Lane. Matthew Miller had painted several rooms before she moved in and he was waiting with transport to help move her furniture and bits and pieces. As soon as everything was in place, she went at once to thank Eric and invite him for Sunday lunch as soon as he was well enough, The future looked good. She was earning a generous wage, with work she enjoyed, a workforce that was pleasant and a kindly boss – plus a house all to herself. Bliss.

Valmai and Gwilym would continue to look after Sadie. Again, because of Rhys not an ideal arrangement but there was no alternative and there was no doubt they loved her and gave her the care she needed. Sadie ran to greet her each evening full of what she had done during the day and turned, time and again, to wave to her grandparents and promise to 'See you tomorrow' as they left for their new home in School Lane.

Twice, Matthew Miller called to make sure they were settled with everything they needed, and besides him there was a regular trail of visitors bringing an assortment of gifts, including a load of firewood and plants for the garden. But there was still no sign of David Gorse.

One day when she and Sadie arrived home, Matthew was digging the garden. 'Can't stop,' he said as she stepped out of her car. 'I know you're busy. I'll just gather my tools and run.'

'Stay and have a cup of tea at least,' she said, laughing at his pretence at running away.

'Another time,' he promised. 'When there's more time.' Pulling faces, waving at a laughing Sadie, he jumped into his van and drove away. He came several times after that although he was never there when she reached home. The borders were neat and the plants she had been given were in place.

She met Mrs Gorse in the butcher's one day and asked about David.

'Still restless, unable to find suitable work, see.'

'Like Walter Prosser,' Sally commiserated and Mrs Gorse shook her head.

'No, not like Walter. He's just plain lazy.'

What the difference was, Sally didn't ask!

The garden was more or less completed and Sally left a note for Matthew Miller, thanking him, but it was still there when she got home. He had obviously finished and wouldn't be back except for the monthly rent. She found herself looking forward to the end of the month.

It was late June, and the sun was still warm at the end of the day when she stopped on the way home and picked up a few pies and crisps and cakes, having decided that a picnic was a good way to end the day. Sadie going to bed a bit later than usual wouldn't matter on such a perfect day. She was smiling as she called to collect her from the nursery. She had finished early and had arranged with Valmai to collect her herself. When Jennifer, the person in charge, opened the door she frowned. 'Mrs Travis? Is something wrong?'

'No, everything's fine. I finished early today and I've called to collect Sadie myself. I've bought a picnic. She loves to eat out and—' Her voice slowed as Jennifer's hands flew to her mouth and she stared at her in horror.

'But she's already been picked up.'

'Oh, it's all right, Mrs Martin must have forgotten. I'll go and get her. Don't worry.'

'It wasn't Valmai. It was a man who said he was her father. She ran to him, called him Daddy, so I thought it must be all right even though you hadn't told me. He's been ill, hasn't he? He looked very unwell but—' She saw the look of horror on Sally's face and stopped. 'It was all right, wasn't it? He said he was her father, and I thought ...'

Sally felt a cold chill run through her. 'I'll go and see if she's at the Martins'. If not, I'm calling the police,' she said as she ran back to the car.

In shock, Jennifer stared after her then ran inside to hold her other charges as though danger threatened them all. What had she done? She never allowed anyone to collect a child without first having made clear and definite arrangements. But he was her father. It must be all right.

Sally drove like a maniac to Mill Road and burst in to see Gwilym setting the table and no sign of Rhys. 'Where is she?' she demanded. 'Where's my daughter?'

'Sadie? I don't understand. Valmai's just gone to the shops. She said you were meeting her today. What's happened?'

'Your son! That's what happened. He took her from nursery. Where *is* she?' She was crying now, fighting the sobs that came from deep in her throat. She stared at Gwilym. 'Where would he take her? Bristol? To the woman he's living with and his other child? Happy families for everyone except me?' Desperately she looked around as though Sadie would magically appear. 'I'm calling the police,' she said and as she turned to run through the door Valmai appeared. Explanations were confused by Sally's distress but Valmai pleaded with her to wait for a while before involving the police.

'No, I can't! Every moment we wait means she'll be further away from me.'

There was the sound of the gate opening and they all held their breath, but it wasn't Rhys, it was David. 'I've just seen Rhys!' he said.

They all spoke at once, demanding to know when and where. 'On the path leading to the mill. I presumed you knew as he had Sadie with him. He's probably going to your house on School Lane.'

'If he isn't there I'm ringing the police!' Sally said, pushing past him on the way out.

David didn't tell her he already had.

Jimmy was at the gate. 'Your Sadie's at the old mill,' he said. 'Are you going to get her? Can I come?'

She opened the car door for him. 'You better had. You might just stop me killing her father,' she said. She tried to drive sensibly but when the car skidded to a stop outside her house in School Lane, Jimmy said, 'Phew, that was fast! Good fun, mind.' Grabbing his hand, she ran to the mill.

Rhys was standing holding the handle of a pushchair, offering up Sadie's coat, obviously pleading with her to go with him. Sadie was sitting on a blanket with food spread out before her, hugging a new toy, a fluffy blue kitten with a gaudy red and yellow ribbon, under one arm. There was jam on her face and a sticky coconut-covered cake in her other hand.

Seeing Sally, Rhys said, 'Sorry, love. I just had to see her. I hoped to get her back in time for my mother to collect her but she seems determined to get me into trouble. I just wanted to spend a little time with her.'

'How dare you! D'you know what a fright you gave us? That I was on the point of calling the police?'

'You didn't, did you?' Alarm crossed his face in a frown.

'You no longer have the right to "spend a little time" with her,' Sally said, snatching her daughter. 'Get away from her.'

'Please, Sally, I'll soon be able to explain everything.'

'Too late. Now please go. I have to let your parents know she's safe. They'll be terrified something awful has happened.'

'I'll run through the wood and tell them,' Jimmy said. 'I'll be quicker, give you time to calm down. I wouldn't like Sadie to suffer one of your crazy drives!' He ran off laughing.

Slowly, with a very sticky Sadie sitting in the pushchair, chattering about the stories Daddy had told her. Sally walked back to the house.

Rhys stood for a moment watching her, head bowed, a picture of dejection. He looked seriously unwell, she noted through her panic and anger. Then there was the sound of people rushing through the bushes and Sally turned to see him held by several policemen.

'It's all right,' she shouted. 'It's all right. Just a mix-up of arrangements, that's all.'

Without waiting to see what happened, she hurried into the house and locked all the doors.

Ten minutes later a knock at the door heralded the arrival of a policewoman.

'Why did you come? I didn't call you,' Sally said, still hugging her daughter. She was angry but she couldn't accuse Rhys of attempted kidnap, could she? She thought too much of Valmai and Gwilym to do that anyway, and he seemed genuinely sorry that his intention to return her to the nursery was thwarted. 'It was a mix-up, that's all. Rhys collected her from nursery without telling me.'

'I'm glad she wasn't harmed. We always act when a child is in danger and are relieved that this time it was a false alarm. But my colleagues are questioning him about that. I came to make sure you and Sadie are all right.'

'All right? I don't think I'll ever be all right ever again! I'm thankful I have my daughter safe but it's been a very difficult time. Her father, Rhys Martin, has been away, you see, and, well, that's a long story. Then there was the unfortunate choice of childminder for her when I decided to go back to work, and now this.'

'I'll go but I'll come back later to discuss what happened and make sure you and Sadie are all right,' the WPC said.

There was a continuous stream of visitors from then on. Valmai came, and Eric. Amy and Rick came when they heard what had happened, then to her surprise, David.

'David. We haven't seen you for ages. Where have you been?'

'Nowhere, just keeping out of your way. You have so many friends and you didn't need me.'

'Of course we need you. You're a friend too.'

'I wanted to be your only friend. The one you turn to whenever things go wrong,' he said.

'We can't have too many friends, David.'

She began to feel uncomfortable, wondering what he was about to say but to her relief, before he could say any more, there was a knock at the door and she smiled, 'Here's another. I wonder who this will be?'

It was the policewoman back and Sally invited her in as David waved goodbye to Sadie, and left.

'There is another matter you might be able to help with,' the policewoman said after being offered a seat. 'Can you tell us why Rhys ran away two and a half years ago?'

'He thought he was suspected of a series of robberies and was afraid an investigation might prevent him from studying to become a teacher. It sounds far fetched even as I say it,' Sally said, making Sadie more comfortable as the little girl relaxed into her arms.

'If he didn't carry out these robberies, why—'

'He didn't do them! Someone else did! He was afraid he'd be suspected, and I don't know why!' Sally wondered why she was so defensive about the man who had let her down so badly and recently given her such a fright.

'You must know what happened, Sally. Anything you can tell us will help us to find the truth. If he didn't do it.'

'He didn't!'

'Then persuade him to help us, tell us all he knows, or just suspects, then we can clear it up and he needn't be afraid any more.'

Sally looked down at the child in her arms, deeply asleep, her face still covered with jam and strands of coconut. 'Rhys is nothing to do with us any more.' She looked at the policewoman and asked, 'How am I going to clean her up enough to put her to bed without waking her?'

The policewoman took Sadie into her arms while Sally gently undressed her and washed her grubby face and hands, then watched as Sally put her into her cot. Both women stood for a few minutes just looking down at the sleeping child, then the policewoman tiptoed out. She had scribbled her name and the telephone number of the station on a scrap of paper and pointed to it as she quietly went out of the door.

David watched with disappointment as Rhys left the police station and walked towards the railway station. His long strides revealed an anger and he was soon lost to David's sight. He had called the police anonymously, reporting a child abducted from the nursery school. He gave details but refused to give his name. The call box would be of little help, specially as he had run fast past it, up through the narrow lane close by and had been innocently wandering towards it when the police arrived. They stopped him and asked if he'd seen anyone using the phone box but he assured them he was just on his way back from the local farmer's barn where he had been looking at a repair job and had only just arrived in sight of it.

He had always hated Rhys Martin. When they were at school, his friends and Rhys's friends were never together. Scrumping apples and playing rat-tat ginger, knocking doors and running away, and helping themselves to an occasional pint of milk from a doorstep were the things in which both groups indulged but never together. And the unforgivable thing was, David's group were often accused, frequently caught, and Rhys's friends were always believed when they gave their word they were innocent.

When the doors of a small factory were left open by mistake, both groups went inside to explore. No damage was done and they came out feeling daring, almost heroic at their bravery in going inside the dark building, each carrying a small item as a keepsake. David had picked up a fountain pen which he hid in his school satchel.

Rhys was questioned as he lived near and he gave the police David's name together with the rest of the rival group. The pen was found and the five children appeared in the juvenile court. They were given a caution but the incident increased his dislike of Rhys to strong hatred.

There had been a certain notoriety in the events; other pupils nudged one another when he passed and looked at him with awe when the stories were repeated and exaggerated. David enjoyed it and began to dream of becoming someone to whom people looked up to with respect. He broke into a small shop and stole some cigarettes, which he sold to some of the older boys. This, he had explained to his followers, was because she wouldn't let him have some sweets off-ration. He was caught and again appeared in court. This time he was told that if he offended again, he would be sent to borstal. He could still picture Rhys's face as he had laughed.

When he risked taking a purse from the post office counter, he told the police he had seen Rhys do it but Rhys had an alibi.

He hadn't achieved much at school, failing at most subjects except woodwork, at which he was better than average. Rhys excelled at academic subjects and sport so reasons to hate him increased. It was only Eric's patient teaching at the furniture factory that had changed his life. The rivalry between Rhys and himself had begun so long ago, when they were little more than children, but the feeling of resentment towards him hadn't faded with time. Now he knew that when the time was right and Rhys felt safe, with what was hidden in his mother's loft he'd be able to knock him off his pedestal for good.

Before that, he wanted to find out what Rhys was doing in Bristol and who the mysterious woman and child were. Was he planning to have two families, one with Sally and one with the woman in Bristol? At the moment he seemed to have chosen the Bristol woman, and he wondered if Sadie was the sole reason for his occasional visits and not Sally. Now if Sally could consider himself as a suitable stepfather to his daughter, Sadie, wouldn't that be a perfect arrow to shoot? It was worth getting a job to see Rhys's reaction to that!

Chapter Nine

SALLY BECAME INVOLVED with the final preparations for Amy and Rick to move into their new home. The wedding had been rearranged and the second issue of invitations had been sent and acknowledged. The house was finished and there was only its contents to be transformed into a home.

Sally went with Amy on shopping trips to fill the larder and store cupboards. Cleaning materials were chosen, although Amy swore she would have as little to do with them as possible. 'Rick paid someone to clean the house after the workmen had finished,' she said airily. 'I have to admit she did a good job. He couldn't remember her name – she was recommended by someone I believe. Pity, I'd like her to come each week and clean through for me.'

Sally smiled and said nothing, remembering the generous payment she had received, which paid for the extras she needed to furnish her own new home. The experience helped her to guide Amy, who seemed vague about what she needed to do.

'Have you arranged deliveries of bread and milk and coal and groceries?' she asked, and Amy gasped.

'None of those. Oh, thank goodness I've got you as a friend. I'll deal with them today. Won't Rick be impressed at how well I've dealt with it all?' She grinned. 'Not that he'll believe me. He'll see an expert guiding hand in all of this.'

'Come on, let's get the bedding sorted and we need to place the small table ready for that television that's arriving tomorrow. By the window, d'you think?'

'And cushions. We need to throw a few cushions around.'

The place was beginning to look like a home. 'All it needs are a couple of full coffee cups on that table and a magazine or two and it'll look lived in,' Sally said.

'All right, coffee it is and perhaps a few biscuit crumbs?' The two friends sat looking out into the formal garden, glancing about them occasionally, and leaning over to tweak a cushion or adjust the table-cloth on what would be the television table. Everything was ready for the second attempt at marrying, 'Nothing can go wrong this time, can it?' Amy asked.

'With your mother in charge? Nothing would dare!'

Amy smiled and said, 'She might be difficult at times, but she has the money and background to make everything perfect.' Superstitiously she crossed her fingers.

The wedding of Amy and Rick eventually took place on Saturday 15th July.

The weather was doubtful at first but everyone in Mill Road and beyond went to see the couple married. The guests were brought by a variety of cars, most of which were expensive and brought shouts of approval from the young boys who had gathered to enjoy the spectacle. The clothes of the arrivals were discussed in murmurs that were punctuated by the occasional burst of laughter when one of the women guests had trouble with an extra large hat, or tripped when alighting from one of the splendid vehicles.

Amy's mother stepped somewhat unsteadily out of an elegant Bentley with someone they later learned was a distant cousin, called Godfrey. The small church was full, with onlookers crowding around the doorway, 'Like beggars at a feast,' Amy's mother declared loudly. 'It's so common to stand and satisfy their curiosity.'

'I think they've come to wish her well, Dorothy,' her cousin Godfrey replied.

'As long as they don't dirty the cars by leaning on them.' She hardly looked at Rick, who was standing in the porch talking to people in the crowd, but as she passed, she muttered from the side of her mouth, 'Can't you make them go away? They're ruining the effect.'

'Hardly!' he replied, but she had walked on, nose in the air, ignoring the greetings from those already seated.

Dorothy Seaton-Jones wasn't the build to be haughty – she seri-ously lacked the height besides being well rounded and wearing a dress with too many frills in a bright pink. She wore gold shoes, carried a gold handbag and struggled to control a wide-brimmed hat. Her face was rosy, her hair was blonde and even in the extra high heels – the reason for her ungainly exit from the car – she was below the level of her partner's shoulder.

Ushers showed her to her place and she looked around as though wondering who to remove from her presence. Sally smiled as she found a place halfway down beside Valmai and Netta, and settled with a chattering Sadie on her lap. David entered and, seeing her, he moved someone along the row and sat beside her. He spoke to Sadie, whispering something in her ear that made the little girl smile, then showed her a packet of chocolate buttons 'For after, mind,' he said, winking at Sally.

Amy looked lovely in a white dress with a fitted bodice and a skirt that flowed around her slim figure like molten satin. She carried a bouquet of flowers in a pale honey colour that matched the dresses of the bridesmaids. She looked quite at ease, smiling at those in the pews that caught her eye, giving a little wave to Sally and Sadie, who called, 'There's Amy and she's pretty!' to the amusement of the congregation.

Despite earlier fears, the train was held capably by six small bridesmaids who followed her obediently to the altar, where it was quickly arranged around her feet. Amy smiled and reached for Rick's hand. The chief bridesmaid, dressed in a slightly deeper shade of honey, took the bouquet and stepped back. The service could begin.

At once Sally began to feel weepy. The dream, so long held, that she would one day walk down the aisle with Rhys, surrounded by well-wishers, was gone for ever. She hugged Sadie as the little girl watched the proceedings in rapt attention, whispering a question sometimes and waving to people she knew.

David, aware she was upset, handed her a handkerchief. When they stood to sing, he put an arm around her shoulder and for once she was glad he was there.

Coming out of the church, everyone smiling, the photographer dashing around trying to organize people into the groups he needed, there was a sudden hush as Milly Sewell's loud voice said, 'Wearing white? Never! There's no shaming some people.'

Dorothy was just behind her and she gave her an unladylike dig in the back. 'What are you talking about? How dare you suggest that my daughter isn't entitled to marry in white!'

Amy tried in vain to hush her mother, but to no avail. 'I want you to leave this gathering at once,' Dorothy demanded.

'Well, if you don't see anything wrong about having a honeymoon before being churched, then why should I?'

'Talking rubbish you are.' Dorothy pushed the woman again.

Milly laughed. 'You pretending you don't know?'

Every effort was made to stop the argument but convinced she was in the right, and outraged at the interruption on her daughter's big day, Dorothy refused to ignore Milly, now joined by a few others who were enjoying the unexpected interlude.

'There's nothing *to* know! Respectable family we are, not like you, Milly Sewell. Where's your son now? Pretending he doesn't exist like always, are you?'

'What are you talking about?' Milly demanded. 'Talking rubbish you are!' She twiddled a finger in the area of her temple suggesting crazy talk, but Sally, watching her, recognized a hint of fear in those hard, dark eyes that she had never seen before. Surely a woman who took such pleasure in hurting people with criticism couldn't have a secret of her own, could she?

Speculation was forgotten as Amy's little mother suddenly ran at Milly and gave her a push that sent her running tip-tilt. To avoid falling over, her feet were moving faster and faster as she tried to regain balance. A man coming around the corner caught her. Breathless but determined, she turned and shouted back, 'Don't believe me? Where were you on the weekend of their original wedding date, eh?'

'In hospital, which is where you'll be if I get hold of you!'

The photographer finally took control and everyone smiled easily for him while he shuffled people here and there, getting his pictures. The unexpected interlude certainly made the crowd look happy. When the job was done there was no sign of Milly. Sally felt a tinge of pity for the woman. If there was any truth in Dorothy Seaton-Jones's accusations, then she must have suffered, and she knew all about that. Taking opportunities to hurt others might be the only way Milly could hide her own pain. She knew that if a child was involved, the pain never leaves. She still grieved for little Samuel, born and lost to her so soon.

Amy and Rick were embarrassed by the outburst, aware the accusation was true, but more so by Dorothy's behaviour. In the Rolls-Royce on the way to their reception, Amy said, 'When I think about how she's always disapproved of practically everyone, reminding those who cared that she was born to better things. Then to charge at Milly like a demented terrier.'

Rick started to laugh and soon they were both helpless. They were still laughing as they reached their destination and throughout the meal, Rick only had to repeat Amy's description of Dorothy as a demented terrier for them to start all over again.

Dorothy just glared.

With exaggerated politeness, Dorothy asked Rick if he had ever been to Paris before. Struggling not to laugh, avoiding Amy's eyes, he shook his head and said, 'No, Mother-in-law, but I can't wait to see it with my lovely wife. The best way to see Paris is with someone you love, isn't it?'

'Never been? No naughty weekend with a previous girlfriend?' someone asked and Amy's laughter was impossible to contain. Sally, aware of their first, unofficial honeymoon, laughed with them.

Amy's mother went on to say that Paris was too far away, too foreign and had an odd attitude to fidelity and free love. Bournemouth, she insisted, would have been a better choice. Rick and Amy clung together and their laughter was contagious although no one really understood the joke. It set the happy mood for the rest of the day.

Sally had left Sadie with Valmai and shared a car with some relations of Rick as the official guests made their way to the hotel where the reception was being held. The odd events had confused her. It made her wonder whether everyone had a secret or two tucked away, hopefully never to be revealed. Milly Sewell with a son? Dorothy with the temper of a fish wife? Where in her fine education and upbringing had she developed that? Were all her fine ideals and attitude lies too?

David hadn't been invited to the reception but, to her surprise, Eric had. She sat next to him as they helped themselves to a huge selection of food from a large, semi-circular buffet in one corner of a well-appointed room with plenty of small tables and comfortable chairs.

'Can it be true – about Milly Sewell having a son?' she asked as they tackled a plateful of delicious pastries.

Eric smiled. 'It's true. Poor Milly. Her mother refused to allow her to keep him. She's lost touch, of course, but it ruined her life. So bitter and angry. The memories of that time must still be fresh and raw.' He looked at her and smiled. 'I have a daughter, you know.'

'A daughter? Where is she? What happened?'

'My wife thought someone else would make her happier than I could so she left and took my little girl with her.'

'I'm so sorry, Eric. That's another pain that never goes away, like poor Milly's. Losing Samuel was only a short while ago but I'll never forget him, and I sometimes wake up having dreamt he was here and growing up. The shock when the dream fades is indescribable.'

He nodded agreement. I haven't seen my child since she was at school.'

'What is your daughter's name?' she asked.

'Julia. She'd be twenty-six now, twenty-seven at Christmas time. Born when I was thirty-eight.'

He didn't seem to want to say more so Sally changed the sad subject and talked instead about the secret honeymoon that was a secret no longer.

The official honeymoon was a few days in London and soon after they returned, Sally saw Rick as he was driving home from work to where Amy was waiting for him in the house locals still called the Waterstones' house.

'Sally! I'm glad I've met you. Amy would like you to come for Sunday lunch one day soon,' he said. 'She says she needs practice first and would rather try out her skills on a friend!'

She thanked him but refused. 'I can't leave Sadie with Valmai and Gwilym; they give her so much of their time.'

'Oh, it won't be for a few weeks yet, and Sadie will be welcome. In fact it's Sadie who's invited and as a favour is allowed to bring you!' he joked. 'Amy would like Valmai and Gwilym as well. D'you think they'll come?'

Sally shook her head. 'Valmai would love to come but Gwilym never leaves the house, or at least, doesn't go any further than his workshop.'

'I understand he refuses to be fitted with an artificial leg, but why doesn't he use the wheelchair? And surely he can manage crutches? Ask him. We'd be so pleased for them both to be our first guests.'

'The trouble is pride, according to Valmai and Eric. Gwilym used to be a popular sportsman and he can't face anyone in his disabled state.'

'Surely someone can persuade him? The first few times would be embarrassing maybe, but people quickly start to notice the person, not the disability, don't they?'

'Ask him, or better still, persuade Amy to ask him. You never know your luck.'

Of course Gwilym refused. Amy pleaded and Valmai lost patience. Sally waited for the invitation but it was a very long time coming. Amy wasn't brave enough to cook for a large number and having promised so many people an invitation she couldn't just ask a few, so she gave up the idea completely.

Valmai was increasingly upset at Gwilym's refusal to leave the house.

'With young Jimmy desperate for a friend to help him succeed at something at school, you're needed, Gwilym. All that knowledge and you're unwilling to help someone like Jimmy. Then there's our granddaughter. Can't you make an effort for Sadie?'

'Not yet,' he replied. 'Soon, maybe, but not yet.'

'Always the same answer. When is *soon*, for heaven's sake?'

'It's a bit late to start cricket practice. Perhaps next year.' He pushed himself out of the house and into his shed.

One of his crutches was kept in the shed in case he needed to get up and reach something. She took the second one into the shed and placed it beside the first, glaring at him before reaching for her bicycle and heading off to work. He hid his distress. He knew he'd let her down and she deserved more than he'd been able to give.

When a few minutes had passed and he was sure she wouldn't return to continue the tirade, Gwilym took out the artificial leg on which he'd been working, referred to the book with its illustrations, and carried on with the task. He was ready to hide it when he heard the approach of footsteps.

Almost every time Sally returned from work David was near, having brought firewood or some plants, or just with something to report. He sometimes went in and shared a cup of tea and some biscuits – often made by his mother. Mostly he just had a brief word, played with Sadie while she sorted out the meal, then left.

'I know you're busy, I only came to see that you and Sadie are all right,' he'd say as he waved goodbye. One day, a week after Amy and Rick's wedding, he was bursting with news.

'I've got a job!' he said. 'Not what I'd hoped for, not proper carpentry, but it's work.'

'David! I'm so pleased. I'm sure it will lead to better things.'

'Maintenance it is, for a man who owns several boarding houses. The work is humdrum compared with what I do best, the money isn't grand either. But it's a start.'

'Congratulations. I'm so pleased.'

'Are you? Well, you should be. My starting work after all these months is down to you. Seeing how hard you work shamed me, Sally. You have Sadie to consider and what responsibilities have I got? None. I should have got started ages ago.'

'Never mind, you're starting now.'

'Fixing new doors and repairing window frames. Not much of a start.'

'Come on in and have tea with us. We're only having beans on toast but there's bread and butter pudding to follow, thanks to Valmai.'

As they sat and shared the meal set out on a small table near the fire, he talked.

'I realize now that if I want a proper life, with a wife and a home and children one day, I have to make a start, even if the start is a long way from where I want to be. I've been a fool to let the years pass me by feeling sorry for myself. I'm no better than Gwilym who refuses to make the effort to get out of that house, allowing Valmai to work like she does. Worse, in fact, being stronger and younger. One day, I'll be able to care for a wife and she won't have to work. She'll be like Amy with money to spare and freedom to enjoy it.'

He was looking at her strangely and Sally felt uncomfortable. Surely he wasn't expecting her to be a part of his plan? 'Come on, Sadie, time for bath and bed. Pass me Teddy Blue Ribbon, will you, David? Thanks for staying. It makes a change now and again.'

He handed the large teddy given to Sadie by Eric, with the blue ribbon around its neck, and reached for his coat.

'Want any help with the dishes?'

'No thanks, you go. You do enough for us without washing the pots.'

He put on his coat and suddenly leaned over and kissed her cheek before leaving. She locked the door after him and frowned. That was a complication she didn't need.

Unaware of her frown, believing he had taken a couple of steps towards a stronger relationship with her, he was smiling when he went through his door. Rhys had been released by the police for now. But his time would come.

His mother was out and a saucepan on the stove was filled with hot water, keeping his plated supper warm. Ignoring it, he went up into the loft. The package was there undisturbed: the stolen items carrying Rhys's fingerprints and no one else's. If Rhys came back then it wouldn't be long before the evidence was given to the police. With Rhys in prison for theft, Sally would put him out of her mind for good. 'And,' he said aloud, 'I'll be there.'

His new job was poorly paid, but with the occasional theft from unsuspecting people, walking into houses left unlocked while the owner was at the shops or even hanging out clothes in their garden when he felt particularly audacious, meant savings building up. One day, he'd be rich enough not to need this but until then there were always people too stupid to notice the small valuable items he took to unsuspecting dealers, who believed he was a market trader or antiques dealer. And besides, it was fun.

The repairs to various houses gave him added opportunity to search for items that were valuable but unlikely to be missed. Everyone, it seemed, had something of value, something special, often hidden away, their sentimental value no longer entitling them to be seen, but kept in a forgotten corner. Throughout the late summer and as autumn drew near, he added to his savings and by the time Christmas decorations began to be seen in shop windows, he had acquired an encouraging amount. Another year was almost at an end and there was still no sign of Rhys coming home. Perhaps now would be a good time to take his relationship with Sally a stage further.

Valmai, with the minimal information given by Sally, had visited Bristol several times during the past months but had failed to find her son. She tried at the house described to her by Sally and there was no one there who knew him from the photograph she took to show around. One neighbour did remember seeing him but assured her he didn't live there, but used to visit a previous tenant. Valmai wasn't sure whether that information was good news or not. If the woman and her child had moved out and Rhys was no longer seen, it seemed a possibility that they had moved away together. But where?

She went to the café to where letters had been sent one Friday afternoon. She had taken a few days' holiday to concentrate on the search.

'Yes, I know him but he hasn't been here for months,' she was told. She ordered tea and toast and sat, with the photograph on the table beside her, hoping someone would see it and be able to help her. A few people glanced as they passed, curiosity bringing them past the table instead of directly to the door.

'Seen him, have you?' Valmai asked a few times but was rewarded only by a shake of a head. Then as she was leaving a man stopped and asked, 'Looking for Rhys, are you?'

'Yes, he's my son. Please, do you know where he is?'

Another shake of a head then the man said, 'You could try Golden Harp Street. Don't know the number but he was there for a while. Working on the roads he is. Council might help.'

She found the street and knocked on doors until she found someone who remembered him. There was another disappointment as she was told Rhys had moved out after only two weeks.

Valmai thanked the man, left her address in case he should ever see him, and headed for the train station. There was nothing more she could do that day. The council offices would be closed as it was after six o'clock on a Friday evening, but they'd be open on Monday and then she'd find him.

She was almost crying with relief when she knocked on Sally's door.

'I went to that café who held his letters and a man there knew him. He lived in Golden Harp Street for a couple of weeks but has moved again. He works on the roads. On Monday I'll find him.'

Sally didn't disguise her lack of interest. 'Glad I am if you find him, but I don't want to know. He treated me like a fool and whatever the reason, his whereabouts are no longer my concern.'

'But he must be in some sort of trouble, Sally. You saw how ill he looked.'

'Then he should have trusted me. If things went wrong he should have told me. I'd have helped, whatever trouble he was in, but now it's too late. You can see that, can't you?'

Sadly Valmai nodded. She went home feeling distressed and angry. By the time she opened her back gate, anger was the strongest emotion and she was prepared to remind Gwilym how he too had let her down. Voices in the shed halted her and she listened as Gwilym and Jimmy were discussing an imaginary game of cricket. She peeped in and saw the game in progress was on paper.

Gwilym put down the pencil he was using to describe various field positions and with a ball in his hand began demonstrating bowling techniques to a very interested Jimmy, who held another ball and followed Gwilym's guide. Valmai went quietly into the house, anger dissipated, and allowed a few minutes to pass before calling to tell Gwilym she was home. Jimmy shared their meal. As usual, he was unwilling to go home.

On Monday, her last day, she once more set off for Bristol. The council offices were open and helpful staff tried to find her son, but eventually Valmai accepted that the lead that had excited her was taking her nowhere. She spent the day wandering around, trying various firms who might just employ him 'on the roads' but at five o'clock, weary and disheartened she caught the train back home. Time to give up, she decided. Rhys knew where to find them and they'd have to wait until he was ready to explain. Better to keep her job and concentrate on helping Sally and Sadie.

She was calm when she reached home and Gwilym was waiting for her, with the table set and soup simmering on the cooker.

'No luck, love?' he asked, stretching up to kiss her.

'We won't find him until he's ready to be found.'

'I'm sorry. I should be doing the running around, not you.'

She glared at him in rare anger. 'Yes, Gwilym. You should.'

The long-awaited Sunday lunch with Amy and Rick was finally arranged in late November. As expected Gwilym and Valmai had declined the invitation so it was a small party. Amy's mother was the only other guest and when Sally walked in with Sadie, she politely reminded Sally that everything was expensive and new, and the child would have to be watched so no damage was done.

'Her name is Sadie,' Sally said equally politely.

'And she's very welcome,' Amy added, guiding Sally away from her mother into the dining room, where a fire burned and Christmas decorations added to the feeling of excitement. A tree stood in one corner and beneath it brightly packed parcels were stacked amid tinsel and tangled strips of green and red crepe paper. Sadie clung to her mother and stared around her with starry eyes.

'I know it's early, but as it's our first Christmas in our first home, I want it to last as long as possible.'

Despite a few complaints from Dorothy, the occasion went well and it was three o'clock before Sally left. She and Amy shared amused glances as Dorothy brushed imaginary crumbs from the armchairs and tut-tutted about the plates left piled up ready for washing.

Rick walked with them as far as the gate. 'Thanks for coming, Sally. Amy and I enjoyed it very much.'

'You had a few doubts once, didn't you?' Sally whispered. 'But now, anyone can see that you are happy. I'm so glad. Amy is a great person and I'm pleased to have her as a friend.'

'Once we accepted that we were both on the same side regarding her mother's interference, the doubts were gone. We're repainting the bathroom pale blue as we both wanted, losing the dull grey she insisted on. The kitchen will soon be white and yellow, not green. The garden is not what I'd hoped for but it's fine. In the summer it will be a pleasant place to sit, and I can still grow the vegetables I want. Eric, clever man, suggested an allotment. So yes, everything is perfect.'

Sally still needed to do something permanent about childcare. Sadie was three and it would be some time before she was at school. A live-in nanny would be perfect but paying for one wouldn't leave her much spare money.

'You don't need a nanny for twenty-four hours, just the time between nursery ending and either you or me getting home,' Valmai said, and persuaded Sally to agree.

'Thank you. I'm so grateful to you both.'

'I didn't do anything,' Gwilym said, looking down at the blanket that covered his legs. 'I wish I had.'

'Not too late!' Valmai retorted. 'When are you going to start helping young Jimmy? He needs help if he's ever going to succeed at cricket and you're the only one capable of helping the poor boy.'

'It's nearly Christmas. Hardly the weather for cricket!'

'Football then! He only needs a few tips and lots of encouragement. Come on, you know what he has to put up with. It would make such a difference to him, you know that.'

The words were harshly spoken, but Sally knew Valmai wasn't angry – she was trying to shame him into helping himself.

'I'll come to the field with you, whenever you want to go,' she told him. 'The one near the old mill, it's quiet there, and one of Sadie's favourite places. She and I would love to go with you.'

'You mean out of sight, where I won't be a sideshow,' he muttered.

'Oh, you'll be a bit of a curiosity for a while,' Sally agreed, 'but only until people are used to seeing you about again. It's been a long time and people are bound to come up and talk about your situation, but in a kindly way. Get that over with and you'll wonder why you didn't try before.'

'Soon,' he said. 'Come the spring maybe.'

Sally smiled. 'In the spring.'

When she set off for home a little later that evening, Sally heard crying. She went back into the house and said, 'Someone's crying and it sounds like Jimmy.'

Valmai went up and found Jimmy sitting on his back doorway. He looked up and in the slanting light from the kitchen she saw that his face was dirt-streaked and swollen with crying. She went to him and put an arm around him. Sitting beside him, she talked and coaxed him to go with her to where Gwilym was waiting anxiously.

Waving for Sally to go home, blowing a kiss to Sadie, she led the still sobbing boy into the house. He was very cold, wearing only a shirt and some ancient pyjama trousers that were too small. His feet were bare.

'Mam's out and I can't find my pyjamas,' he sobbed. Gathering him into a blanket, Valmai cuddled him, while Gwilym wheeled himself into the kitchen to put milk in a pan to make a hot drink. Half an hour later, Jimmy had been fed, comforted and was fast asleep, warmed by the cosy blanket, the roaring fire and loving care – luxuries he had been managing without for a long time.

When Netta returned at eleven o'clock, Valmai heard her coming along the pavement and from the sound of her footsteps, changing from walking to running, she had suddenly begun to feel guilty.

Netta was surprised to see that her house was in darkness and she wondered whether Walter was already asleep, and whether he had made a meal for Jimmy. 'Poor Jimmy,' she said aloud.

Valmai waited in her doorway and allowed Netta to go upstairs and realize Jimmy wasn't there. She heard a scream and stepped towards her neighbour's back door. 'It's all right. This time!' she shouted over. 'Jimmy is safe with us. What are you doing to the child? Leaving him alone like this?'

'Walter was here. He said he'd stay while I went to see Mam. He promised.'

Netta carried the sleeping Jimmy, still wrapped in the blanket, back to his bed and covered him. She sat beside his bed for the rest of the night, determined that the first thing he'd see on waking was her sitting there, smiling at him, able to reassure him that all was well and it would never happen again.

A week later, when frost covered the ground in a sparkling reminder that winter was about to descend, Jimmy disappeared.

Rows were constant. When both Netta and Walter were at home there was either silence that was palpable and more than Jimmy could cope with at such a young age, or shouting matches that drove him from the house. On this particular night he heard blows being struck and the sound of his mother throwing china. He dressed in as many clothes as he could squeeze on to his skinny frame and, when the couple eventually went into their separate bedrooms, he crept downstairs. He dragged a couple of blankets with him, which he wrapped around his shoulders and tied with string around his waist. Two carrier bags were filled with as much food as he could carry and he left, heading first for the mill.

In the morning, his mother left early, shouting to Walter, telling him she would be out for the day and to stay with Jimmy. An hour later, neither of them having checked on Jimmy, Walter too left the house.

Valmai went to Netta's house at lunchtime that Saturday wondering where Jimmy was as he had promised to come to the shed to help make a pull-along duck for Sadie. The back door was wide open and she called then went inside. Everything was in disarray.

Pots and pans were piled up ready to wash, dirty plates were every-where, many broken and left where they had fallen. The grate was filled with cold ashes and the temperature suggested it hadn't been lit for a long time. Alarmed she ran upstairs and looked in each room. They had all gone. Why hadn't she been told? Something was seri-ously wrong.

She ran back to tell Gwilym and he told her they had to call the police. She ran to the phone box and dialled 999 and waited, staring up and down the road hoping to see the three of them walking back with explanations.

The police searched the house and before they had finished, Walter came back.

'She told me I was to stay and mind the boy,' he said. 'No one tells me what to do. He's her kid not mine.'

'What d'you mean?' Valmai asked. 'Of course he's yours.'

'I didn't want him. She did and I'm not staying home while she goes out and has fun. What sort of a man d'you take me for?'

'Where is your wife, sir?' one of the policemen asked.

Walter shrugged. 'Says she's visiting her mother.'

'The address?' Walter gave it, the information was passed on and he was then asked, 'And the boy? Did he go with her?'

Walter shrugged again.

Police were sent to Netta's parents' home and at once a search was on for Jimmy. Neither parent knew where he could be. The day passed and no one saw or heard from him.

When Sally heard about Jimmy's disappearance she went at once to the mill after telling the police it was his favourite place.

With a powerful torch she nervously entered the building, calling his name as she climbed the precarious steps to the top floor. He wasn't there. His friends were contacted but no one had any idea of where he might be.

Hiding in a tree that was covered in a thick coat of ivy that concealed him completely, Jimmy watched. When first Sally then the police had searched the mill and gone away, he crept down and settled to sleep in the top room, safe from more searchers at least until morning.

Chapter Ten

THE PEOPLE CONCERNED about Jimmy didn't expect to sleep. Throughout the evening searches were made of outhouses and barns. Torches patterned the air as more and more people joined in the worrying exploration of every place they could think of where a small boy could hide. So far no one had suggested any danger or harm, only that he had run away and was hiding.

People were increasing in number as news of the missing boy spread and they went off in different directions with policemen making notes of where they went. Rick went back to the mill in case Jimmy had returned after the earlier search.

As he heard him coming, calling his name, and seen the torch flashing from side to side, Jimmy ran from the mill, grabbing his bag of food – some of which he dropped – and went back to the invisible safety of the ivy-covered tree. He thought the branches would never stop moving, especially as he disturbed them to try and retrieve the food he had unfortunately dropped, but by the time Rick came out of the mill again, nothing was moving and there was no sound to betray his presence, so close to where he stood.

Unable to just wait, Sally thought of David. He would surely help. Leaving Valmai to stay with Sadie, who was blissfully asleep, Sally ran to where David lived with his mother and asked if he would help them find the boy. She knew that he walked the fields and woods day and night and he'd know of places no one else had considered.

'Sorry I am,' Mrs Gorse said, 'but he's out. Never one to stay in, he goes out walking and watching wildlife most nights. I'll tell him if he comes back before I go to sleep but he never comes in very early.'

She chattered on, making excuses for David's inability to help, and promised to tell him the moment he came home. 'He'll come straight away when he knows, sure to.'

Sally walked away and on impulse knocked on the door of the local teacher, Joy Laker. Joy offered to come at once. 'Wait and we'll go in the car,' she said. 'That way we can search a bit further away.' She went to the drive and stared about her in astonishment. 'My car! It's gone!'

Sally waited while Joy rang the local police, then Joy shrugged. 'I'll come anyway. An extra pair of eyes will help.' They hurried back to Sally's house in School Lane. 'Such a nuisance about the car. I need it tomorrow to go and see my mother. And it might be damaged.'

'Maybe it's been taken by someone too lazy to walk home. Borrowed, not stolen.'

'I hope so.'

Eric stood and looked down the lane towards the mill. 'I still think he might be around there somewhere,' he told PC Harvey. 'He knows the place well and he'd have found a dozen places to hide.'

'Shall we go for another look? It's getting late and he might have fallen asleep thinking we've finished searching until tomorrow.'

Eric patted his pockets. 'I'd like to go on my own. I think I've an idea how to coax him out. Just give me an hour, will you?'

The policeman conferred with the others and they agreed to stay away from the mill for an hour and leave Eric to try and persuade the boy to show himself. 'I'll wait within calling distance, in case there's been an accident and you need help,' the constable promised.

Eric gathered dry grasses and small kindling wood and soon had a fire burning. He took from his pockets a few small potatoes and, wrapped in greaseproof paper, a couple of meat pies. He had known as soon as he had learned of Jimmy's disappearance that food would be the best way to tempt him from hiding. Once the fire had a heart he placed the potatoes in the glowing ash and sat and waited, his ears alert for the first sound.

Just out of sight but as patient and aware as Eric, PC Harvey also listened to the night. Voices were heard occasionally, calling to others as the search moved around them. A rustling sound gave brief hope as a fox ambled past him. He heard the fox rustling some paper, then the unmistakable lip-smacking sound of it eating. Lucky fox, he'd found a morsel for his supper.

In the tree, safely out of sight, Jimmy tried to stretch his stiff limbs. Tiredness was making his eyes droop. The cold night air was seeping into his body and shivers warned of worse to come. He tightened the duffel coat tighter around him but it no longer made any difference. If only they'd go away so he could get into the mill again. Worst of all, he was hungry. He had dropped his sandwiches and the chocolate bar as he'd climbed into the ivy and every time he decided to go down and look for them, a faint sound, a voice or the rustling of feet pushing through the dead grasses stopped him. Now they had been enjoyed by a fox.

Then he smelt smoke and his eyes opened wide. Someone was at the mill. Could it be Eric? It had to be. No one else would be there on such a cold night. More cautiously than the fox, he moved down from the tree. Eric, just a distorted silhouette, was sitting beside the fire, stirring the ashes with a stick. Without turning his head, he said, 'Hello, boy, come for some supper, have you?'

'Yeah. The fox pinched mine.'

'Take one of these pies. That'll warm you up. Then I think we'd better go home.' Constable Harvey was smiling as he watched the boy biting huge mouthfuls of the welcome food.

'Taters aren't cooked, are they?'

'Not yet. Perhaps we'll finish them off tomorrow.'

With Jimmy eating a second pie, a partly cooked potato in the other fist as a hand-warmer and Eric's arm around his shoulders, the man and the boy walked back to Mill Road after telling the relieved police all was well.

Walter came running out of the house shouting and raging against Eric.

'What have you done to the boy? Where did you take him? Evil you are, Eric Thomas, always thought you were a bit funny in the head and—'

He was stopped as Netta pushed him out of the way and hugged Jimmy. 'Shut up!' she said, and Jimmy tensed. Surely they weren't going to start arguing straight away?

'Are you all right? We've been so worried. Why did you go away?'

'Fed up with the rows. And I know they're my fault,' Jimmy said, trying to hold back sobs. 'I try to please Dad but he hates me.'

'What rubbish you talk,' she soothed. 'We both love you very much.'

Walter was still shouting at Eric. 'Keep away from my son. Right? Spending time with children like my Jimmy. You're weird! No wonder your wife and daughter left.'

'The police were with me all the time,' Eric said, his eyes wide with shock. 'I'd never harm Jimmy, or any other child.'

Constable Harvey came then and led a still protesting Walter inside, where he warned the man against repeating unconfirmed and nonsensical accusations about the man who found his son and brought him safely home.

It was very gradually that the crowds dispersed, everyone wanting to talk about the events of the day and the surprising rescue by old Eric. When Sally was going into her house to allow Valmai to go home, David appeared.

'What's happened? Have they found him?' He showed relief to be told the boy was back with his parents. 'Up in the wood the other side of the park I was, watching a family of badgers. Sorry I wasn't there when you needed me.'

When Joy Laker reached her house, the car was back in her drive, almost precisely where she had parked it after coming home from school. Almost but not exactly.

When Valmai reached home Gwilym was upset, although relieved to know Jimmy was safe. 'I should have been helping. I should have been out there with the others,' he said.

Valmai knew that sympathy hadn't persuaded him to get out and face the world and her new method just might, so she said. 'Yes, you should have been there.' Then, leaving him to settle on the day bed in the living room, she went upstairs without another word. She hated treating him like this, but sympathy was too convenient an excuse for him not to try.

Childcare workers and a woman police officer called on Netta and Walter, and Joy Laker, as Jimmy's teacher, gave him more of her time. She went to talk to Netta and Walter and tried to make them see what their arguments were doing to a boy who couldn't understand but could only accept blame for their misery. None of these visits were discussed outside the privacy of their house and Valmai could only hope that some good would come out of them. Jimmy was neglected by being in the middle of two very unhappy people and how could he not blame himself?

Jimmy still hesitated before walking into the house. He felt happier when his mother was there but more and more often these days she was not. The table would be covered with newspapers and dirty plates where Walter had made food for himself. Jimmy had to wait until his mother came home from work and the time she arrived was becoming later and later. He had brought home a picture he had made, nothing special, except he had painted it with a design of clouds and the glow of sun across the sea. 'Dad,' he said hesitantly, 'Miss Laker said this was good. What d'you think?'

'What's it supposed to be? It's a picture with nothing going on. That's a strange one. She was being kind to you, son. You're better off doing sums and things if you ask me.'

Jimmy nodded, 'Yeah, none of us did anything special. Just messing about.' He'd long ago decided it was best if he agreed. 'I'd better leave it to show Mam, though.'

He couldn't decide which was worse, the rows and his mother there, or this long wait with his uncommunicative father who had eyes and ears only for the newspapers, the radio or the television. He cut a slice of bread and jam and went up to his room. If he noticed he had gone, Walter didn't acknowledge the fact.

Jimmy put the painting on the table beside the bed, stared at it and wondered whether his father was right and he shouldn't waste his time on things no one wanted. Perhaps he'd give it away, but who would want it? Perhaps the box he was making in woodwork would please him. Or maybe the teacher would like it – if he could manage to finish the lid.

David's new job of maintenance for a firm responsible for several houses and other properties meant he had to travel and after a few weeks of getting about on his bike, the manager accepted that his work and reliability were satisfactory and gave him the use of a van. Fortunately it was a popular model, and there were many to be seen, unnoticeable, just what he liked. With the name of the firm emblazoned on its side and with no encouragement to keep it clean, he felt able to travel around in it, with mud partially disguising the number plate, and find a few houses to rob.

He made sure to walk far away from where he parked the van and what he took were often not missed for a long time and in many cases never reported to the police. He was conscientious about the work he was given but sometimes he was so tired he parked up and dozed. It was on one such occasion that Sally saw him.

She stopped and asked if he was all right and he happily assured her he was, now she had appeared. She asked about his mother and said, 'Why don't you bring her to the house for coffee on Sunday morning? Sadie loves company and we haven't seen her apart from the night Jimmy was missing.'

'Mam won't come, she's busy all morning preparing her famous roast dinner,' he said, 'but I will. See you about half ten?'

'Bother,' she muttered. Now she'd have to invite a few more or he'd get the wrong idea and she didn't want any more complications in her life. She smiled then. She was like a teenager fighting off unwanted suitors. But it wasn't really funny; she had the eerie feeling that friend though he was, David could make a nasty enemy.

David's savings were growing. Thanks to his mother's generosity he didn't pay anything to the home, she having decided he needed a few months to get on his feet. One evening he left the van and walked and found an uninhabited house at the end of a lane ten miles from home. With the aid of his torch he peered inside and saw there were several paintings that to his inexperienced eye looked as though they might be valuable. The place was locked, the windows secured but it was a simple task for him to enter. Trained as a carpenter, he was adept at removing locks, which he then replaced.

He put three paintings in the van, hidden by the tools and materials he carried, and drove away. How could he learn of their value and how, if they were worth something, could he sell them? Perhaps he'd do better to wait and claim a reward. Although that would be risky; he might have left evidence of being in the house. Unless …

The next day, he called on Sally and told her how he had helped the police and nearly caught a burglar.

'I saw a car drive away, see, and curious, I went to see what was along the lane. There was this house and the door was open and I went inside and looked around. Then I relocked the door and went to call the police.'

'That could have been dangerous. You should be careful,' she said. 'Did they find the paintings?'

'The police didn't. I did! They were hidden in the hedge – the thieves probably planned to pick them up later. No one was caught though,' he added.

A few days later, having been told by a dealer how much he'd have paid for the paintings, David found the house again. What a pity I couldn't get Rhys's fingerprints on a few things in that house, he mused. That would finish him for good.

Milly saw the postman about to take letters to Valmai and to Netta and Walter. 'Here,' she said, holding out her hand. 'Save yourself a few paces. I'm just going to call on them both. It's about a Bring and Buy on Saturday. Tell your wife, will you?' The postman thanked her and hurried on.

Milly glanced at the envelopes and smiled in satisfaction. One was for Valmai and Gwilym and the postmark was Bristol. It must be from that runaway son of theirs.

'Hello, Valmai, any chance of a cup of tea?' she called as she went through the gate. 'Letter here from your son. Lovely to hear, even if he never comes home, isn't it?'

Valmai snatched the envelope and glared at Milly, who was smiling innocently.

'From your Rhys, is it?'

'I don't know till I open it.'

'Don't tell me it's been so long you've forgotten his handwriting. Sad that is.'

'What's sad is you nosing into other people's business!'

'No tea then? Never mind.' Still smiling, Milly went back to the gate. She stopped and poked her head into the shed, 'Letter from your Rhys, Gwilym. Still writing care of that café, are you? No proper address yet?'

'He's fine, and we're well aware of where he is and what he's doing.'

'I bet poor Sally wishes she felt the same.'

Gwilym moved even closer to the bench, making sure his legs were hidden, and turned back to the wood he was planing.

Milly went to call on one of her friends and asked, 'Fancy a trip to Bristol? Do a bit of Christmas shopping? There's a nice little café I've heard of where we can have a spot of lunch.'

Sally's job kept her busy although she felt guilty about the time she spent away from Sadie, and the reduced hours Valmai worked to help them. Sadie was content and chattered happily whenever they were alone, about all she had been doing at Granny's. For the time being Sally had to accept the arrangements and get on with securing her place in the business she enjoyed.

She was building up a reputation for making clever choices, wise distribution of stock and for buying at the best prices. In December she was given a rise in pay. Time, she decided, to start 1962 right by making proper arrangements for Sadie and give Valmai the chance to return to the full number of hours she needed to work. Getting her life on a firm base would please them all.

She would make enquiries about a qualified childminder to stay in the house. She began with an advertisement in the local paper and also approached an agency. This time, no matter how long it took, she had to make sure she found the right person.

Jimmy spent a lot of time with Gwilym. Sometimes Eric was there but he only stayed when either Valmai or Netta came too. Walter's outburst the night he had found Jimmy still worried him, even though the police had been there all the time and Walter was aware of this. He had spent a lot of time at the mill with the boy and he was afraid that a few words at the wrong time and in the hearing of the wrong people would mean he'd be in serious – albeit undeserved – trouble.

The headboard Gwilym had made for Sally had been much admired during the time it had been in the workshop and he had since made three more, with Eric's help. Now, in between making two rocking cradles, ordered by one of the shops in Barry, they spent odd moments making tree ornaments, which Jimmy helped them to paint.

Jimmy came in one afternoon proudly showing them the box he had made at school. The sides had been recessed inside, near the top, to support a lid. 'It needs a little knob to open it, but I broke the one I was making and we didn't have time for another try,' he explained.

'It's beautifully made, young Jimmy. Well done!'

'Better than I could have done at your age,' Eric added.

'Come back when you've shown your father and we'll sort out a finial for the lid. Well done indeed!' And as Jimmy went off to show his father, hoping for at least a little praise, Gwilym began marking out an acorn to act as a handle to go in the centre of the lid.

Walter hardly glanced at the box being proudly held up by his son. 'Wasting time fiddling about with stuff like that,' he said. 'You should stay away from Gwilym and that Eric. Fiddling about with wood won't get you far. Fiddling with stuff no one wants, painting weird pictures, I don't know what that school is thinking of.'

'But you do like it, Dad?'

'Yes, it's fine. Now shush, boy, I'm listening to the TV.'

Jimmy didn't bother to show him his end-of-term report.

The acorn was carved by Jimmy with Gwilym encouraging and Valmai holding her breath as the boy managed with the sharp tools. It was fixed in place and Jimmy said, 'Dad won't want it, he doesn't like me fiddling with stuff like this. I thought I'd give it to Miss Laker as a Christmas present.'

'Better check with Mam and Dad first. I think they'll love it, it's really well made,' Valmai said.

She was waiting when Netta arrived back from work and at once she said. 'Your Jimmy has made a beautiful box and he should be praised for doing it. Your Walter won't bother, but really, Netta, you must.'

Netta went in and said all the right things; it was wonderful, he was so clever, but all the time she was glancing at Walter and hardly looked at it. Jimmy went out that night and threw it in the leat, where it floated for a while then sank and disappeared into the silt.

He spent hours at the mill despite the cold weather, clearing the leat and struggling to ease the penstock so it could be raised and lowered. What it needed, Eric had explained when they discussed it, was some thick cart grease. 'Even then,' Eric went on, 'I doubt if it will work, not after all the years of neglect.'

Surprisingly it was David Gorse who helped, by providing grease to use on the neglected gates. Jimmy found a tin that was still half full which David had thrown away and he took it to the mill and spent a happy afternoon working to free the rusted metal.

Milly Sewell and her friend Mavis were in Bristol. They stopped at the café Milly had learned was the postal address for Rhys and talked about him loudly, hoping to attract some comments. The man behind the counter stared at them occasionally but said nothing. An hour later they left, Milly disappointed. They hadn't gone far on their way to the shopping centre that her luck changed. Coming out of a wallpaper and paint shop was Rhys. With him, sharing his laughter about something, were a woman and a young girl. The woman she didn't recognize at first, but then Rhys called, 'Come on, Julia Thomas, we'll be late for the pictures at this rate. A real slow coach she is, your mother,' he said to the little girl.

Milly stared, frowning until she was convinced that she knew who the young woman was. 'Well I never!' she muttered to Mavis. 'Fancy that! Rhys Martin and Eric's daughter. Who'd have believed it?'

Milly spent the journey home wondering about the best way of using her exciting new knowledge. Should she tell Eric? Or would it be more fun to tell Valmai and that workshy husband of hers, idling his time in that shed instead of facing the world and getting a proper job? What she really needed was an audience and the following morning she found one.

She was making her way to Valmai and Gwilym's house, intending to just hint that she had news of their son, and when she reached the front gate laughter led her to the shed in the back garden. Eric was there, and Jimmy was showing them a small tree Eric had made for a nativity scene which was minus its top. 'The chisel slipped, Uncle Gwilym. I saw it slip and snap the top off. And he's done it before.' Jimmy was laughing as he held the two pieces together.

'It just shows that even the best of us can make a mistake.' Gwilym said, winking at Eric.

'Now, Jimmy.' Eric said, 'will you have another go at sanding this figure's arms so they look like a pair?'

Milly stood for a moment watching the two men and the boy working together, then, as Valmai came to join them, she said, 'I saw your daughter yesterday, Eric. Looking well, isn't she?'

'Julia? You saw Julia? Where is she? How is she?' Eric was shaken. He dropped what he was doing and stared at Milly's smiling face.

'Oh, she's fine and very happy from what I saw. With Rhys she was, her and the little girl. Was she another poor woman your Rhys abandoned then went back to, Gwilym?'

'Julia? Are you sure? And a child? I don't understand,' Eric said.

'What's to understand? Loves and leaves them, doesn't he, your Rhys?' she said, looking at Valmai.

Questions came thick and fast, voices increasing in volume as Milly teased them with half-complete replies. Jimmy went to stand beside Valmai and reached for her hand, afraid that the questions would turn into rows. Not here, he pleaded with an unrecognized God. If they row here I'll have nowhere to go.

Milly smiled at a white-faced Valmai and held up her hands in protest. 'Stop. Please. I'll tell you all I know if you'll give me a chance.'

Valmai moved closer to Gwilym and stared at her. 'Stop enjoying this and tell us what you know, if it's the truth you're telling and not a pack of vicious lies, Milly Sewell.'

She released Jimmy's hand and, unnoticed, he moved away, out of the door and back to his empty house. Walter was asleep in the armchair, the television was on, the fire was out, and he went up to his room. He opened his bedroom window and listened to the voices raised in anger. Now there was nowhere to go.

In the workshop, Milly was still holding court, pleased with the way the news was greeted.

'I went for a day out and saw your Rhys and he was with a woman.' She paused for effect. 'And when I recognized Eric's daughter Julia I was too surprised to say anything. I just watched as they walked off with a dear little girl. I thought I must be dreaming, but it was Rhys all right and the woman he was with was your daughter, Eric.'

'How can you know? She was a schoolgirl when you last saw her.'

'You know what it's like to see photographs of babies and know straight away who they are. There's always something that doesn't change. That thick hair and those big blue eyes. Even after all this time there was no doubt. Your Julia is with Rhys Martin living in Bristol, there was no mistake. All this time he's been missing and poor Sally's been coping with his daughter on her own.' She turned to Valmai. 'Protecting him you've been, and Eric not told where his daughter is. Shame on you, Valmai. All this time he's been with Julia Thomas, or whatever her name is now. If they're married it would be Martin, wouldn't it, Gwilym?'

'Of course he isn't married! Eric, she's mistaken. Rhys and Sally have an understanding. He'll be back soon and then we'll hear the truth.'

'Shall I tell Sally or would you like to give her the sad news?' Milly said with false sympathy.

'Keep away from her, d'you hear? This is a distortion of the facts, something you do very well, Milly Sewell. Now go away and leave us to deal with any problems we have in our own way.'

Milly waved and left, smiling at the shouted remarks from Gwilym's workshop that followed her. She didn't care if she had been mistaken; she'd had her fun.

Next door, Jimmy covered his ears.

'Eric,' Gwilym pleaded. 'Believe us, we know nothing about this and I for one don't think it's true.' He reached out and patted Eric's shoulder. Eric moved away, his face white as he stared at Gwilym and Valmai in disbelief. 'You knew. All this time you knew Rhys was with Julia and didn't tell me.'

'No, Eric, we'd have told you. It isn't true. It can't be.' Valmai was adamant, desperate for him to believe her.

'Milly might have seen Rhys; she's clever enough to find out where he lives. Sally no longer tries to keep it a secret,' Gwilym said. 'She might have seen someone resembling your daughter, Eric, but after all this time, how can she be certain it was her? She was a child when she left. Pigtails and missing some teeth. No, I'm sure Rhys isn't with Julia. He'd have told us if he'd found her. He wouldn't keep that to himself, whatever his reason for staying away.'

'In fact, if he learned of her whereabouts the very first thing he'd do would be to tell you, knowing how much you want to see her. You know Rhys well enough to believe that.'

Eric put down the chisel he'd been gripping as though for support and walked out of the shed. Valmai called after him but he didn't look back.

Gwilym called after him. 'Come back, man. This is what Milly wanted, for us to fall out.' He stared at Valmai, speechless; the sound of departing footsteps and the closing gate punctuated the silence.

'I'll have to find Sally as soon as she gets home,' Valmai said tear-fully. 'She mustn't hear this from Milly, true or false.' She went to collect a jacket and set off on her bicycle, firstly to work at the hotel, then to wait at the house in School Lane for Sally's return.

Gwilym reached under the bench in the cupboard used for assorted offcuts of wood and pulled out the almost completed leg. Could he? If he could master it, with the aid of two crutches he had to get out, and stop leaving all this to Valmai. The harness was almost completed and he stood to try it on with trembling limbs. After half an hour of trying to walk around in the workshop – which was all he had imagined doing when he decided to make it – he threw it back into its hiding place. It was no use, he couldn't do it. It isn't agoraphobia, he told himself, it's a fear of falling flat on my stupid face!

He stared at the cupboard, which was hiding his puny attempt at mobility and promised himself he'd try again. Tomorrow.

More important now was where was Jimmy? He'd probably been frightened by the raised voices here, at the place he always came to avoid the rows at home. He kicked at the cupboard door with his good leg and cursed his rotten luck at being hit by a car that didn't stop. He and Eric on the same day, but Eric got off lightly. Although, he admitted, he had been more fortunate, having Valmai and, until two years ago, a son too. Eric's wife had left him years before, leaving him with a mountain of debts and had taken his daughter with her. Even losing a leg, he was the lucky one.

He was still staring into space when Valmai was due home. Slowly he went down the path to the kitchen to peel potatoes and set the table for their meal. He called from the back garden gate but Jimmy either didn't hear or chose not to answer.

Valmai found Sally at home about to bath Sadie. 'Sally, love, come and sit down a minute, will you? There's something I need to tell you.'

'Rhys? Has something happened? Is he all right?'

'It's some story from Milly. Loves a bit of gossip and what she can't find she makes up.' Sally was staring at her, waiting, and she went on. 'She went to Bristol, to the café where you sent letters and somewhere near there she says she saw Rhys with a woman and a little girl and the woman was Eric's daughter, Julia.'

Sally's shoulders drooped. 'I saw her too but of course I didn't recognize her. I've never met her. I couldn't describe her; all I remember was the shock and disbelief. I did see the little girl though – about seven I'd guess.' She paused, staring into space then asked, 'Does Eric know?'

'It can't be Julia. How could Milly recognize her after seeing her last as a schoolgirl? It's vicious nonsense. Poor Eric was very upset. She chooses her time well does Milly. He went off convinced that Gwilym and I have known all along, that we kept Julia's whereabouts from him.'

'What will you do?'

Valmai shrugged. 'Go and find him? Make him tell us the truth? It's time all this came to an end.'

Sally shook her head. 'No, not me. I'm sorry, Valmai but I want nothing more to do with Rhys and his secrets.'

'If only Gwilym was mobile.' She sighed as she stood to leave. 'I'll have to go on my own.'

'You could take Eric?'

'I'll ask. Oh, Sally, love, there are many times when I miss having Gwilym to support me and this is one of them.'

Eric was at the mill. Winter was warning of darker and colder days to come. The trees were skeletal and the sound of their branches touching was a harsh sound compared with the months when leaves softened their caress. He had made a fire, a brave attempt to brighten the day and his mood. If Milly was right, Julia had been near enough to visit all these years. He could understand why she couldn't come when she was small, but surely she must have been curious? Why hadn't she come to find him? Ask what had happened? Why had she never been in touch? Her mother must have told her stories that had made him into a villain.

'Eric? Any taters? I've got some biscuits.'

'Go away, Jimmy, your father told you to stay away from me.'

'He didn't mean it, he just likes arguing. Want a biscuit? Custard creams and some ginger nuts.'

'Sorry, Jimmy. I have to go.' He kicked the ashes apart and reached down to get a can of water he always left nearby and drenched the remains of the fire. Leaving Jimmy still offering the bag of biscuits, he walked away to go and see Sally.

'All right, go! I don't care. I'm off to see Rick and Amy.' Red-faced with hurt and disappointment, convinced that no one in the whole world cared for him, Jimmy ran along the path to Mill Road and knocked furiously on the door of the Waterstones' house.

'Can I come in? I'm freezing. I've got some biscuits, ginger nuts, they're my favourites. I saved some for you though.'

Sally opened the door and stood aside for Eric to enter. 'Come and sit close to the fire. There's a pot of tea just made and I'll make us some toast.'

'You've heard?' he asked.

'D'you think it really was Julia who Milly saw? Is she the one Rhys left Sadie and me for?'

'If it was Julia, she would be twenty-six. Old enough to come and find me.'

'You can't think that. You don't know what her mother told her about you. She might have told her you were – she might have told her you were dead.'

'Dead, or so evil she had to be saved from me?'

'Valmai wants to go and find Rhys and find out for certain. I do think it's unlikely though. There's no address but it's the same area so they should be found. Will you go with her?'

'Best not. Until I know why she hasn't tried to find me I'd better stay away. If it's true, there's a daughter too. A granddaughter I'll probably never know. I don't want to risk her walking away again. I'll wait until Valmai talks to them. She and Gwilym are good friends. They understood my outburst when Milly dropped her bombshell.'

Gwilym struggled with the leather fastening and tested his weight on the carved leg. He had been making a rocking horse and that had made it easier to disguise the leg as he carved it and also explained the order for quality leather he had added to what he had needed for saddle and bridle and reins. He walked around the shed using both sticks. He had to get around better than in the chair. Even with the care taken to design the work area there were still places he needed help to reach.

He was concentrating so deeply on the rhythm and balance of walking that he didn't hear Valmai come in.

'Gwilym!' she gasped. And he pushed himself back to the bench and sat down, the artificial leg sticking out awkwardly in front of him.

'Don't say anything. Just don't say anything,' he muttered. 'I've tried but it isn't going to work.'

'But it seems fine.'

'It was only for moving about in the shed, not for going out,' he said firmly. 'Don't think I'll be walking around because I won't.'

'Let me see what you can do. Please, Gwilym,' she added, as he turned his head away.

'Tomorrow,' he replied.

'Always tomorrow,' she sighed. She walked on down the path and went into the kitchen. Her eyes were shining with hope. It was a stupid idea to make himself a leg when he could be fitted with a professional, custom-made limb and have help learning to cope with it. But perhaps it was really going to happen. She was humming cheerfully when she filled the kettle and put the potatoes on to boil.

Gwilym stared at the door for a long time after she had gone. He was in a prison but one to which he held the key. If only he were brave enough to turn it.

The meal was ready to serve and still Gwilym hadn't appeared. Valmai looked up at the shed where the light still shone. He must have been finishing off something. He wasn't one to leave a job unfinished. Each stage had to be completed before he'd put the work aside. She slipped on a coat and walked up.

There was no sound from inside and she opened the door and saw that his chair was empty. She frowned. Surely he hadn't stepped outside to try out the amateur leg? It wouldn't be safe. There was a slight frost and he could so easily slip. Waving the torch around, calling his name, she went along the path towards the pavement but there was no sign of him.

Netta heard her calling and came out. 'What's up, Valmai? Don't tell me your Gwilym's gone walkabout?' she joked.

'Yes, he has. He made himself a stupid wooden leg and he's gone out. Where can he be? He can't have gone far.'

'I'll get a torch and go along the road a bit. You go back and look around the shed. He might have just stepped outside.'

'He'd have heard me calling.'

'Go anyway. Start at the beginning and I'll go along the road.'

He was behind the shed, lying on the ground, his good leg twisted underneath him, his face, in the light of the trembling torch, like that of a very old man.

'Netta!' she called. 'Go to the phone box and ring for an ambulance. Hurry!'

Chapter Eleven

WITH GWILYM IN hospital, thoughts of finding Rhys were pushed aside. Valmai visited him daily and continued to work the usual hours at the hotel. She was frightened at the damage he had done to his healthy leg but also hopeful that after this stupidity he would finally accept the need for a properly fitted false limb.

Sally called at the hospital too and sometimes brought Sadie to wave to her grandfather through the window. His bedside table was always covered with treats and most of these he passed on to Eric when he came.

For Eric the delay in searching for his daughter was painful but he had promised Valmai he wouldn't go on his own. To find the money to travel there and stay a night or two, which is what he hoped to do, would have meant giving up his room for a week. 'Sleeping at the mill in December is not allowed,' Valmai had warned. 'If you try, I'll tell the police you're a vagrant and need locking up!'

He smiled, knowing she was joking but he agreed to wait.

Valmai knew she should offer him a room with her and Gwilym, even if only for the winter months, but with only two bedrooms and one large living room, it wouldn't have been very convenient and Eric would have regretted the loss of his privacy. The second bedroom was still for Rhys.

David seemed amused by the latest rumours. He laughed at the story of Rhys and Eric's daughter being together to his mother and people he met, but to Sally he showed nothing but sympathy. He visited her often, taking small gifts for Sadie and sometimes calling and suggesting a walk. He put Sadie on his shoulders and they spent time in the park and walking through the woods, where he would point out where various animals lived and invent stories about their lives.

Sadie greeted him with excitement and Sally too began to feel a warmth towards him she hadn't expected. With Christmas almost upon them, they went shopping and bought a few presents, laughing as they hid from each other the surprises that would be revealed on Christmas Day. He waited outside a bookshop while Sally went in to buy something for Sadie and Mrs Gorse, and also outside the men's clothing shop, where Rick worked, to buy a gift for him.

David often put an arm around her shoulders as they crossed a road or when he shepherded them into yet another shop. It seemed natural, and she didn't edge away from his occasional embrace. It was the season that made the difference, she decided. There was a willingness to share, a need to belong and the warmth that was Christmas changed people for the better. Every day was filled with moments of happiness. Strangers shared their plans and the shops were crowded with people who smiled more readily. There was an unusual politeness.

It was this mood, this excitement, she mused, that had made the difference in the way she felt about David, a happiness in sharing that she hadn't known for a very long time. Everything was fun and for an hour or two Sally could forget the hurt she suffered by Rhys's mysterious behaviour and revel in the joy of the season and friends with whom to share it. She enjoyed making plans, preparing for guests, cooking, buying party clothes for herself and Sadie. Money, she admitted to David, made a big difference.

They went back to the house in School Lane loaded with parcels one afternoon and as Sally took off her coat and filled the kettle, David ran upstairs with the parcels. As he walked slowly back down again he looked serious.

'I've enjoyed today, Sally love. I want more days like this; you, Sadie and me.' He looked at her, assessing her mood, then moved towards her and put his arms around her. 'Tell me you feel the same. We've both been lonely too long. You know I love you and little Sadie. I know we can be happy together now Rhys is out of your life and unable to ruin things ever again.'

His arms felt so comforting, the words touching her heart, and when he mentioned Rhys she tried not to feel anything but indifference. His kiss warmed her and the need for this closeness was strong. Then Sadie called, insisting she was 'hungry for a cake', and the mood faded, although the look in David's eyes didn't change. He kissed her again lightly then went to see what the shopping bags offered for the hungry little girl. 'Doughnut or currant cake?' he asked.

'Yes, please, David. Both!' Sadie said with a laugh.

Sally's mind was in turmoil as a picture of Rhys came and went, being replaced by the smiling face of David. During these terrible months he was always there when she needed him and asked nothing in return. She wondered if she would – could – forget Rhys and accept David. Something inside her at that moment as she watched her daughter laughing, looking up at him, grew in strength and she thought she might.

Eric still felt uneasy spending time with Jimmy but he didn't want the boy to think he no longer had a friend. He knew Jimmy was unsettled and guessed he was likely to run away again if things became intolerable in the Prosser household. He wanted to keep an eye on him to make sure that if he did, he'd be there and able to help.

He was sitting in the workshop one afternoon finishing a rocking horse Gwilym was making. It was a long job and he did some of the work every day in between other smaller pieces. Jimmy talked about a book he was reading about a boy who had an adventure travelling, and working when he needed money. 'He used a compass,' he said. 'How does that help?'

Eric explained about following a course and he also promised to get him one. 'You'll enjoy the book even more if you can see the way he's travelling,' he said, 'and you follow his route on a map.'

'So if he wanted to go from here to the seaside, he'd go south?'

Eric laughed. 'You wouldn't need a compass for that. From here to the seaside you could catch a bus and be home for supper!'

'It must be a long way. I've never been there,' he surprised him by saying.

Amy and Rick had heard the latest on the Rhys saga and they called on Sally one evening. As Valmai wasn't free to go, they offered to take Sally and Eric to Bristol.

'We won't intrude,' Rick promised, 'we'll just drop you off where you want to be and pick you up later.'

'It isn't such a great favour,' Amy admitted. 'I'm longing for the excuse to visit more shops. This is our first Christmas and Mummy isn't coming. She's going to Bournemouth to stay with cousin Godfrey.'

'Three cheers for cousin Godfrey,' Rick said. 'We're going to have the best Christmas ever. Breakfast in bed, a long walk in the morning, followed by a late lunch, then a party for friends on Boxing Day to finish off the turkey.'

'We've decorated the whole house in a way that will horrify my mother,' Amy added. 'Using every colour and shade known to man, streamers and balloons and more glitter than you've ever seen in your life.'

When they were leaving, Amy told her friend that they were happier than they'd ever imagined. 'Mummy caused a few problems at the beginning, insisting on us following her advice. Now, half the fun is learning to outwit her. Wicked, isn't it?'

'We love her of course,' Rick added quickly, 'and we'd never deliberately hurt her feelings, but we need to make her see that our ways are different from hers.'

'She hasn't visited for a while. There was her illness and hospital, the convalescence in Bournemouth with cousin Godfrey. Since then we've had to visit her. When she does come she'll be surprised at the changes we've already made to her carefully designed decor. Cheerful blue instead of the drab grey she ordered for the bathroom and the kitchen is now a cheerful yellow. The drab curtains too have been put aside and new ones chosen. Poor Mum, she will insist that she knows best.'

'But she'll soon see that the house is ours, Amy's and mine, and we want everything to represent our taste, not chosen from the books on design she'd buried herself in for months.'

David's mother loved Christmas and although there would be only the two of them and David would be out for most of the day, she decided to decorate a tree and put up some coloured lights. The trimmings, as she called them, were stored in the loft and, impatient once she had made up her mind, she was unable to wait for David to come home so struggled in with the ladder and went up herself.

There was no light up there and with the aid of a torch she searched the assorted boxes until she found the lights and baubles to hang on the tree. Now she needed the artificial tree. It was as she pulled aside some old mats and a chair with a broken seat that she found David's treasure. She gasped with delight. He was always buying antiques. Perhaps these were for her Christmas present. He rarely bought something new, always something old and beautiful.

She pushed the tree down on to the landing, carefully carried down the box of fragile baubles then went back and brought down the picture and the silver vase. She spent a happy couple of hours cleaning them, then put them back, carefully rewrapped, so David's surprise wouldn't be spoilt.

When he came home, David was alarmed when he saw the tree dressed in the bright decorations. 'Mam! Have you been up in the loft? You shouldn't do things like that. Why didn't you wait for me?'

'I remembered where they were, I didn't have to search,' she said, hoping he wouldn't notice the difference in the way the secret gifts had been wrapped. 'It didn't take more than a minute or two.'

Later, David made the excuse of going up and making sure there were no more trimmings they could use and he was relieved to see the picture and bowl still wrapped and in the same place as he'd left them.

Sally arranged a day when she and Eric would go to Bristol and one week before Christmas, on Monday 18th, they went. Sally directed them to the place where she had seen Rhys with the woman who, in the unlikely event of Milly being right, was Eric's daughter. Amy and Rick waited in the car when they walked up the steps and knocked at the door. There was no reply and going around to the back they knocked again but no one came. The thin curtains were drawn but no light showed. The place looked deserted.

Hiding the disappointment they all felt, they got back in the car and went to spend a few hours enjoying the shops. Sadie loved the displays and shouted in excitement as they went into each new store. Rick carried her part of the time as, from her pushchair, down among shopping bags and people's knees, she couldn't see what was going on and protested loudly to let them know.

Before they left to drive home, Rick took them back to the house where Rhys had apparently lived and Eric walked around again to find nothing had changed. The place looked abandoned. 'They might be away for Christmas,' Eric said. 'I'll have to be patient until the New Year.'

'Sorry, Eric, I should have faced them when I came first instead of running away.'

'Don't worry. After so long, what's another few days?'

'Look, we aren't in a hurry to get home, shall we go somewhere and eat?' Rick suggested. 'Sadie will sleep in the car going home if she's tired and we can call it a pre-Christmas treat.'

They chose a small restaurant and it was almost ten o'clock when they reached home. Sally, carrying her shopping with a sleeping Sadie over her shoulder, opened the front door and stood to wave as Eric, Amy and Rick drove away. Then a figure materialized a few feet away.

'Please, Sally, can I come in?' Rhys asked.

Sally threw the shopping bags inside, went in after them and without a word, closed the door.

She knew that was wrong. She should have allowed him in and given him the chance to tell her about the woman. If it was Eric's daughter he needed to know. She had let Eric down again by shutting the door against Rhys. She put Sadie down and went outside, but there was no sign of him. Why had she acted so selfishly? Why hadn't she thought about Eric before slamming the door?

Jimmy was on his bed, lying on his front, propped up on his elbows with his hands over his ears. Even with his hands pressed tightly as he could, he could still hear them arguing. His father's low rumbling voice in counterpoint to the high-pitched shrieking of his mother's. The book in front of him was one lent to him by Rick and it was an interesting story, but the shouting from the kitchen made it impossible to concentrate. If only he had somewhere to go he'd be out of here as fast as his feet could take him.

Eric was no longer his friend. Recently he'd often refused to go for a walk with him, even when he wanted to show him where the badgers had run, leaving tufts of their hair on the wire fencing. Nobody likes me, he thought glumly. Dad's right and I'm useless. It was only eight o'clock but, still fully dressed, he slid between the sheets. He pressed his head into the pillow and brought another over his other ear but still the noise went on. Then there was a sudden and louder sound. Plates smashed, and what sounded like a table being overturned. He dug deeper into the covers and closed his eyes tight as though that could help to obliterate the sounds from below.

Then there was silence that was as unnerving as the noise and he got out of bed and went on to the landing. The voices were still to be heard but quieter now. His mother's voice was the easiest to hear and she was telling his father to go.

'I'm not going anywhere!' Walter raised his voice again. 'If anyone leaves it's going to be you and you can take that useless boy with you.' Jimmy heard the back door open and slam closed and the sound of his mother's slippered feet running down the path.

He didn't wait to hear any more. He grabbed his clothes, the blankets packed ready for when he had to leave, and when he heard his father go into the living room and turn on the television very loud he went cautiously down, stole the contents of his mother's purse, then filled a bag with food and a bottle of pop and left the house, staggering under his load.

He was surprised at how cold it was. He'd been under the bed covers fully dressed and the contrast hit him with a shock. Frost sparked on the fences and on patches of damp on the road. He wondered where his mam had gone. Why hadn't she waited for him, he wondered sadly. Forgot I was there, like she usually does when she and Dad argue.

He'd have preferred it if his father had been the one to leave and for a moment he hesitated and wondered whether his dad might be all right without anyone to argue with. But then, he decided sadly, he'd still have me, 'that useless boy', to shout at. He hurried on. Tomorrow he'd go and see Valmai and Gwilym – they'd know what to do – but for tonight he'd go and seek comfort in the old mill. He patted his shoulder bag. Food, drink and paper and matches to light a fire. He'd be all right until morning.

Rhys went to his parents' house and having heard about Gwilym's accident asked to be allowed to stay. 'This is still your home, Rhys,' Valmai said, but she was uneasy. She felt that by allowing him to stay she was letting Sally down, but what else could she do? He was her son and she couldn't send him away. Specially with so many questions needing answers. 'You can't use your room, mind. Netta's in there. She and Walter have had a serious falling out. You can sleep here on your dad's chair.' He didn't sleep, but sat beside the fire and tried to prepare the words he needed to say to Sally, if she ever allowed him to say them. She had to be the first one to hear his story. Then he'd tell his parents and ask them all to forgive him or at least to understand.

He and Julia had left the house in Bristol for the Christmas period. He hoped they wouldn't be going back. She had taken her daughter and gone to spend Christmas with a friend in West Wales for a week. He had decided that the time had come to explain all that had happened. Would Sally understand? Would she even allow him to tell his story?

Netta was surprised to see Rhys there when she went downstairs early the next morning. His eyes were closed and she tiptoed past him and filled the kettle as quietly as she could. But he followed her into the kitchen and began putting cups out on a tray.

'I've got your room, Rhys, I'm sorry.'

'Don't be. I'm a big boy now, Auntie Netta,' he said, using the name he'd used all his life. 'If things hadn't gone so terribly wrong, I'd be married with a home of my own by now.'

Netta didn't ask for an explanation; this was not her business. 'Uncle Walter and I have had too many rows. I couldn't stand it any longer.'

'Where's Jimmy?'

'Still asleep. I'll go and fetch him and give him breakfast a bit later. Best to let him sleep while he can and I don't want to go and wake up Walter and start more rows.'

They heard Valmai coming down the stairs and Rhys looked towards the door ready to greet her. 'Mam, I'll explain when I've spoken to Sally. She needs to be told before anyone else.'

Valmai shrugged. 'What about you, Netta, are you going back to see to Jimmy? Frightened he'll be and wondering where you are.'

'Will you go and fetch him? Please, Val. I just can't face the man. He'll only start off again. Bring Jimmy here and before the end of the day I'll have decided what to do.'

'Of course I'll fetch Jimmy. And you can stay as long as you need to. Just get things settled once and for all, for Jimmy's sake as well as yours.'

Rhys drank some tea and then left. He walked to the house on School Lane and looked up at the windows, shining in the sudden brightness of an early morning sun. There were lights on in one bedroom and below. At the side, a shaft of light shone from between partially open curtains in what was probably the kitchen. He followed the path around to the back door and knocked.

He heard voices within and the soft giggle of a child. A pang of pain pierced him as he thought about what he had done to his daughter. The voices stopped and the door opened a crack.

'Sally, please, let me talk to you. I want to see you and Sadie. I have to explain. Please.' The door closed without Sally uttering a word.

'Damn! I've done it again!' she gasped aloud. What is the matter with me? I've let Eric down again! He deserves to know whether or not the woman was his daughter. What sort of a friend am I that I could miss the chance of finding the answer, twice? Then she excused herself by remembering that she had to get to work and before then get Sadie ready and taken to the nursery. Now Rhys was here. Eric would soon learn the truth. Her not opening the door wouldn't change anything. Rhys owed everyone an explanation and she didn't need to mess up her day to help him. Now was a stupid time to knock on her door. Satisfied for the moment that the blame was with Rhys, she hurriedly prepared for the start of the day. 'Come on, lazy bones,' she called to Sadie. 'Time to get ready for nursery.'

David was there as she went to her car and she almost didn't see him. The man at the edge of her sight she presumed to be Rhys and she got into the car and slammed the door, turned on the engine and was moving off when he reached the driver's door. 'Sally, wait!'

She switched off the engine. 'David. I'm sorry. I thought it was Rhys.'

'He's back?' David was surprised. 'I don't know how he can face you. Wants more money, does he? Or more time?'

'I don't know. I didn't give him a chance to tell me.' She smiled up at him. 'Let's forget Rhys, shall we? He's no longer a part of my life and he doesn't appear to want to be part of Sadie's either.'

'That's fine by me!' He leaned into the car and kissed her cheek. 'Sally, I was going to ask if you were free for an hour, lunchtime maybe? Or can you leave early? With only days to go I haven't bought anything for Mam and I know she would like a dressing gown. Now how can I choose a dressing gown? I don't know what size or what colour she'd like. I was hoping you'd help.'

'Can you meet me in Cardiff, near the office, at three? I'll have an hour but I'll have to go back to the office. We'll find something in an hour, surely.'

'Thank you.' Smiling, he waved her off. 'I can't wait,' he shouted. Rhys was back and he'd keep coming back. It was time to play his trump card and get rid of him for good. Taking Sally away from him might be easier than he'd thought. But if Rhys no longer wanted her, if he'd found someone else, that would be different. He didn't want her if Rhys didn't. There was no fun in that.

Netta kept putting off going back into her house and it was Valmai who, at half past eight, went to wake Jimmy and bring him back to give him breakfast. Walter was sleeping, slack-mouthed, on a couch and the place smelled unpleasantly of stale food and beer and cigarette smoke. There was no sign of Jimmy. Giving Walter a prod to rouse him she told him she was going to wake his son and ran up the stairs. Jimmy's room was empty. She looked in the other bedroom and ran down, alarm growing by the second. 'Walter! Where's Jimmy? He hasn't gone to school without breakfast, has he?'

'Still in bed. Never gets up in time unless he's called.'

'And you didn't think to call him!' She looked at the clock. It was almost nine o'clock. 'Walter, he isn't here! For heaven's sake, man, he's only eleven and you don't know where he is! When did he go? He could have walked out some time during the night and he didn't knock on my door, so where would he go?'

'He'll be all right. On his way to school, sure to be.' But he looked concerned. His eyes, bleary and watery, had widened in alarm.

'Walter, wake up! It's cold out there. We don't know how long he's been out there. We have to find him!'

Valmai appeared then, and guessed from the expression on their faces that once again Jimmy had run away. 'Where will you look?' she shouted. 'What if he isn't at school? What then? Proud of yourself, are you? Driving a child out because of your idleness and foul temper. Shamed you should be, Walter Prosser. Shamed.'

'Us you mean. It isn't only me. He's running away because of US!'

'And who can blame him,' Netta whispered, looking at Valmai in fright. 'It's winter – he can't be sleeping out in this, can he?' She grabbed her purse and ran to the phone box. The children would be filing into their classes and she asked the secretary to phone back and let her know if Jimmy Prosser was present. She tapped her fingers impatiently on the phone as she waited for the call, shushing away someone who came wanting to use it. She willed him to be there and that he hadn't wandered off somewhere. The weather wasn't seriously cold but the temperature was low enough for a night out to be dangerous for a young boy. She kept picturing the old mill, imagining Jimmy sleeping then slipping into unconsciousness and – the terrifying thoughts stopped there as the phone rang.

No, Jimmy wasn't at school.

Jimmy hadn't slept well. The floor never lost its chill, the blankets too were cold to the touch and his nose seemed like a piece of ice that didn't belong to his face. As dawn broke he rose, checked his compass and began to walk south. The money he had taken from his mother's purse would last a few days, then he'd go to the police, give a false name and he'd be taken to a children's home where there'd be lots of friends and no one calling him useless.

Rhys went at once to look for the boy. Firstly to the mill where there was no sign of him although a few apple cores suggested he – or someone else – had stayed there for a while. He looked around the place where he had spent many hours as a child; friends and imagination was all they had needed. The paddles on the waterwheel were obviously being cleaned. Piles of moss and water weed stood on the bank of the stream and several of the paddles had been scraped clean. The water was moving sluggishly and grease was visible on the moving parts of the pen-stock which had once controlled the water to the wheel along the leat. Jimmy's work, he guessed. Spending time here to escape the rows at home, he'd have been glad of something to pass the time. Poor lonely, frightened little boy.

He walked through the woods, searching each of the many places he had played in years before. The hollow ash where they'd left messages for other gang members, the hazel tree that drooped and made a good hiding place, but with the leaves fallen from the trees they were no longer any use for concealment. Some evergreens offered hope but yielded no sign of Jimmy being there recently. He went back to the house to see if anyone else had been more fortunate.

Eric was there and he nodded with little friendliness at Rhys, before turning away.

'Eric, I have to talk to you.'

'Jimmy's missing. He's the priority now.'

'But I have things to tell you.'

'Forget Eric and tell *me* where you've looked,' Walter said, glaring at Eric.

Ignoring him, Rhys said, 'Eric, I have to talk to you.'

'Later!'

An hour later, having faced accusations from everyone for his neglect of his son, Walter's face had lost its anger. He looked deflated, and more than a little afraid. He had washed hurriedly and had already walked the streets following the route Jimmy would normally take to school. He had asked the teacher to talk to Jimmy's friends and ask them for suggestions as to where he might have gone. He rejoined the others in Valmai's house.

'I've searched the mill and the woods around,' Rhys told them now. 'I doubt if he's gone far. He's probably nearby, punishing someone, making them worry.'

'But we have to find him. He can't survive in this weather,' Netta wailed.

'I think I might find him,' Eric said. 'If he hears my voice I think he'd come out for me.'

'Stay away from my son!' Walter snapped. 'You're probably the reason why he ran away.' Shocked, Eric sat down on the chair normally used by Valmai and stared unseeing at the ashes of the fire.

Valmai came and put a hand on his shoulder. 'Talking through his hat as usual. Ignore him,' she said loudly, glaring at the man.

'But I know I'm the one to find him. He'll come if he hears me,' Eric said anxiously. 'Every minute he's out there in this weather, the more dangerous it becomes.'

'Stay away. I'm warning you.' Walter muttered. He knew he was being stupid but guilt and something more, jealousy of Eric, made him keep up his ridiculous attack. *He* had to find his son, not Eric.

He went out and leaned on the wall, staring over the fields, then went back inside.

Rhys was returning to the house when he heard raised voices. Sally and his mother were having a disagreement, Sally insistent and his mother pleading. He quickly gathered that if he stayed, Sally and Sadie would not spend Christmas Day with his parents. He had caused them all enough misery. It was time Rhys left.

Gathering his few belongings he slipped away unnoticed by anyone and walked towards the bus stop to start his journey to a lonely Christmas.

Jimmy saw a shed near the path he was taking across a field, and he pushed through the hedge and went inside. He was hungry and cold and wrapping the blankets around him, he searched in his bag for something to eat.

'Clear off!' a voice near him growled and he leapt up in alarm. There was no sign of anyone and he began to think of ghosts and monsters. The voice came again and this time, a man who had been sleeping in a corner wrapped in sacks, sat up. 'Clear off!' he repeated. 'If the farmer saw you coming he'll send us both on our way and I've slept here for a week.' He looked at the bag. 'Got any food?'

Jimmy offered him some biscuits. 'You a tramp?' he asked. The man crawled across and snatched the bag. 'Go home, you stupid boy. Got a home, haven't you?' When Jimmy nodded, he said, 'Thought so. Well, go on then. What are you doing out here disturbing the likes of me, eh? Go on, clear off!'

As Jimmy ran from the building, the man snatched the blankets from him. 'You won't need these, got plenty at home. Go on, clear off.'

Jimmy hurried away and, afraid to sit and eat the food he had left in case the tramp appeared or the farmer he'd warned him about, he went to the road and waited for a bus. He didn't know which way he needed to go to reach the seaside but as soon as a bus appeared he got on. The pocket in which he'd put the money was empty. It must have fallen as he ran away from the tramp. 'No bus fare, no bus ride,' the conductor told him. 'Sorry, son. Far from home, are you?'

'No, not far,' Jimmy said.

'Best you get back there. It's getting colder and you aren't exactly well dressed, are you?'

At least he didn't say they'd be worried, Jimmy thought with a sigh. He stopped and looked around him. He had to go back. There was no choice with the money gone and no blankets. He looked at the compass and tried to find a path or road that would take him north. If he could manage to find his way back, he'd make a shelter and stay at the mill. One day when he was old enough he'd live there and forget he ever had parents. That would please them. They can shout at each other all day, he thought, and they'll be glad not to have me hanging around.

The police came several times and promised to do everything they could to find the boy. 'How long has he been missing this time?' the constable asked.

'We don't know,' Netta wailed, glaring at her husband. '*He* was supposed to be looking after him and he didn't know he wasn't in his bed. Call yourself a father?' she shouted at Walter.

'Netta, make us all some tea,' Valmai demanded imperiously. 'Stop shouting at each other and think.'

China rattled and water was poured into the kettle but Netta's hands were shaking and it was Eric who took over the task. 'I'm not touching anything he's made,' Walter muttered. Netta threw a cushion at him and told him to get out. Walter looked threatening and began to rise out of the chair. Netta pushed him back and Valmai tried to hold them apart.

The constable took over. 'Go now, and ask anyone you can think of to come and help,' he told Walter. He coaxed him up out of his chair, handed him his coat and pushed him firmly out of the door. 'Right. What next?'

'Somebody should go and talk to the farmer. There are lots of barns and places where he might be.'

'We're already on to that,' Constable Harvey assured her.

Netta shivered. 'Oh, why did I walk out last night? Why did I leave him in the hands of that idle, useless husband of mine? I should have taken Jimmy and gone years ago. If anything's happened to my boy, I'll—'

'Here, drink this, then we'll ring the school again in case he got there late.'

The police had already arranged for the school to let them know if Jimmy turned up but the constable said nothing to Netta. Better give her that small hope for a while longer.

Unaware of the missing child, David was waiting for Sally outside her office. He linked arms and held her close. 'Where first?' he asked. 'Cup of tea and a cake?' Laughing happily they went into a smart café offering mince pies and Christmas cake and sat making plans for Christmas.

'I know you'll want to be with Valmai and Gwilym on Christmas Day – they'll be feeling the absence of that son of theirs and Sadie will cheer them up. But what about Boxing Day? Mam would love it if you and Sadie came to us.'

'You're right we'll be with the Martins on Christmas Day and we've arranged something on Boxing Day – lunch with Amy and Rick,' she said.

'And what about Christmas Eve?'

Soon it was all arranged and Sally admitted to herself that the pleasure she displayed was really relief at not being in the house where Rhys might find her. 'It will be perfect if I can manage to avoid seeing Rhys.'

Words that warmed David's heart.

Gwilym was brought home by ambulance that afternoon and as the light began to fade and there was still no sign of Jimmy, Eric said, 'Say what you like, Walter, but I'm going to find the boy. I know he'll come if he sees me and I know the area where he'll be hiding. I've told the police and they've searched several times but I know he'll come out for me. He talked about going to the seaside. He told me he'd never been. Imagine that, Gwilym, eleven years old and the coast only a few miles away and Walter's never taken him there.'

Walter began to bluster and threaten but with Constable Harvey following, Eric set off for the mill. Walter followed, resentment against Eric stronger than fear for the boy's safety.

Before they reached the part of the path from where they had a first sight of the ruined building, Eric stopped and listened. 'Can you hear something?'

Constable Harvey shook his head. He couldn't hear anything except the wind in the trees.

'I can hear the water. He's got the wheel turning! Hurry, he's sure to be still there.'

Harvey and Eric ran, with Walter struggling to catch up. Eric pointed towards the derelict room where he had often slept and they both called and listened. There was only the sound of the stream. Eric went to look at the wheel and there was Jimmy, half in the water, his face red with blood, his eyes closed. 'Jimmy!' Eric called, running down to him.

'Why were you so long?' Jimmy murmured.

He had been trying to release the wheel and his arm had caught in a split plank of wood. Eric eased him out of his coat and wrapped the boy in his own. Walter arrived as Eric stood in the stream, holding Jimmy in his arms. He angrily demanded that Eric came away and left him to help his son. He leaned over and began to pull Eric aside and the wheel moved, slightly, but threateningly.

The bank was slippery and was already marked where the boy had struggled as his sleeve had caught in the weak piece of wood. Eric pushed Walter away and Walter tried to respond by pushing him towards the water. Jimmy was in danger of falling into the stream, now deeper due to his efforts to clean it. Eric eased the boy up the slippery bank where willing hands lifted him to safety, then he turned and grabbed Walter by the scruff of his pants and the collar of his shirt and threw him in the deep water of the stream. He went back to Jimmy and said, 'Sorry, son, but I've wanted to do that for a very long time.'

Jimmy's eyes were closing and Eric called for the constable to help him. Together they carried Jimmy home with Walter behind, shivering, trying to hold back sobs of anguish. 'Sorry, son,' he was muttering. 'Sorry.'

'I knew you'd find me,' he heard Jimmy say to Eric. 'I knew you'd come.'

'That was the worst thing of all, Jimmy knowing Eric would find him and not me,' Walter told Netta later, but his anger against Eric hadn't eased.

Chapter Twelve

JIMMY BECAME HYSTERICAL when Eric tried to carry him back into his own house and pleaded to go to Valmai and Gwilym. It was there that they waited for the doctor, while someone went to find Netta, who was preparing a meal for him and filling hot water bottles to put in his bed.

There was no apparent injury except some grazing on his arm and the danger was mostly from the chill of lying half in half out of the icy-cold stream. Valmai made him comfortable on the couch beside a roaring fire, surrounded by cushions and covered in blankets. Netta sat beside him and a distressed Walter hovered around outside.

Two days later they were confident of his recovery and Netta went to the post office where, during the summer, the rooms above the shop were rented to visitors. It was agreed that she and Jimmy could stay there. She went back to Valmai and told Jimmy he needn't go back to the house.

Making sure Walter wasn't there, Netta went with Valmai to gather all she would need and during her search she found the rent book. She looked at it and gasped.

'Look at this! Walter hasn't been paying the rent! I've left the money out every week and he hasn't been paying it. We're in serious arrears, Valmai, and unless I can find the money we'll lose the house.' As she had been at work all day, she had been leaving the money in the book for Walter to give to the collector. Whatever he'd been doing with the weekly amount, it hadn't paid their rent. 'I can't pay this off and rent the room for Jimmy and me. Oh, Valmai, what shall we do? I can't go back to how it was. Jimmy wouldn't cope and he doesn't deserve it.'

'Lock the doors so Walter can't go back in, and stay with us until everything is sorted. It'll be a squash but Jimmy won't mind that and Rhys has gone back to Bristol.'

'What about Gwilym?'

'As long as he has privacy when he needs it he'll be happy to have you and Jimmy staying with us.'

Walter had stayed with friends, Roy and Mildred, for two nights but knew he had to go back to the house. He had a little money, enough to get some food, and there was fuel for the fire. He'd be all right until Netta relented and came home.

It was a shock to find it locked. The back door for which he had a key had been bolted inside. He couldn't get in and at once he became angry. Locked out of his own home? How dare she?

He went back to the friends where he had stayed, expecting sympathy and perhaps help breaking into his house but instead Roy and his wife both shook their heads.

'Sorry, Walter, but we are on Netta's side in this. You've treated her and Jimmy disgracefully. We feel sorry for Netta, supporting you in idleness and putting up with your treatment of her and your son. Sort yourself out, man. We can't help you.'

Walter walked away, his shoulders drooped in embarrassment. They were only saying what he knew was true. Every time he thought of Jimmy he felt a swell of shame. He'd been selfish and ill-tempered and he cringed as he thought of all the months he had sat there allowing Netta to earn the money, some of which he had wasted on eating in cafés, drinking at the pub, even treating strangers, just for company with people who, for the price of a pint, would offer false sympathy and assure him he was justified in not accepting a job he didn't want. Netta paid for everything. He had money in his pockets, more than he'd needed, so why work? But he had to do something. He couldn't cope without Netta and Jimmy.

His immediate problem was where he could live until he had sorted his life out. He went to the boarding house and the first person he saw was Eric. 'This is your fault,' he shouted. 'Stealing my son's affections and who knows what besides. I ought to have the police on you.'

The landlady came out and ushered him away. 'Sorry I am, but

Christmas or not there's no room here for the likes of you, Walter Prosser.'

Walter walked away, still shouting at Eric even after the landlady closed the door.

'I'll find somewhere better than that place. I don't want to share a roof with you, Eric Thomas.'

But where? He wasn't going to sleep at the mill like Eric had done on occasions. He wasn't a useless layabout who was content to live like a tramp! 'Useless layabout' were the words that he repeated in his mind and as he walked the street the rhythm matched his stride. That's what I am, he admitted bitterly. I got away with it for too long. How can I start again? And where can I stay tonight?

Feeling sorry for himself, he turned without thinking along the path leading to the mill. When he realized where he was going he turned and almost ran back to the street. Not that! Never would he sink that low. He went back to the road and looked at shop windows where advertisements were placed.

He found a small house advertising bed and breakfast and although they weren't happy to have a visitor staying over the Christmas period, he took out some money and they grudgingly agreed to rent him a room only. No food. He went to the shops and, spending as little as possible, bought what he thought he would need for the few days he intended staying there.

He took out his wallet and counted the notes. If he put what he had left into the rent book it might just be enough to avoid serious trouble. Paying for the room hadn't left much in his pocket though.

He'd been stupid, keeping back the rent just to show off to his friends, bringing out notes and joking about how well he managed without working, with a wife to look after him. Telling them they were fools. They had laughed, thought him an amusing fellow, but they were at home with their families now, whereas he had been left with nothing and when he'd complained, there had been no sympathy for him, only derisive comments. After Christmas, he'd persuade Netta to let him go home. What he had to do was get work and pay the rest of the debt as fast as he could.

Guilt was still balanced against resentment and self-pity. He patted the wallet in his pocket. He'd need to spend a little more. After all, he had to eat. And he wanted a drink and the company that went with it. That wasn't unreasonable. Netta couldn't expect him to stay in that room and not see another soul all over Christmas. Convincing himself he was justified, he took two pounds more from the wallet.

Christmas came and went but it lacked the usual joyful feeling: Walter alone in his room, listening to the sounds of laughter and the tempting smell of food, thinking of Netta sharing the days with Valmai and Gwilym. He walked past the house several times and saw Jimmy with Sally and Sadie, who called laden with gifts and good wishes. To his annoyance, Eric stayed on Christmas Day and again on Boxing day. Several friends called to wish them well and Netta and Jimmy paid visits to others.

All the time Netta was trying to decide what to do. She needed to provide a home, a proper home, for herself and Jimmy. But how, if they lost the house?

For Sally Christmas was happier than she'd hoped. Visiting Valmai and sharing part of the day with Netta and Jimmy and Eric made it a party, much enjoyed by Sadie, although as Sally was aware of underlying tension, guessing the reason, she didn't stay as long as planned. She had been constantly watching the door, afraid of Walter appearing and causing trouble, or Rhys coming back and having to stay with him for a while for Sadie's sake. But there was no sign of either. She almost ran in relief as she finally left the house.

Rhys should at least have been honest enough to tell her the truth, not leave her hanging on hoping for some miraculous return to how they had been. Even little Samuel, born in such tragic circumstances, had been unwanted by him. He must have been horrified, wondering how to tell his new love how Samuel had been conceived. No wonder he'd muttered anxiously about the possibility of an abortion. Now, it was all heartbreakingly obvious.

She wondered if he would ever return to Tre Melin or would just visit his parents briefly, after dark, afraid she'd demand repayment of the money she had given him over all these months.

David's mother had welcomed her to tea on Christmas Eve and there were gifts under the tree for herself and Sadie. Mrs Gorse had gone to a lot of trouble to make them feel at home, cooking and setting the table with as much decoration and sparkle as it would hold and still leave room for them to eat. David went with her to

Amy and Rick's on Boxing Day and they went for a walk several times during the holiday weekend. Every time she returned home though, there was a fear that Rhys would be waiting for her. What would she say? Would he tell her the truth at last? Or would her instinct to cut him out of her life make her close the door against him again?

A note pushed through Valmai's door a few days after Christmas was addressed to Netta. While Jimmy was with Gwilym and Eric in the workshop, she showed Valmai.

'Walter's gone,' she said, her voice emotional as she handed Valmai the note. 'He doesn't say where, just that a part of the arrears has been paid and he'll send the rest as soon as he finds a job. He hopes Jimmy and I will go back home.'

'I'm pleased, Netta. You need to go back. It's your home and all your things are there and for Jimmy's sake I hope you can stay.'

'But where's Walter? What'll happen to him? I know he was making us unhappy but I feel like I've abandoned him.'

'I'll ask around. He won't have gone far,' Valmai promised. 'Now, what about us going in and lighting the fire and making sure the place is cosy again.'

'And tidy! That would be a change.'

Together they cleaned the neglected house and lit the fire and soon the place looked like it always had, until Walter had lost his job and willingly given up hope of another.

'That factory closing, that's what changed him,' Valmai said. 'It changed the lives of everyone who worked there.'

'It wasn't only the closing of the factory that changed him,' Netta said. 'He used that for an excuse to settle into a life of idleness, with failure an excuse for bad temper and irritability. It's every man's dream, not having to work.'

'Not every man. Most of the men found other work and were thankful to start earning again.'

'Him and that David Gorse, they've been happy to waste their days.'

'I can't argue with that. I blame David's mother, mind. Keeping a man who's twenty-four, it's a disgrace. I don't know what he lives on. She's a pensioner after all.'

'David was always a bit light-fingered as a boy. Perhaps he's still the same?'

Netta and Jimmy were walking along Mill Street when they saw Walter approaching. At once Jimmy ran off and he disappeared into the boarding house where Eric lived.

Walter started to run towards her, waving his arms. Netta stood her ground.

'Get the boy out of there – that man is up to no good with him.'

'Go away. Jimmy's my responsibility.'

'But it's Eric who's upsetting him. He drove his wife and daughter away, remember.'

'Wrong. It's you that causes him to keep running away, not Eric. He's a kind man and worth a dozen of you.'

'I don't like the man.'

'Still looking for someone to blame?'

'Keep him away from my boy!'

Ignoring him. Netta walked on.

David was happy. Sally and Sadie had spent a lot of the Christmas holiday with him and his mother. Affection was strong and growing. He liked her company and he felt proud walking with her holding his arm, but the greatest joy was knowing he had beaten Rhys Martin and stolen his girl. And his daughter too! What more could he ask of life?

He knew Rhys wasn't staying with his mother, which was worrying, and perhaps winning Sally would be only a brief moment of satisfaction. Rhys staying away at Christmas suggested he'd found someone else and again he thought with distaste of Sally being Rhys Martin's cast off. People thinking he was second choice? Second best? That wasn't what he wanted, not at all. He'd miss her, but he'd drop her at once if this were the case. No one was going to feel sorry for David Gorse. He'd still enjoy seeing him arrested though. He went up into the loft to reassure himself that the hidden evidence was still there.

Mrs Gorse had been puzzled when she wasn't given the bowl and the painting for her Christmas present. Could he have forgotten? It had been there for quite a long time. The scarf he had given her was very pretty but she waited in vain for her real gift, the beautiful bowl and the charming picture. When she saw him coming out of the loft she asked, 'Any secrets up there, David?'

He stared for a moment then shook his head. 'No secrets, Mam, just a lot of rubbish which I'll clear out one day.'

It was her birthday in January – that must be it; he was keeping the special surprises for her fiftieth birthday. Smiling, she gave him a hug then toddled off to start preparing supper. A nice piece of steak for him, that was his favourite. Expensive but he deserved the best.

As soon as the offices opened, Walter went to look for a job. Any job, he told himself. He wouldn't be proud. Whatever was offered he would accept. Then Netta would take him back. To his shame he was half hoping they had nothing to offer him, but after a brief interview he was given a job in the packing department of a factory just a few miles away. He was smiling as he went back to Tre Melin. It wasn't very well paid but wasn't arduous either; he could manage to do that for a few weeks, until something better turned up. If he really disliked it, it would be easy to get himself sacked.

David was also looking for work, something better paid and more impressive than a repair man for a few properties. If he and Sally were to make a life together, he needed to impress her with his endeavours. He put on his smartest suit, a white shirt and a silk tie. He swaggered in and explained that he was looking for something in middle management. He wasn't sure what that meant but it sounded better than 'I'm an unemployed factory worker.'

He was given the address of a small factory where an office clerk was needed and an appointment was made. Seriously unimpressed, David went, told them he was looking for something with better prospects and walked away. This wasn't going to be easy.

Then his luck changed and he was interviewed for the position of carpenter with a small building firm. He demonstrated his knowledge and mentioned his intention of marrying. That was an incentive for a young man to find regular work and implied he would be a reliable employee. Although he hadn't been in employment for two and a half years, his reference from his previous job supported that, and he was given a month's trial.

Tonight he would tell Sally and ask her to marry him. They could live with Mam for a while, or perhaps they'd live in the house she rented in School Lane. He daydreamed happily all the way home. Then he saw Rhys.

Rhys had walked into his father's workshop unannounced. Gwilym's reaction was shock, not at seeing his son but at how thin and ill he looked. But he showed no pleasure at his appearance; he just stared at him as though at a stranger.

'Hello, Dad. Sorry I didn't stay for Christmas. There were things I had to finish. Now they're done and I can come home, once I've been to the police and sorted out any accusations they have. I didn't do the—'

'Don't tell me, son,' Gwilym interrupted angrily. 'It's Sally who should hear what you have to say. Then your mother and I will listen. Sally first. Right?'

'Of course. I was only going to tell you I didn't burgle any houses. I've never stolen anything in my life.'

Gwilym stared at him, his eyes cold. 'Haven't you? That's something you'll need to talk to Sally about, too! There are many ways of stealing.'

'But I'll—'

Again Gwilym interrupted him. 'Talk to Sally. Not me or your mother. It's Sally who needs to understand why you took money – not stole it, took it. If there's a difference I don't know it.'

'I'll go to the house and wait for her.'

'Best you do. Don't come here until you've spoken to her, right?'

Rhys nodded and went out. Gwilym put down the plane he was holding and sat, head bowed, wondering what possible explanation Rhys could find for the disgraceful way he had behaved towards Sally and their daughter, Sadie. Whatever had been happening, Rhys was so thin and gaunt, it can't have been pleasant. Perhaps he'd been too hasty? But no. Sally was entitled to hear what he had to say before the rest of them. He doubted if it would be convincing.

David had followed Rhys from a distance and saw that he hadn't stayed long with Gwilym. He'd be going to wait for Sally. She was meeting Sadie herself today, so he'd go to the nursery and walk back with her. Better if he were there when they met.

He watched from the shadows as Sadie came out with Sally. They were holding hands and Sadie was chattering, presumably about her day, and Sally was bending over slightly to listen above all the noise created by the other children. He stepped forward and asked. 'Did you have a good day, Sadie?'

Sally looked up and smiled. 'This is a nice surprise, David.'

'I've come to tell you I have a job.'

'Marvellous! I'm so pleased. I know you weren't happy doing unsatisfactory repairs for a boss who didn't want to pay for a decent job.'

'You understand me so well.' He leaned over and kissed her cheek, then bent to kiss the top of Sadie's head.

'What is the new job?' she asked. He explained about the work on building sites and made it sound as though his carving skills would be valued, rather than fixing ready-made roofing timbers with several other men.

'Rhys is back,' he told her as they drew near to School Lane. She stopped and stared at him. 'Sally, don't let him wriggle out of what he's done. He'll have prepared some story hoping you're willing to believe it. Nothing can excuse what he did to you and Sadie, and,' he whispered softly, 'to dear little Samuel.'

'I don't want to see him.'

'Then don't, love. Come back with me. Mam'll give Sadie something nice to eat and we can stay until we think Rhys has given up hope.'

They went to see a delighted Mrs Gorse who opened biscuits and tinned ham and raided the fridge and in a short time the table was filled with salads, meats, cheeses and a huge plateful of bread and butter. Sadie chattered away and they enjoyed a pleasant hour.

When they walked back to the house, there was no sign of Rhys, and David stood outside for a while, after listening to keys turn and bolts thrust home. Before walking away he went around the house to check the back in case Rhys was waiting for him to leave. There was no sign of him, but he almost tripped over a man's glove. It might be Rhys's and that might be handy. He picked it up, using a handkerchief to grasp it.

He smiled into the darkness. Satisfied, he went off, not back home, but into the fields. Time for another burglary perhaps? Although the coincidence might be too much for the police to accept, it would be too obvious. Instead, he'd just break into a house and drop it. Disturb the larder, as though Rhys had stayed there. He didn't seem to have anywhere else to go.

Walter watched from the darkness of the fir trees on the drive as the man passed him. There was a flicker of a torch and he saw the man's face. David Gorse! He watched as the window was opened and he saw David look around before getting in. So that's the game, is it? Everyone suspecting Rhys Martin and David showing how easy it was. He slipped back into the fir trees edging the drive of the house. He wanted to make sure. Carefully he placed a branch on the dark drive and waited, hoping David, if it was he, would trip.

He held his breath as he heard the sound of the window sliding back down, then David walked calmly back towards the gate. He stifled laughter as he saw him trip and issue a couple of loud expletives. No doubt at all. That was David Gorse.

He'd say nothing until tomorrow, when news of the robbery came out, then he'd tell the police what he had seen. Honest, upright citizen that he was. That would be a start towards getting the Martins on his side, a first step towards Netta letting him come back home.

David went home, and although it was very late, in her bedroom, unable to sleep after the excitement of Sally and Sadie's visit, Mrs Gorse glanced at the clock. She rose and went down. 'I couldn't sleep, David, shall I make us a cup of cocoa? That might settle me and you look frozen and in need of something warm.'

When his mother finally slept, David went up into the loft to check once more on his evidence. He eased the wrapping paper away and almost shouted in dismay. The silver bowl shone and the picture too was as clean as any seen in a gallery. They had been cleaned. His stupid mother had found them and polished them, removing any evidence of Rhys's fingerprints.

He eventually calmed down. Rhys wouldn't know and the threat would be enough to keep him away from Sally. The police would still be interested and he could leave them somewhere to implicate Rhys.

To Walter's surprise nothing was said about a break-in the following day and he went back to the house. No lights. The tenants were still not home. Well, he'd noted the time and the details; he could wait.

Stories about the break-in spread two days later. 'Not exactly a burglary. Apparently someone had broken in and had taken only food,' Valmai was told.

'Some poor homeless wanderer,' Netta said, when Valmai shared the news and the two women stared at each other.

'Could it have been your Rhys?'

Valmai shook her head. 'Eric told me he was staying at a small hotel on Cardiff Road. I doubt if he's so hard up that he'd steal food. He'd come to us before he did something as stupid as that.'

Gwilym was listening and he nodded agreement. He didn't feel that he knew his son any more, but he was convinced that he wouldn't have broken into a house.

'Whatever's wrong, Rhys wouldn't steal anything,' he said to Valmai, later. He'd said nothing to her about Rhys's brief visit, waiting anxiously to learn that his son had offered explanations to Sally. He was curious about the delay. Had Sally refused to listen to him? Or simply not believed him? Who could blame her, he thought sadly.

When the police came and asked where they could find him, he told them where his son could be found. There was nothing to hide and pretending he didn't know would have been a foolish move. When they heard that Rhys was at the police station, rumours abounded and soon everyone was convinced that he was under arrest. Gwilym knew then that he had to do something, and fast.

Contingency plans had been made and the information he needed gathered. He was anxious about what he had to do but determined that this time he would do something to help. That night, when Valmai was asleep, Gwilym struggled to get out of the house using the wheelchair, his crutches across his knees.

He found the journey very tiring; the exercises he'd been doing hadn't really prepared him for the effort needed. Cutting across the fields, via the regularly used paths and on past the old mill, he reached School Lane and went into the house where Freddie Carter lived. He knew the man was away from home and also knew that Freddie rarely locked the door, even when he was staying with his daughter in Bath.

He opened the door, planning to pick up one or two things then leave them in the garden as though the thief had been interrupted. With his crutches, he moved into the living room and there, snoring, sprawled across the couch, was Freddie. Tucking a couple of silver ornaments in his pocket, taking a silver framed photograph in another pocket, he backed quietly out and, leaving the door open, he struggled back to the mill. He left all he had taken, then slowly, painfully, made his way back home. His leg was aching after the short walk using crutches and his arms were trembling with fatigue. He wondered if he'd be able to get up the path and back into the house before dawn broke.

As far as he could tell no one had seen him. With Rhys in custody, the robbery would make it plain to the police that someone else was responsible.

He got out of the chair and was about to collapse on to the day bed when he saw to his consternation that someone was in the room. 'Valmai?'

'Can you tell me how you can move about so well while all this time you've insisted that you can't go further than the shed? You've been out for hours, Gwilym. Where have you been?'

Valmai was sitting in the armchair, barely visible in the dark room. 'This is what you've been planning, is it? Robbery? So you go to prison instead of Rhys?'

He flopped into the bed and wondered if the pain would ever go away. 'No,' he said, trying not to show his discomfort. 'Not that. I thought that if there was a burglary Rhys couldn't have done, the police might start looking for someone else. I thought of this a long time ago, and I've been waiting for an opportunity. With Rhys held by the police he has a perfect alibi.'

'But he hasn't, they released him hours ago. He's back in the hotel long since.'

Recriminations followed as Valmai made Gwilym promise to go back to the hospital and get help to become mobile once again. It was Valmai who ran back to Freddie's house and replaced all the items Gwilym had taken. Freddie snored happily on.

The following day the police came again. Freddie had insisted that, although nothing had been stolen, someone had been in his house. Things had been moved and the door had been left wide open. PC Harvey warned him about locking doors and left, convinced the man had been mistaken. Still, it might be worth having a chat to Rhys Martin again.

'Where are you staying now?' he asked when he saw Rhys later that day. 'Back with your parents?'

'No, I have a room in a hotel.'

He gave the name and the constable asked, 'Out late last night, weren't you? Someone said you were down by the old mill. Funny how that place attracts people. You were there last night, weren't you?'

'Not me. I like the comfort of a warm bed. It's David Gorse who likes wandering at night.'

Walter also alerted the police to David Gorse's night-time wanderings. They were aware of the many times he had been seen crossing the fields during the hours of darkness. He'd been stopped on several occasions and had even shared his flask of coffee with a policeman once or twice. He had explained that he watched wildlife, particularly badgers. 'And as dawn breaks all goes still and utterly quiet, then the stillness is broken by birdsong as one by one they wake,' he said. 'The morning chorus in the spring is magical; well worth getting up early for, you ought to try it,' he had enthused.

Harvey laughed. 'As a constable used to working every shift man can devise, the nights hold no secrets from me.'

Although they doubted the man was responsible for the burglaries, a woman police constable was sent to talk to David's mother.

'Come in, dear,' Mrs Gorse said, opening the door wide in welcome. 'Sit down in that chair near the fire and I'll make us a nice cup of tea.' She was always pleased to greet visitors and opened tins to offer cakes and biscuit, chatting all the time.

'Your son spends a lot of time out in the fields, doesn't he? Keen on wildlife, I believe.'

'Yes, but it's not the real reason he walks around at night. He can't sleep, see. He can't get work. He comes in very quiet, like, tries not to disturb me. I did hear him come in the other night and I got up and made us a nice cup of cocoa.' She sighed. 'He's never slept properly since the factory closed and he lost his job. Loved that job he did.'

'Such a shame about the factory closing, wasn't it? Men lost more than their jobs when the place closed down. More than two years some have been out of work. Your David working now, is he?'

'Yes, got a job on the buildings. Not a proper use of his talents, mind, but he's very friendly with Sally Travis and needs more money than I can spare him.' She leaned closer and said confidentially, 'I'm hoping he'll settle down and marry.'

'You'll miss him. I expect he spoils you.'

'Yes he does.' She placed the tray on a small table and again the confidential whisper. 'I'll be fifty in a couple of weeks and I think I've found the present he bought for me. It's a beautiful silver bowl. He loves nice things and never buys anything new. Prefers the old quality stuff.'

'How exciting. Can I see it, d'you think?'

Mrs Gorse looked doubtful for a moment, then said, 'It's up in the loft, mind, but we can easily get the ladder in. David gets cross but I've done it once or twice, searching for the Christmas trimmings, that's how I know it's there.'

The ladder was put in place and they went up and into the loft, a powerful torch helping them to find the bowl and the painting. When they took them down, the policewoman went out to make a call. 'I have to report every couple of hours,' she said in explanation. 'Leave them there while I make my call and I'll come back and we can have a good look. You are lucky to have such a generous son. What about another cup of tea?'

They were sitting drinking their second cup of tea when there was a knock at the door. 'It's one of my colleagues. I'll answer it.'

The two officers asked permission to search the loft, which she willingly gave, unaware of the implications. Then a van arrived and the stolen items plus other pieces they had confiscated were put in and the men left a now tearful Mrs Gorse, cursing her own stupidity, waiting with the WPC for news of David's arrest.

*

Rhys had returned to Bristol once more, and it was at the end of January when he came home again. This time Valmai encouraged Sally to listen to his explanation.

'You have to hear what he has to say, love, then decide whether or not you believe him. Either way you can then rebuild your life and forget you ever loved him. But you have to listen.'

Valmai stayed with Sadie and he took her to a small public house where they sat near a roaring fire with the low murmur of conversations, the clink of glasses and the clack-clack of dominoes around them. The peaceful sounds were enough to offer privacy and Rhys took a deep breath and began.

'I borrowed a car and a friend was teaching me to drive. I was involved in an accident that was entirely my fault. My lack of experience meant I had reacted more slowly than an experienced driver might. The person I hit was Eric's daughter, Julia and her little girl.

'Julia suffered nothing more than bruising, but the child had serious injuries to her legs. It was thought at first that she might not walk again. Knowing how the loss of a limb had affected Dad, I had to help.'

'Why didn't you tell me?'

'If you'd refused – and you'd have been entitled to do so – I couldn't have helped. My going to prison wouldn't have done anything to help little Erica to walk again. Money could. My error, your money which you were trusting me with. I'd never have earned enough to pay for the treatment she needed. There were specialists who could help her more than what was already being done but the money was needed quickly if she stood a chance and the treatment was beyond Julia's ability to pay, so I offered to cover all the expenses myself.'

He reached into his pocket and took out an envelope. 'At first I thought I could earn enough by my own efforts, but although I've been doing two jobs for most of the time, I couldn't. I left college and did more unpleasant but better paid jobs – three for a long time. And—' He offered her the envelope '—these extra months were to pay back what I owe you. It isn't all there but I intend to pay you back the remainder in two months' time.'

Sally was speechless. 'Why didn't you tell me?' was all she could say.

Later, when most of the details had been discussed, they walked home and told it all again, to Valmai and Gwilym.

'Does Eric know where his daughter lives?' Valmai asked once she understood most of what had happened. 'He deserves to know that she's all right, he deserves at least that.'

'Julia's mother filled her head with terrible stories about Eric. She believes he was a cruel, uncaring husband who wasn't interested in his daughter.'

'She wasn't told about the debts her mother left him with, I suppose? How he sold everything he possessed, including his house, to pay them off? Or how he finally paid them just a few weeks before the factory closed?' She stared at her son. '1 hope you told her.'

'Or how he slept at the mill for a week so he could buy a teddy for Sadie?' Sally added. 'I hope you told her all this.'

'I've told her everything I know about Eric and I've persuaded her to come here next week and meet him.'

'Not at that awful boarding house!' Valmai said at once. 'Eric will come to us and they'll meet here.'

Eric was nervous as he sat in Valmai and Gwilym's living room waiting for his daughter to arrive. After twenty years how could he not be anxious? She had been brought up on her mother's version of what happened, making him the villain. Whatever Rhys had since told her might have made her curious but it wouldn't guarantee her believing that he was the innocent party in her mother's lies. Her story, perfected over the years, would be too embedded to be changed by anything he could say, he thought, as the clock ticked and they waited for the snick of the gate.

To his surprise she didn't look that much different. Older, of course, but as he stared at her the face became as familiar as the photograph he still looked at almost daily. And beside her, holding her hand and looked around at the row of strange faces was his granddaughter. He opened his arms and the little girl went to him and still looking up at his smiling face, asked, 'Why are you crying?'

'What's your name?' Eric asked and was shaken when she said, 'I'm Erica, are you my granddad?'

'Granddad Eric,' he replied, smiling at them all. He looked at the stranger who was his daughter and asked, 'Why did you call her Erica?'

'I always wondered what you were like. I even went to find you once at the only address I had, but the people there didn't know where you were.'

Rhys and his parents went out, Gwilym determinedly using his wheelchair to leave the house and garden for only the second time since his accident, Rhys pushing occasionally, Eric and his family following. They went to the pub, where others were planning to join them. The news had spread and curiosity brought everyone who knew Eric there to hear the exciting story of the reunion.

Amy and Rick, with her disapproving mother, were there. Netta and an embarrassed Walter were there and conversations filled the place with noise and laughter but for most of the time Eric and Julia and a chattering Erica were oblivious to the rest. They talked and laughed as they learned of each other's lives in the years they had been apart.

Mrs Seaton-Jones was sitting with Amy and Rick and she shocked them by announcing that she believed they should move. She had been looking around her at the people in groups and clearly disapproved of them all.

'This isn't the place for you. It's full of thieves and delinquents. Even that nice David Gorse has turned to crime. This place hasn't the right ambience for families like ours, Amy. Where's that tramp living now? And the boy you tried to befriend? The one who was always missing from school.'

'Eric Thomas and Jimmy are both fine, Mummy.'

Rick pointed to where Eric and Julia sat. 'In fact, Mother–in-law, we'll be joining Eric and his daughter later, when we've given them a chance to talk. Rhys found Eric's daughter and they've met for the first time for twenty years. Quite an event.'

'Yes, I heard! Rhys found her when he was in Bristol where he's been spending money he was stealing from Sally.'

Rick made an excuse and went to talk to Gwilym and Amy followed. Mrs Seaton-Jones leaned towards Netta. 'I hear that you and your husband are separating. Such a pity. Families are so important,' she announced. 'I stay with my daughter and her husband every weekend. They're my family and we should be together. Don't you agree?'

Netta shook her head. 'No, Dorothy, a young couple need time together to get to know each other and make plans.'

'But I'm family and their plans include me. That's the kind of family we are, d'you see.'

'I wonder if they see it like that? I had my mother-in-law living with us for eight long years and because of it, Walter expected me to be not a wife but an extra mother. Spoilt he was and so was our marriage. What I didn't do, she did. He didn't lift a finger. Me trying to outdo his mother in the way I cared for him. Her determined to show she knew best.'

'It isn't like that with us,' Dorothy defended, but she sounded less sure. 'Come on, Amy dear, it's time we went home.' She reached out an arm and Rick came across to help her out of her seat.

On the way home Amy and Rick allowed Mrs Seaton-Jones to march ahead. Once there, she turned and asked, 'Am I a nuisance, coming every weekend?'

'Of course you aren't a nuisance, Mummy. We look forward to seeing you, don't we, darling?'

'That common Netta woman, she has no idea how a decent family lives.'

Rick didn't go in immediately, but held Amy's arm and leaned on their gate.

'Darling, what can we do?' he wailed. 'I think we missed our chance there. Imagine having her here every weekend for ever!'

'There's only one alternative that I can see.'

'Tell me. Please, whatever it is, tell me.'

'We can convince her that cousin Godfrey needs her more than we do.'

'All right. We'll try writing to him, then we'll tell her he needs company.'

They stopped and kissed until Mrs Seaton-Jones turned and called, 'Not in public, Amy! What are you thinking of? It's so—' Her final words were lost in their laughter. Later that evening, to their surprise, she broached the subject herself.

'I've been neglecting cousin Godfrey,' she said. She looked at them with her shrewd eyes. 'And I've been spending too much time with you.' She raised hands to ward off disagreement. 'Much as you need my support.'

'Whatever you think is best, Mummy,' Amy said, avoiding looking at Rick.

'Perhaps if you have more time to yourselves there'll be less of this embarrassing kissing in public!'

After a long discussion, which included Jimmy on many occasions, Walter went home. He wasn't allowed in the bedroom, but made to sleep on the couch in which he had idled away so many days. 'You have to earn your place,' Netta insisted firmly. 'Keep your job and help make the house a home, then one day maybe we'll be a family again.'

Rhys came back from Bristol in February and repaid the last of the money he owed to Sally. He was still thin and pale, but the weariness had left his eyes. He came to see Sally and Sadie, who was proud of her tiny two-wheeled bicycle with stabilizers, which she called stable riders, at the back.

'Everyone seems to have settled down,' he said one day as they sat and picnicked at the mill. 'Amy and Rick have persuaded her mother that they'd be better on their own, Walter is trying so hard to be good to persuade Netta he's a changed man that it's comical to see him. And Eric. He's so happy he wants nothing more of life. Julia and Erica visit every week, staying with Mam and Dad, while I sleep on the couch. A full house suits Mam, she loves looking after people. Dad is meeting with consultants preparing for proper treatment and an artificial leg.' He looked at her fondly. 'There's only you and me to get ourselves sorted.'

'I love you, Rhys, I always have, but I'm still a bit raw. Mistrustful. It will take time to forget how dishonest you were. You should have trusted me.'

'I know, but it seemed such a risk. Julia's a widow, her husband died of influenza just months after Erica was born. There was no one else to help her. Erica wouldn't be the lively active little girl she is now if you'd refused. I took a chance, hoping that when you knew the story you'd forgive me.'

'One day, when I learn to cope with the fact you didn't trust me.' She smiled at him.

'Soon,' he pleaded. 'I want to be a part of Sadie's life, so she'll forget the years I wasn't here.'

'Come on, Daddy.' Sadie called. 'Come and see my bike again. It's got stable riders an' everything.'

'Stable riders?' he asked.

She watched as Rhys pushed his daughter over the steep parts of the path and listened as their voices and the laughter echoed back. 'Soon,' she said aloud. 'Very soon.'